THE
ICOSAHEDRA
KEY

AND OTHER TAILS!

by

B. JE JONES

Front cover image: "face to face : D" by Jasper Zhao
https://www.artstation.com/eijihsoahz
Book design by Bashiri Je Jones

Contact info for author:

bashirijejones@yahoo.com

Acknowledgments

Of course, first let me say thank you, to you! What you hold in your hand or more likely on your tablet is a project I have been working on for a few years now. It is my fondest wish that you are entertained by what I have birthed into existence.

To my mother Barbara Jones for whom none of this would have been possible. Through my whole life you have fostered my dreams and gave me the space to grow into the man I am... A unique and odd creation like no other!

To my baba, gone these past several years, Dr. Ibin Saidi Liwaru, half of the reason I am a "special" person is because of your love and wisdom. Love you.

To my family: my brothers and sister, James, Ben, Jason, and Angela. I know you have all to some degree or another questioned my life path but you have all been supportive no matter where I have journeyed and for that I love you and I wish for you all the happiness that the world can provide you.

To my dear friends I love you all but a special thanks must go to Dan Nakamura, my brother Jamaal Jenkins, the discerning Kevin Kurihara, Goose and Pan and Britt, Wen, the Mad Hatter Alyn Lewis and my sister Lisa, my inspiring brother Aron Lee, and my high school D&D group: Cedric, Rommel, Maurice, Patrick, Pete, and Chris... Yes, I am a nerd and proud of it! Special shoutouts to Bill Owen my first DM, and Dr. Winn who made us all read Dune! Also, shoutouts to George, Mary, Jim, and the beloved and not forgotten Bobby McGee. Some of the best adults a kid could grow up around.

Thanks to Milton, you weren't my father, but you were an exceptional role model to be around and you are missed.

To my nieces and nephews...dream big...dream often...dream out loud until all your dreams come true!

And finally, with all my heart, my feline companions throughout the years to present: Chico, Gin-gin and Latay-latay, Little Pony, you were some of the best cats ever born and thank you for sharing your lives with me; and to my lil guy, who just turned one, Raggamuffin...cats are amazing.

To you all, the ones I have mentioned and the ones I have not, you have inspired me, and I thank you from the center of my glorious and glowing heart!

Table of Contents

The Alchemist

Bubble,
Bubble,
This and That
Spoil the child
And create the brat,
The brew is mild
To some is wild
The Alchemist creates
And begins to make
His creation of chemicals,
His lifeless child,
His potential dream,
His blatant style,
To all is
To all not
The Alchemist creates
What some cannot.
by Bashiri Je Jones...age 16

The Silent Sitter

The Silent Sitter sat
in the seat next to me.
His paling pallid presence
felt in mystery.

A strange storm steals and thunders
the frozen fragile frames
of windows waxed and washed
in mist from coldest seas

the warp of wood
and the wheel wound right
the prow of ships
silhouette the night

and, the quiet widow prays
in candles that light away
the melancholy chill
of memories that play and spill
making minutes mince and stray

grey tones of ancient stones
leech red rimmed rust
from ingots of iron forged
dripping tears to cobblestones
filling cracks of mud and dust

bells blossom and peel
floating bodies, flotsam, and keel
stones rounded by the sea;

a piece of quartz?
an old man's knee?;

a lone seagull
with wounded wing;
a missing eye;
a piece of string

neither night nor day seen in these fogs of grey

which,
with misted fingers reach
through quiet drenched wet streets

silent in the settling
in wind's watchful wail
still the quiet's nettling
spun a mortal tale

the silent sitter sat
in the seat next to me
my greatest wish the sound
as the sitter
silent
leaves.

The Lake

January 03, 1946

Re: BOB ERVIN HOWARD, transfer of care

TO: Head of Psychiatry

John Dibble General Hospital

Menlo Park, California

The patient/prisoner is identified as one "BOB ERVIN HOWARDS".

We have discovered this information is inaccurate. There are no records on either side of the South Pacific conflict of any soldier or outside contractor by this name. It was suggested the name could be a play on a late American writer's name.

Along with this my preliminary analysis and whatever documentation that has been generated, also included is a recording, the only evidence thus far that Mr. HOWARD can speak. After this recorded interview, my beliefs that Mr. HOWARD has some background in literature, namely with another deceased author, the poet Edgar Allan Poe. Though I am not trained classically with literature or poetry my colleagues have filled in the gaps. It was immediately remarked that parts this poem, for lack of a better word, bore striking similarities to the style used by E.A. Poe. Mr. HOWARD, in this recording, uses a mix of various techniques from basic rhyming to complex alliteration, which hints at a past where the patient had some experience with higher levels of education. The "poem" itself could be mere theatrics. A rehearsed planned act, written and memorized, yet this seems highly improbable for the only outcome would be confinement, in one facility or another.

MR. HOWARD presents acute signs of not only physical deprivations. He has obviously suffered a traumatic incident which has left him borderline catatonic at some instance, and then only later to swing cross the spectrum to a manic state in others. He is monitored 24 hours a day and is generally kept in confinement to avoid any further "altercations"(see case file). No matter his state, MR. HOWARD is non-verbal(the authorities found him wandering the city have said when asked he gave the above name then said no more), but since we can confirm he has no physical impairments that would exclude him from verbal communication, I have taken to recording our sessions in the off chance he may give a statement or information deemed important. On the morning October 30, 1945 MR. HOWARD began to speak. I do not know what inspired this, or what inner block had fallen briefly allowing him to regain his speaking ability. In rare cases an individual's neurosis may exhibit compulsions that go beyond regular classifications. It is apparent Mr. HOWARD suffers from horrific delusions and is assuredly a paranoid schizophrenic. Whether these are prior conditions remains for further observation and diagnosis to determine.

Though my colleagues and I have not ruled this out, there seems to be no physical sign the patient suffered any head trauma which may have affected the Wernicke's area, and inversely his language comprehension, resulting in Wernicke's aphasia. Mr. HOWARD follows verbal directions with no difficulties, minus his observed manic. His behaviors run counterintuitive with a diagnosis of aphasia(though they could later be classified as a new category of this condition).

The patient has some connection to the entertainment field, for at points during the session Mr. Howard appeared to demonstrate ventriloquism, with his voice sounding from different areas of the room, his lips were completely unmoving at these times. This leaves me to believe he has been trained in theatrics either professionally or has achieved his abilities naturally through self-education. I can further confirm this is the case with Mr. HOWARD, for several times throughout the recording he caused objects to fall or move, by some undetectable wires or some other method, and once created the effect in the air of a drifting coil of black smoke. This would suggest more than adequate proficiency in sleight of hand and pick pocketing. Please tell your staff to keep an eye on their possessions around him, especially all flammables: lighters, matches, cigarettes, etc.

I recommend Mr. HOWARD be committed to a long term care facility and perhaps with proper medication and treatment, an initial trial of ELECTROCONVULSIVE THERAPY to balance his behavior with daily regimen of SODIUM PENTHOHAL and/or MEPHENESIN, MR. HOWARD could potentially find freedom from the demons that possess him. Currently we are unable to offer such treatment at this facility and are assured shortly this facility with return to its prewar operations.

(**note: throughout the recording especially towards the end there are certain audio artifacts or anomalies. We apologize but this was something beyond our control as the new audio equipment had been recently provided by a special medical investigation unit the United States Army Medical Research Laboratories at the Aberdeen Proving Ground out of Edgewood Arsenal, Maryland. All further inquiries should be directed to their operations. We were to record Mr. HOWARD's sessions with equipment which had only arrived recently after Mr. Howard's arrival. We were assured we need only plug in the microphones and press "record".)

Yours sincerely,

Dr. Donald Petersen,

M.D.
4th General Hospital
Manila, Philippines

DP:h

"Our bodies on the beach,
Our ship a smoldering wreck,
The jungle watched loud and deep,
The grit of sand on our cheeks.
Of a thousand islands
Fate had granted one.

"With what breath we had we stumbled,
Under a sun that grew and rumbled,
Into a deep and loud obscene
Till not a living man was seen.

"Immediately the jungle closed its grasp,
Heavy wet,
A living mass.
Of things that bit,
That stung,
That roared,
Far worse was the water that poured
From the sky in tearing sheets.
From eyes as soldiers weep
For our fallen not found.
The truth of a war so proud.
The rich invading smell of hot metal and oil
Forging young men for war.

"Separated, we were.

"Lost, for none knew
Of the fate of ship and crew.
Set upon by enemy in air
Without mere moments to spare
Then next awakened still breathing.
We survivors ventured into this seething
Steamy beating sea of evening
Of a verdant sick and weaving.
Its tendrils crossed our broken hearts.

"Chance of help uncertain
With the closing of its curtain.
Its curtains of waxy greens.

"Days passed.
One to next.
Falling forward our only quest
But never fast
In this held morass
So, like a dream descending.
A constant day unending.
Of a hope we kept pretending.
Pretending we would go home.

"Of our trail there was none to follow
For our hellish trek erased by morrow,
Our dead it quickly swallowed.
This coiling broiling nest of serpents
Which feed on light and water,
And life that quickly rotted
When life was there departed,
Yet the vessel still remained.

"One by one,
Ripped and ruined,
Undone by this journey of consuming,
It was slow, our recognition
The changing of our position
From oppression heat and hell,
From tight and closely held,
To an opening sun kissed swell,
To a downward stretch of land.

"And there below,
Amongst Herculean stones,
A welcome sight we came across.

"The jungle had unclenched its grasp
Into an area we could pass.

"Our haunted trance dawned understanding,
Of this new world we saw expanding,
A forgotten dream commanding
We awoke from our hypnotic wake;
In the heart of an ancient kingdom,
At the edge of an ancient lake.

"Clear, so clear
As if no reflection could appear
Of a sky now seen blue above.

"On our knees we kneeled and trembled,
Our deprivations marked resembled.
Resembled pleading worshipers assembled,
Assembled at the feet of God.
Blue and green and teal,
Those ancient still waters revealed.

Revealed a bottom devoid of murk
Nor any creatures that swam or lurked,
Water more inviting than a lover's arms.

"Charmed,
Quickly we set to work,
To quench the thirst which perched
In our throats that stung and hurt,
From the taste of the rotted earth,
And the fetid air we'd found.

"To quench the fire made
By the jungle and its blaze.
Stoked and fed while in its cage
Its maze of deepest green.

"Our fingers broke....
The still waters.

"Then....they came.

"Walking...
Never talking.
Lithe gentle creatures stalking.
Stalking us victims of the mocking
Jungle and its creeping deep.
Of exotic features pure,
They spoke without a word.
Green eyed and brown of skin
They invited us all in.
They welcomed us with ease
But filled with fear we seized
To accept their welcome hands.

"Yet our hunger did not retreat
And quickly we joined their feast,
A meal of exotic treats.
Mostly sour, yet often sweet
Such succulent bits of meat
That we sucked between our teeth.

"Time seemed to slow.
Bitter honey in the snow,
Sweet but not to know
Of the bitter fall in Spring.
The thaw the light would bring
As the amber drop ripped free.
Night finally raised her hand
As I was guided by a plan,
By a maiden's open hand,
Into a jungle now more friend
Than foe.

"But....
I paused.
Holding a moment
Freezing when Mother has called.
Sensing some disturbance
A change in the air,
That made her whisper admonishments
'Son, you must take care!'

"I released the maiden's hand
And the opium of her presence ran
And a cloud upon my eyes...
Lifted!
And I was no longer blind.

"Dead all around me.
At the lake's edge...dead.
The water reflecting what couldn't be said.
My comrades in arms
Dressed and ready
Like hogs on the farm.
'Steady'
I thought to myself.
Heady
The scented remains of our repast.

"I recognized others.
All our fallen brothers.
Brothers I had left behind
As they had withered and died,
But now,
Obviously saved
From the jungle's decaying dismay.

"Here they all were!
And next to them
Racks!
Set above fires
That smoldered and cracked.
That gave off sweet smoke.
That caused me to choke.
Then to invoke
All my stomach contained,
From the feast of these folk.

"No fiends!
Some twisted and sick walking disease.
Feeding dark gods, they could never appease
While wearing faces

Like you and me.

"I spun.
Fleeing in fright
As the true face of my hosts
Came into sight.

"Misshapen and lurching,
Arms too long for their frames.
Brows massive and heavy,
Heads covered in dark manes.
Round swollen bellies.
Eyes set too wide apart.
Skin painted in tattoos
Of the darkest of arts.
Some primordial race
That had been lost and forgotten,
Who never knew wheel
And were more like the haunted,
And the cursed.
Who have not been saved
By the sacrifices
Man had to make.
Being blessed with a rise
Evolving to find
A path free of the mire
While other creatures expired.
Finding Gods
And Goddesses
More like us.
Who offered us blessings
And thrones we could touch.

"These lake living things had none
At least none no sane human could love.

"No Buddha or Moses.
Nor sacred red roses.
They even stood removed
From that garden of two,
And the first act
The serpent issued.

"From the damned I ran
Clutching my life.
In my waking right hand
Clutching my knife.
The jungle played
Toyed with my soul.
Guiding me on a path I could not control.
The green opened,
And said to me...behold!

"Covered in vines,
Encircled by trees,
Shined the face of a god
That offered no peace.
It rose high against the hill
Carved from a strange glistening stone.
Larger than life, surrounded by bones.
What light there was danced,
Stars trapped under its skin.

"Impossible!

"Something so massive should not yet be undiscovered
At least by recent spy planes
In their passes and hovers.
But here it was!

"Here It was!

"'It' was all it could be.
Devoid of physiognomy like she or he
My mind sought to define
But the more I sought
The steeper the climb.
Coils obscuring.
Parts of it stirring.
Folding fat wrinkles of flesh.
Scales or pustules or tiny sharp horns.
A thing still maturing
Yet to be born.
Frozen in some amoebic state.
A gestating embryo in space.
I couldn't tell!
The eyes!
Deep and black,
An unwanted sky.

"It saw me!

"I was sure,
Feeling its presence
In the tears which had blurred,
Clouding my vision
From this holy sight,
Worshiped by monsters
That preyed on the night.
Prayed, to some thing
No heaven had made.

"Screaming.
Writhing.

Barely even breathing.
I flew into jungle,
A fell into evening.
For how long
I do not suppose,
Finally,
I awoke from my nightmare,
Madness and tatters my clothes.
Not much more I can tell you
This was all that was shown.
The answers you seek
Are not mine to hold.
But this I can answer.
Never to go
And drink from the waters
Where no reflection may grow.
Nor eat with the people,
Who worship dead bones
Of an ancient deity
Who rests in repose...
Waiting and watching
To steal back its throne."

CATS

The Bodhisattva Mittens

Opposable thumbs.

One of the physical keystones to the evolution and rise of humankind. Earth's most dominant sentient species.

Opposable thumbs.

Now, there are mixed opinions as to how big, or how little, the evolution of opposable thumbs for *Homo sapien's* ancestors was in terms of the creation of a truly sentient species. Cognizant and self-aware. Some postulate that without the opposable thumb humans would have never developed tools and the brain capacity to use said tools.

Others stated if humanity had evolved with only four fingers and no thumbs it would mean only that the tools would be different, yet the brain would have developed more, or less, the same. The trajectory of sentience is unerring.

Felis sapien. Common relative *Felis catus.* All agree, on one level or another, that their birth into sentience began with opposable thumbs, and after that things accelerated.

By the year 2047 genetics had become rather advanced. Advanced enough that many things could be manipulated and created. Mostly the genetic market was made up predominantly of human self-enhancements, and enhancements to a fetus's genetics in utero. The rest of the market was divided into genetic improvements to food and food production, and the cloning of domesticated animals.

In 2050 the movie, "The Big Miss", dominated the box offices, and its biggest selling point was an adorable and quirky chihuahua pitbull mix named "Alexander".

Alexander was so popular that demands for his species grew exponentially. Not wanting to miss out on the potential profits, the film producers decided to clone the star of their film and offered up clones for an exorbitant amount. Over 10,000 of these clones sold. It was a huge windfall.

For the modern pet owner it became a status symbol to have one's pet genetically modified and/or altered, and the pinnacle was to genetically create, completely from paws to claws, your pet and have it born into an artificial womb in a sterile and well-lit lab. Height, fur length and texture, eye color, immunities to allergens and built-in scent blockers to deter fleas and ticks, and other creepy crawlies which lived off blood, all options in a pet's creation.

Frederick Kerry. He was a financial wizard, born from wealth; and a fond owner of a few select *Felis catus* with high price tags and higher pedigrees. He could have anything, and there was nothing he couldn't have made, within reason and the limitations of technology. He was a man of particular and rumored peculiar tastes. A chronic bachelor, he would often date serially, preferring female companions overall. All were under legal restrictions, signed NDAs, in terms of discussion during, or after, regarding the nature of relationship and his proclivities if any, sexual or otherwise. All would admit, legally, that, he "loved" cats.

Garden.

Was her name. The first of her kind, created to appease a powerful man's desires.

Large for her species and the breeds she was blended from. Short hair that ran gold-blond to white. A longer than average tail, but more sinuous, prehensile, more like a monkey's than a cat's tail.   Large eyes, cobalt blue with flecks of golds and deep browns.

All this made her special and the most expensive feline yet created, but it was two key genetic upgrades which set her apart from all others making her a potential Eve of feline proportions.

These upgrades: a slightly enlarged frontal lobe; and...small hands with opposable thumbs.

They say Kerry was happier than anyone had ever seen him. He got into the habit of throwing parties to show off his "Garden". Many guests witnessed the no expense lavishness he heaped on his "pet".

This was considered the beginning of *Felis sapien.*

Over the next few years, others created their own Garden's, but authorities, fearing unchecked genetic manipulation of domestic species, set new limitations on how much could and should be manipulated genetically...and after allegations were put against Frederick Kerry, and his relationship with his pet, the trend died out, and years later Garden and others like her followed suit.

Yet, this was enough. Possibly, some form of animalistic jealousy sparked *Felis catus* to make its own natural genetic leap, as over the preceding decades more and more of this species naturally developed opposable thumbs and small fingers to match. It didn't end there. Those cute little meows which had bordered on actual words like "momma" or "I love you" suddenly became clear and unmistakable. Baby talk from kitties slowly became the norm.

It could not be doubted *Felis catus* was evolving rapidly, when they went from 4 leg-walkers to 2 leg beginning the transformation to *Felis sapien.*

It was cute. It was novel. It was exciting. Other pet owners looked to their canine companions, searching for similar natural genetic upgrades. Who wouldn't find Fido cuter if he suddenly could speak when spoken to? They weren't so lucky as man's best friend remained as such: obedient and dumb to death. Some say, it was the close indoor relationship *Felis catus' shared* with humans that was the truest of sparks for their awakening. Perhaps canines were too dependent on humankind.

The Earth entered a new era, and a percentage of humankind wasn't particularly happy about it.

It wasn't easy for some to share what had been given over to them by a divine creator, or a coincidental universe.

Many humans believed *Felis sapien* was the height of "cool" and novel. But the open door to share the world humanity had known, that started with glassy eyes and wide grins at these new beings, didn't stay open. Some humans felt vastly inept and slow when compared to the new intelligent cats, who naturally showed more flare and wit than most humans.

Humans still owned cats.

This naturally led to the emancipation of all domesticated felines, sentient or not. Some humans were not comfortable being called "slave owners" solely because of their possession of unenlightened felines whom they loved.

In a bold action, as a species, *Felis sapien* bought Africa and parts of Indonesia and South America. "Bought" might be too strong a word. More like "bartered" for control through donations and direct negotiations. Almost overnight the trade, legal and illegal, of cats large and small was completely stopped. The barbaric custom of ripping apart, especially the large cats, for medicinal and procreative cures was nixed. Some countries sought to stop this but failed and were compensated financially to accept the inevitable. Lions and tigers were saved, oh my! Bears weren't so lucky.

It was only natural that *Felis sapien* started to adopt human qualities, and concepts of justice and social customs.

The world began to see its first human and cat couples, which led many to question laws regarding bestiality and cross species mating, if possible. Misplaced fears of cat-human hybrids taking over the world had purists, on all sides, rallying in front of government houses and courts of law all over the world.

"Keep your paws to yourself!"

"Cross-species love is a SIN!"

"Fur is murder! Of the human species!"

The sale of cat toys, hairbrushes, shampoos and conditioners, hair dyes and hair treatments increased as *Felis sapiens* became consumers. Even hair loss products specifically for felines became a thing. Hair loss for a *Felis sapien* could be devastating.

Pets...they started to own pets. Birds and dogs, even fish as strange as that was, but only as strange as humans that ate pork yet owned pet pigs. Mostly *Felis catus* had a fondness for primate species. It became common to see a cat person walking about with a small monkey on a leash. As this trend began, it was met with smiles and laughter, until it was commented their choice of pets may be a direct statement about humans having owned their kind in the past.

Humans owned them before sentience, now were they trying to own humanity's cousins?

Smiles soon turned to frowns.

Felis sapien. Average height 3.5' tall. Average weight 44.5 lbs. Like its less evolved cousin, *Felis catus*, they have eyes of varying shades and hues. Hair running the gambit from short to long, and every color except green and purple, excepted when dyed my choice.

It was known that Mittens' ancestors had Persian ancestry but from there it was anyone's guess his exact lineage. Born full furred under an auspicious moon, though one man's auspicious moon is another's bad moon rising, Mittens was an avid student and devoted to solving the social ills of both feline and human.

It surprised most humans that Mittens was who he was, but in human history, though rare, it was something which occurred every few generations: the birth of one special being above many, if not all.

Moses...Krsna...Zoroaster...Jesus...the Prophet Elijah and Mohammed. Blessed humans who represented the great unknown and the even greater creator, commonly called God. Sent to save, redeem, and awaken all humanity...and more.

A few religions, and even more philosophies, claimed Mittens as their own, but only the Buddha's teachings seemed to be most like those of Mittens.

The Bodhisattva Mittens was coined and stuck.

Humanity was divided. God was theirs solely...wasn't He?

It was hard, almost impossible, for some to accept...a God cat?! A tailed messiah. A divine being, all powerful, all knowing, and covered in fur.

It had been too long since human's Creator, with a capital "C", had made His/Her presence known with burning bushes or bearded prophets with water bending skills!

Mittens' following grew with both feline and human. He was invited by humans and his kind, to speak and teach, to spread his brand of truth. He met with many leaders, both political and religious. He was a media darling with one Oscar winning bio pic and several best sellers, written by followers and detractors. Then the threats began, and soon attempts on his life, but miraculously the would-be assassins would have their plans thwarted, mostly by luck.

Mittens owned no homes and wandered here and there. Whim often guided him to different places and people, so itinerary created by his most devoted followers more than not fell to pieces. He was sometimes hard to find for those that sought him most. Usually the arrogant self-entitled wealthy socialites and sociopaths who collected unique experiences to justify their vain lives and material lusts found it difficult to gain his presence.

Many sought him out to debate, to attempt to disprove his teachings, but showed their own weaknesses as the Bodhisattva Mittens kindly shined a clear wisdom on their ignorance. Most debates ended with one more follower for the feline prophet.

Mars had a civil war.

Mars for more than 150 years had been an outpost, a colony, for a small population of humans and an even smaller population of *Felis sapien*. Mars biggest contribution to Earth was minerals. The right piece of Martian soil could make anyone rich. Almost inevitable for conflicts. Corporate warfare turned into out-and-out war. Red blood spilling on red soil. Things got worse as those on Earth became divided along party and socioeconomic lines.

The Bodhisattva Mittens felt drawn to the red planet, to knit the tear between those at war. His launch into space was the biggest event and was watched by almost everyone.

He never made it.

One moment his ship was being tracked and monitored by agencies both private and public. Next...gone.

The assassins finally succeeded. A cleverly created incidence...a corrupt piece of data...a faulty panel...and Mittens was lost. Space that day was colder.

Were they trying to stop the efforts by Mittens to end the war, or simply trying to stop him and his growing religion? The real answer was anyone's guess.

The war on Mars ended in the aftermath, as the worlds mourned.

There were inquiries, investigations, trials and a few executions, with no real culprits discovered, just rumors of powerful people, human and feline, who either liked their bodhisattvas to be human or who enjoyed materialistic lives with rich saucers of milk, fresh exotic fish, and the finest hair brushes money could buy without worrying about the turmoil and the strife a fellow cat could bring by saying and doing too much.

You couldn't have a modern religion without at least one martyr!

Mittens, with his cute little nose, was that martyr.

The days and weeks following his assassination Mittens appeared, like a resurrected messiah, to a few of his followers and to one or two large gatherings of the faithful. A perfect being, now unflawed by flesh.

The cold at the loss of Mittens was replaced with a fiery devotion. Wealthy benefactors shed their wealth in waves of adoration to create schools and temples, each adorned with statues and images of the hirsute Bodhisattva, thus to honor their fallen savior and spread his legacy from now to the end of time.

His adopted symbol, a simple outline drawing of a pair of knitted wool mittens, spread everywhere his message lived and grew, and on parting his followers would say to one another "Don't forget your mittens."

The Bodhisattva Mittens would not be forgotten. Two days of the year became holidays dedicated to his life and death, and on those days, it became customary to wear mittens and to gift friends and family shiny jingling toys, and hair products, and to sit down to a meal of fresh fish.

On the tenth anniversary of his death a meeting of nations occurred to raise a monument to Mittens' legacy and the gifts he had given to both felines and humans. It was a huge celebration and at the event the crowd reached over a million sentient beings in attendance, both human and cat alike. And there...something strange, happened.

In a large open space, a large mass of small dark and light furry shapes scurried. The crowds drew back, a few screamed, not knowing to what good or ill this wriggling mass of fur could bring.

The mass of small creatures pulled together, and then, unmistakably, they started to form a shape from their gathering. Little bodies climbing on one another. Little limbs clutching and holding. They quickly built a three-dimensional shape of a figure sitting.

A stunned gasp went up through the crowd for the small furry shapes had created a large and very realistic image of the Bodhisattva Mittens. People cheered or wept. Some of his most devoted fell to their knees.

This lasted for more than a minute as the image of this miraculous event was cast into the mediasphere by those in attendance, and within this short span most started to see what these small creatures were.

Mice.

Mus sapien. Common relative *Mus musculus*, had reached sentience nearly 2700 years ago, well before Felis catus, and as advised by the Buddha Shakyamuni had kept their existence secret. The Buddha prophesied one day another group of sentient creatures would first start the path to acceptance with humankind, and one among them would be of the Dharma, born to free all, furred and unfurred alike.

They recognized Mittens as the one the Buddha had spoken of.

They were filled with joy and secretly met with Mittens. It was hard to set aside their fears, for Mittens' ancestors were quite fond of eating their ancestors. Many a *Mus musculus* died as they were batted about by paws and scratched, bitten and held, then dropped to scurry for safety only to be snatched up again for the whole process to repeat. Death could take hours. It was an experience both utterly horrific and traumatic to say the least.

Mittens had been expecting them and offered immediate acceptance to their species. He already knew his death was approaching so he then told them what they must do at the tenth anniversary of his death.

As quickly as they had recreated a physical representation of the great teacher amongst the throng of celebrants, they then disassembled and moved to create another shape, this one flat and two dimensional. One word. Large, and very clear.

"Hello."

Starfish, The Wizard, The Water Square & the Castle by The Sea

Starfish lived in the Castle by the Sea.

She was a serving girl and her days and most of her nights were filled with the menial tasks of serving the knights and knaves, the lords and ladies, the princes and princesses, and the king and queen of the Castle by the Sea.

Starfish's skin smelled like dried salt and old cooking oil, which was not necessarily a bad thing. Her weathered clothing, off-colored rags of gray and brown, on the other hand, smelled bad. At the mercy of the damp, her garb smelled slightly off, and when the rains grew heavy her smell was fit company for wet mongrel dogs. She still smelled better than certain areas in the Castle by the Sea.

She could be found most often drawing water from the water cells, large opened and sealed rooms filled with fresh water brought from afar; or, basting roasting birds over open flames that licked at her small fingers; or, wringing water soaked linens with water saturated hands, valleyed and dimpled; or, fighting for scraps with dogs with her small fists with rough, scraped knuckles; or, perhaps, pulling some slimy dead thing from the surf and jagged dark rocks that surrounded most of the castle on its north and west sides.

The Castle by the Sea was an old castle, and the mist, and the wind, and the sea and all its water crept in and through every opening, every crack, and every crevice. The old stones were black and wet most times, and for every hallway and chamber filled with light and warmth, even more stood dark and dank, cold and empty.

Starfish lived in constant fear for these were the dark portals and tunnels she had to use to serve those who lived in the Castle by the Sea.

In their well-lit wanderings, the royals of the castle did not enjoy the sight of a starfish walking amongst them.

"Aren't you supposed to be under a rock somewhere?!!"

Traveling through her underworld, Starfish could arrive and appear by secret passages and secret doors to deliver sweets and treats, drinks and treasures upon summoned command.

One would think for little Starfish nothing more could add to her life of fear and servitude, but people have been wrong before.

Her fear was deepened by the smiling faces of the cruel and callous royals, who appeared pleasant and sweet like shining echoes of heavenly things. Yet when errors were perceived, when things were misplaced or broken, when days did not dawn sunny, which they never did for the Castle by the Sea, they wielded vicious hands and razored tongues to berate and belittle dear little Starfish.

In a better world, Starfish would have at least been able to turn for comfort to those who lived as she did, serve as she did... but no! They too, were mostly unkind, or ambivalent, having long ago lost the battle to be better people.

Starfish had known the taste of fear long before she had known the taste of milk.

...but of all the people she feared most in the Castle by the Sea...Starfish feared most the Wizard in his keep.

Once a week, often at night, Starfish was summoned to serve him... and most dreadful, and most terrible, and most fearful of all ...she believed she was beginning to learn his magic!

It began when he first arrived to serve the King and Queen, and the other royals of the castle. In this time of strife, when more fishermen's boats came back empty of both fish and men; when the whisperings of the smaller lords and ladies had begun to resemble the faint unsettling rumbles of dissent; when more and more reports of raids by masked and cloaked marauders were coming from the edges of the kingdom, he had come, and on that first night, Starfish was summoned.

It continued from this first night, a new dark path, and its way fully opened when the Wizard began to teach her...the Game, in the second week of his stay.

And these words he spoke first.

"This is a pawn."

The Wizard's palm cradled a carved dark stone, long as Starfish's longest finger, wider at one end and narrower at the other...the widest end was perfectly flat while the narrow end was rounded.

"My lord? What is a...pa-on?" her nervousness made her use of the new word come out strange.

"What is a pawn? That is a very, very, very important question," he replied with a wicked smile, his scraggly white hair once more falling before his right eye. "But to answer truthfully and completely, one must first answer many other questions. Like, for instance, the Board, what is it and how does it affect the Game? Or, how can you play a game when you don't know what's at stake or even, the etiquette of play? You see, for children, games are fun, cheerful, delightful adventures they engage in, until they outgrow them."

Starfish had only ever played one game before, and in the playing there had been no delight, no cheer, no fun. Starfish did not like games, and even more she did not trust those who wished to engage her in them.

The Wizard continued.

"But for the grown, for those invested in trade, land, and for those seeking gold or power...even for those seeking magic!"

Starfish's eyes freeze when she peers into his, fear seeping into her, locking her in place.

"...games can be dangerous....and amazing! Games can be keys to success and wealth, or keys to failure and poverty!

"My Master taught me the Game when I first began to learn from him, and he had learned it from his Master, and so on and so forth for thousands of years. Master to student! ...an unending chain that can either stop us from flying ....or stop us from flying too far away!

"You cannot solve the puzzle of the pawn until you understand all the other pieces in the Game. Then and then only... when the time is right, I will ask, 'What is a pawn?' ...and you will answer!"

Thus went their first conversation, and more did follow. The Wizard demanded only for Starfish to listen, learn the game, and to speak only when spoken to.

Her dreams changed.

It began, in the third month of the Wizard's visitation to the Castle by the Sea. That night, their time together had begun as usual, and then changed when the Wizard rose from his gnarled throne-like chair made from driftwood pardoned by the sea. He moved slowly across the fur covered stone floor to a set of large dark wood chests, banded in dusky bands of pitted and strong rocksteel. He then opened the largest chests, and drew from their depths...

...the bucket, and the rope.

Starfish had begun to doubt her fears of the Wizard and his magic, and of their time sitting at the Board. The bucket and the rope, these new things, pulled her fear back from the depths from which it had begun to settle. He handed these new things to her.

"I need you to draw some water..."

Fetching water was not a new chore, and she knew immediately the closest water room to visit for the task. Arranging the coils and coils of the thin rope over her shoulders, the scratchy fibers grazed her cheek; she picked up the bucket and started to retreat from the Wizard's cell.

"...from the Water Square."

The heavy bucket tumbled to the floor. The sound it made, though muted by the thick fur, still covered the small gasp which escaped Starfish's lips.

The Water Square!

It was rumored that thousands of years, the Castle by the Sea did not exist...but instead, there was solely a rocky island, and at its center a vast opening in the rocks leading down,

down to a rocky chamber constantly fed by the sea and the crashing waves. Legend says the Water Square was built around this opening making the way down much deeper, and then the Castle by the Sea was built around the Water Square making it even deeper still.

The Water Square was a cold place. It was quiet, silent except for the distant crashing waves below and the steady gurgle of liquid coming from the pipes that fed into it.

The Water Square was a convenient place to send human waste and refuse to be consumed by the turbulent water below. Roughly carved holes in the surrounding walls of the square allowed for metal pipes to pipe merry and muddy slurries of foul oils and food from the alchemist labs and kitchens, to weep and wash a river of excrement, and other "unwanted" things, down and away from the royal lives. Once, or more than once, Starfish and a few other smaller servants were required to go into those pipes to free obstructions. No worse job within the Castle by the Sea existed in Starfish's experiences.

She was wrong.

A balustrade surrounded the dark opening and it would take a tall man fifty long strides to reach the stone rail overlooking the watery pit from the four walls which surrounded it. And, if that man could walk on air, it would take him sixty or more strides to reach the rail on the other side.

It had taken only a short time in her young life for Starfish to learn all the pathways to use so as to avoid the Water Square and its haunted regions in her services in the Castle by the Sea, and it was because of this knowledge she immediately knew the quickest way to it.

Her fear made the journey longer.

At one corner of the Water Square a section of the floor and railings stretched out into the open air over the void and the waters below. Here it is said, the rare condemned man or woman, or child, was given to the water below.

What they say was true.

Whether the condemned were condemned by punishment or pleasure, Starfish did not know.

They also say at the bottom of the Water Square, deep below the raging spoiled waters lived the Water People.

Of this, Starfish did not know the truth.

Starfish swung the bucket out and then down over the railing, as she began to lower it. The bucket quickly descended through her experienced hands. In moments, the buckets descent halted as it breached the foul waters below. She had not yet reached womanhood, so owned none of the height and strength that would-be granted her in her season. Yet, she was strong, and where she lacked strength, she made up with mind. Starfish weaved the rope through and around the railings, so she simply had to walk around the square a few times to see the bucket's return. Tying off the end of the rope, Starfish slowly returned to the walkway where the bucket hung swinging. She dreaded the bucket's contents but feared the Wizard's wrath even more. She hastened her steps.

The water in the bucket had a skin of a black, oily substance floating on its surface which cast distorted rainbows up into the eyes of Starfish's gaze. At least two meters of the rope was covered in the substance. It smelled of rot and foul sulfur.

Starfish did her best to keep the substance from staining her too much during her journey back to the Wizard's keep, but later was beaten by the head servant for ruining her clothing and fouling the air.

A third of her visits to the Wizard now ended with her being commanded to go to the Water Square. Sometimes to draw "water"... and, sometimes... sent to send things down in the bucket that didn't return when she retrieved it.

Starfish learned to protect her clothes and her hands much better.

Then, she had the dream.

The dream was neither complex nor long. In the dream a beautiful man and woman stood over Starfish. Their skin was like her skin, a warm light brown minus the dirt. Starfish once imagined that the dirt on her was in some places as old as she, for as the lowest of the low she has never known clean as the royals have known clean. The two in the dream seemed not to care and looked on her with kindness and love in their eyes.

The dream ended too soon.

Once there was an incredibly old servant. His skin also had been like hers. He was kind. His eyes held the same look as the couple. He died when he offended a young knight who then pushed him down a flight of stairs in the Grand Hall. The Grand Hall was full at the time with feasters in full fury. Almost everyone laughed.

Starfish did not.

She had been named Starfish because it was said she was found amongst the rocks. She thought perhaps the man and the woman from her dream could've been her parents, yet she believed this to be an impossibility, for in her mind they could have only been beings of magic. She was not.

And, this is when she first began to fear the Game was more, and that she was secretly being taught magic.

...but why?

Cod was a mean boy. A very, very mean boy. One of the oldest among the serving boys, he was also the tallest and had started to grow his whiskers, so he commanded more respect, and more fear. Starfish tried to avoid Cod, just like the Water Square, but recently, the things and people she wished to avoid, she, for unknown reasons, could not.

Over the past few days, in the fifth month of the Wizard's habitation, Starfish crossed paths with Cod more often than she liked, and more frequently than she ever had before. Each time she was lucky to walk away with no more than a cuff to the back of the head. She never cried. She knew better than to show tears to the likes of Cod.

Then, something changed in her life, and afterwards, Cod bothered her no more.

It was the day after Starfish found the kitten.

A storm had grown out of the North, heavy and thick with rain and wind, thunder and lightning, which cracked the sky covered sea like a hand of a royal lashing out after being awakened too soon after just falling asleep. Starfish was returning from another evening spent with the Wizard. Today's lesson had been about the Knight. A piece for the Board shaped like the head of a large horse, which Starfish found strange.

"Shouldn't it be shaped like a knight?" she thought to herself.

"Perhaps. Now the Knight's piece is known to most people, and strangely enough, it moves like a knight, though it looks like a horse. Stiff, repetitive, and unforgiving. See the Knight in your mind. What do you see?"

The Wizard rose from his chair and tried to straighten his crooked body. In a bad attempt at imitation he then marched in place, raising his arms, fists clenched and pumping in the air.

"The Knight. Left, right, left, always better at going forwards yet not so quick at direction change, which is why, in the Game, they can move twice in one direction and only once in another

"The Tower is sometimes called a Rook. The Tower has more movement and size. While the Knight does not have its reach, it makes up for it by at least being able to change direction. The Rook cannot when it moves. Life gives the Knight this ability. A wall cannot decide to turn. Only people can turn a wall. A knight tries to be a wall, protective, but always remembers it's a man...or woman in rare instances!

"A knight is only as good as his king and queen. Only as good as his heart. For the greatest knights, every sweep of their razor-edged swords is an expression of their heart and their attempt to protect the kingdom. The Board.

"Do you know what a 'crook' is?"

"No," Starfish answered attentively.

"As you should! A crook is a tool used by herders, and little do you who live on an island know of such people as herders. In places where the land is big enough and green enough men will gather their animals to let them roam free on this land: to eat; to have children; and to grow fat. After a time, the animal's number grows quite large, and these large groups of animals are called herds. And the men who protect them and live by their lives, are called herders. These herders use a crook. A crook is like a staff with a hook on one end, and a crook has only one goal. To control. To fight the other animals, that would harm their herds, with the hard and uncompromising edge of the crook. Or, it can be used to control the herd, who are gently guided by the hook of the crook and brought back into the fold.

"Sometimes, an animal in the herd that does not respond to the gentle control of the crook gets the hard and uncompromising edge instead!"

The Wizard laughed.

"Interesting how similar the two words are....rook and crook! Don't you think?"

She left tired, but glad, for the bucket and rope had not appeared this night. Arriving at the great kitchen Starfish ducked behind the stacks. Crawling through the kegs and sacks in the giant kitchen's giant larder she arrived at her "home".

Her home. Two or more years ago, Starfish and a few other servants had been tasked with giving the giant kitchen a giant cleaning. Starfish was the best at getting into small and hard to reach places. That is when she found it.

Nestled behind the rows of stacked kegs and sacks, behind the boxes and bins, a flaw existed in the wall of the large kitchen. A flaw, large enough for a large sack, or a small girl, to enter.

Starfish had not had much chance to use her home, mostly she slept in the crowded servant's quarters, three large rooms that shared one common room for eating, but lately this unachieved desire to rest in her hidden hidey hole had been realized. Not once, but more than once. Most of the servants, having connected Starfish to the Wizard and the Wizard's wants, were so loathed to find her when ordered to, for in finding her they might find themselves in the Wizard's presence, that they no longer sought Starfish out. Now, if she was ever summoned by anyone other than the Wizard, they just simply sent someone else to fulfill the demanded task.

Starfish's home was a pile of straw covered by a few abandoned burlap sacks, and by touch alone she settled herself down into it. Reaching down into the straw she pulled out her few belongings: a broken mirror; a small empty bottle colored a midnight purple; a small candle and a few broken fire sticks to light it. It was when she lit the candle, she noticed the movement below the straw layers.

She froze.

Immediately she thought the rats had once again returned to the kitchen, but if that were the case it would be short lived.

Four weeks prior, Starfish...had made a move in the Game of her own life, after spending her first full night in her home. She would have enjoyed that first night if it had not been for the rats, and by morning time she had devised a plan to deal with them. Catching three of the many rats that ran wild in the kitchen, at night or even day, she then set them free in the private chambers of the princesses and princes. What followed were the screams and the crashing of furniture as royals came face to snout with the creeping pests.

Games can be delightful.

By the end of the week most of the rats in the Castle by the Sea had been killed or had run off to hide in darker places.

In her home, the straw parted in front of Starfish to reveal a set of sea green jade eyes. Starfish remained still as more of the straw fell away and there before her sat something she'd never seen before. A cat. A baby cat. A kitten! From what

Starfish knew there had been no cats in the Castle by the Sea in an exceptionally long time. It was rumored, long-ago the Castle by the Sea used to house many cats of all sizes and varieties, and that their numbers were so great at one time that even on the shore amongst the rocks for every three pincer ladened crab you would find at least one cat.

The kitten's fur was long and the color of light sea mist, and its tail was long and expressive like a banner in the wind.

Starfish felt something explode inside of her as her mouth opened wide and the corners of her mouth tried to touch her ears.

She was happy, and the thing on her face was a smile.

The next day, Starfish carried her happiness with her...this was a mistake!

"What are you smiling for?!!!"

It was Cod. Thinking she was alone walking in the corridor, Starfish had tried on her new smile, but in the servant corridors you are never alone for long.

"I know you've been hiding somewhere," Cod vehemently spat in her face. Cod slammed his hands onto her shoulders. Cod was strong and pushed Starfish against the wall where her head hit the stones with a resounding knock. Rainbow edged dots of light danced across her sight as she heard him say.

"I'm going to find your secret."

Then he was gone, and Starfish found herself the owner of a new fear.

The kitten! Hers...but not hers.

The royals had taught her about ownership and about people called "Masters". Who treat "pets" to games where death is the best part of the game, and when a good pet died it was with fear in its eyes, lips curled back with rage and confusion. Cod was very much like them. Starfish could not let Cod find the kitten. She did not own the kitten, but its life was so precious to her, even after only one night, that she must protect it.

All day Starfish wove a path of service in the Castle by the Sea, so that no one could say where she was at any given moment with any certainty. With each step she tried to treat Cod like a piece from the Game, envisioning which pieces she could move against him to defend her position, but her life was not exactly the Game and any pieces on her meager board were few and perhaps powerless.

Yet, left with only a pocket full of a servant's hopes and dreams, Starfish chose to see her board as full and filled with powerful pieces, and she moved them accordingly in her mind, and there, in her mind's eye, her Bishop removed Cod from the Board.

And, so it also went, for the living, breathing, and stalking subject of her real world, named "Cod".

He was caught with gold and silver taken from the Temple's altar plates. Offerings for those above. Starfish could never imagine why anyone above her suffering and fear, the Gods, could want for such mortal trinkets. She believed maybe Cod had felt the same way.

They cast his body into the sea in four parts, one piece thrown in each direction. His head was cast into the Water Square, and for months after, Starfish on her missions with the bucket and rope, feared with each returning bucketful an eyeless salt puckered head of a the mean serving boy once named "Cod", would be found bobbing on its surface.

"Why can the Queen move like both the Tower and the Bishop, and yet the King, whom all assumes to be more powerful than the Queen, cannot?"

The Wizard didn't wait for an answer. He continued.

"Every King in his way is a slave, bound by the demands of the kingdom. When the King travels, he travels with more, many more members of the kingdom than the Queen. Sometimes a king will not travel at all without his army around him. By their movements alone the King and Queen on the Board have elements, aspects, of both the Tower and the Bishop. What does the Tower represent?"

"The Tower represents the World."

"And, what does the Bishop represent?"

Starfish remained silent, for truly she didn't know. The Wizard waited.

"The Gods?"

"Yes and no. The Bishop represents the Temple. The Bishop represents the Divine, the Unseen. The Tower and the Bishop. The material and immaterial, the earthly and the divine, that which can be broken and that which can never be broken. When the two are balanced, the broken can be mended and that which was unbreakable may snap like a twig. In your case, little Starfish, they would crack like a gull's egg!

"But. This still doesn't explain why the Queen moves like a blade across the Board.

"Some men are born with a little magic. Most have none. I was lucky. But all women, every single one, is born with some

[59]

magic. They say magic comes from the Father through the hands of the Mother. Thus, is the gift magnified in all women.

"Most women burn their magic away...by feeding their petty desires and even smaller hatreds; by accepting their offspring's ignorance with open arms; by loving bad men. And for the ones who keep their ember of magic alive through this maelstrom, they can become something else. Something better or...They can become monsters, just like the wickedest of men. Will you be most women, my little Starfish?"

One evening the Game lasted longer than usual between Starfish and the Wizard. Minutes passed as the Wizard studied the Board in silence, and then into that silence he began to speak. Not to Starfish, but to the pieces.

The Wizard held conversation with the pieces for quite some time. There were moments of laughter and anger, and then into that understanding, agreement, and gratitude finally appeared, and the Wizard's conversation with the stone pieces ended.

Starfish was silent. To her ears the Wizard had only spoken to himself, but she was sure the Wizard was not holding a conversation with himself solely.

"When the student has fully grasped the foundations of the Game, it may be possible, and I do say 'may be possible', for one to speak and converse with the pieces, to hear their voices...if they're made of stone, and the older the stone the better. My Master and his Master before him called it Stone Speaking.

"Actually, it's more like stone listening. The more you listen, the more you understand, and, eventually, you can speak the language of Stone. If you have the heart, you can be a vessel for the power such a gift could bring."

Returning home in the evening to the kitten and her bed of straw, Starfish's path through the Castle by the Sea wandered, and she was surprised and shocked as she found herself before the arches which led to the Water Square. Slowly she moved out onto the hard stone that surrounded the heart of the chamber. Arriving at the stone rail, Starfish moved quickly to place her hands upon the cold hard surface. Before she could let this small bit of courage fail her, Starfish sent her thoughts into the stones of the Water Square and the water below. And quickly...she was answered!

From the rigid core of the hard stones a reply echoed through her whole being.

She ran in terror, for expecting a voice of darkness, of cold, or nothing at all, there had been a warmth and kindness, and most horrific and disconcerting, a sense of recognition in the answering.

The darkness and watery stones knew who she was.

For Starfish, this was the final proof magic and life had been exchanged between herself and the Wizard. She was no longer a child of sunshine and light. Starfish had been marked, and something loomed unseen above her, and she shivered under its long shadow.

The royal fleet set sail at high tide. The Castle by the Sea was in turmoil. The news was bad. The main port, an island two weeks to the east, had been taken. A main contingent of knights along with those lords hungry for glory, and favor, had been ordered by the King to action.

The King's army.

Half of the army would join with half of the royal fleet to regain the port. The other halves would set out to begin dealing with raiders assaulting the islands at the kingdom's furthest most boundaries. The sun was a red spot on horizon, and the royal fleet, silhouetted in its light, eventually vanished into its brightness and rage.

Starfish was confused as she only half watched the royal fleet. Enjoying a stolen moment when all eyes were commanded to watch the army and the royal fleet departing on their missions, Starfish barely noticed the group of boats disappearing beyond the waves. She had greater concerns.

Nine months had passed since the Wizard had made his home in the Castle by the Sea, and now magic surrounded Starfish like a familiar cloak. She felt... powerful! ...and afraid! She should be afraid. While passing old stones, now more often than not, they would speak to her. She tried not to listen. She began to discover everywhere she looked in the Castle by the Sea, on walls and steps and ceilings and floors, she could see hidden and disguised images of a strange creature worked within the crafted and chiseled stones. Sometimes the creature was large. Sometimes it was ridiculously small, but Starfish knew, the strange creature, if it existed at all, would have to be huge. Mammoth! Gargantuan. So, she was afraid, but also not afraid!

This was only part of her current confusion. The other part: Why would the Wizard give her magic?!!!

Her times awake, Starfish's thoughts were devoted to the Game and this question. The Wizard had given her power. He'd given her a gift!

But she was Starfish! Servant, rock baby, pipe cleaner, whipping boy, the should-be-under-a-rock-girl! Power was never meant to kiss her fingertips let alone drape its arm around her in hidden protection.

She was different. With more time for herself, she was cleaner. Her matted hair was now combed and thicker. Walking, she rounded her shoulders less. The fear that had bent her head and eyes and body down was growing lighter. Starfish did not go unnoticed. Everyone could see the change. The deference to which the other servants treated her had now spread to the royals. In their minds, it too was best to view Starfish and Wizard as one, and no one called on the Wizard except for the King and Queen, and then only as a last measure, so now most dared not to breathe her name.

The Game had grown more intense, different. Nightly, Starfish fought longer and harder to maintain her pieces' dominance on the Board, but the greatest difference was the Wizard had to fight longer and harder too! The Wizard did more and more Stone Speaking, and Starfish, heard more and more from the stones till his conversations were no more hidden to her than the flame on the tip of the candle she lit at night.

It was on a night when both Starfish and the Wizard fought long and hard, and both of their kings were in retreat on the Board, when the Wizard asked, "Do you know where this board and its pieces comes from?"

"Yes, from here," Starfish answered.

The Wizard was surprised, yet not, "And how do you know this?"

"I recognized the stones from which this set is made. This dark blue stone can only be found here, on our shores. The white pieces are encrusted from shells from this shore also."

The Wizard waited.

Starfish continued.

"The stones told me more...They are old. Very old, and all they have ever known is this island. They were crafted by a man with gentle hands who chose each stone lovingly from amongst the shore rocks. He was a king... but not like this king."

The Wizard moved his last bishop. He had made a mistake. Small and tiny, still its appearance to Starfish was huge and glaring, sunrise on a darkened battlefield. The Wizard immediately realized his mistake.

Starfish capitalized on it.

"Checkmate."

The Wizard was pleased.

"Well done, little Starfish... well done."

Twelve days passed in the Castle by the Sea following the great fleet's departure, and the streets of the village and the halls of the castle ran quiet with silence. Here and there behind wood and thatch, stone and timber, laughter and music could be heard, people playing at being at ease, but a pall hung over everything. Many sought to hide from it, ignorantly thinking that whatever this air which laid across the island of the Castle by the Sea would pass them by because the windows were shuttered, and the doors were closed and bolted. This was no mist kept out by walls. No common chill in the air easily defended by locks.

Fear had washed ashore unseen in the night, and amongst the rocks it lay fat and ghostly pale.

The Wizard was busy.

The royals knew what lay upon them gold and steel could avail not. This was magic. This was power warped and whipped into service.

Starfish, taught by the Game and the Wizard, could see accurately that if the situation was on the Board only three pieces could act: the King, the Queen... and the Bishop. The King and Queen of the Castle by the Sea had already turned to the Temple and had received in return plates full of prayers and demands for more gold.

Now they turned to the only human representation of the Bishop left to them. The Wizard.

Starfish spent the day to herself. The Wizard, as part of her training in the Game, had taught her to read. It wasn't magic, reading, but in a strange way it was to Starfish. With the kitten, who was soon to be too old to be called such, and a book she had found in an old storage room the stones of the castle had guided her to, Starfish spent her day reading.

The book was old but had been lovingly cared for, in its use and hiding. Wrapped in a piece of old silk and a length of water-proofed leather it had survived its time in waiting quite well. The book was a collection of stories and records of a kingdom...a kingdom which ruled from a castle by the sea. A kingdom which could not be the one she lived in. The people in the book had such light and life. Even after all these centuries their lives shone from the pages.

Starfish learned a new word.

Noble.

The Game that evening started late, and Starfish felt for some odd reason... this would be the last game she played as Starfish. Whatever doom which had reached the Castle by the Sea on the tide, would have exacted its price by this time tomorrow.

Starfish didn't know how she knew this. The stones had said nothing, but she knew.

She and the Wizard battled well into the night and reached a place where, in this battle, there would be no victor. It was a stalemate, and the dawn was but a few hours away. The Wizard sighed, and for the first time in Starfish's eyes, he looked tired. She thought perhaps there was something that could be done to avert this judgment upon the castle and its people. The Wizard being a wizard read her mind like an open book.

"For this castle... and these self-proclaimed royals... nothing can be done."

The Wizard reached into his wizard garb and drew something from within it. He kept it hidden within his hands. After a moment of stillness, he placed the object in the center of the Board. It was about the same size as all the other game pieces, but it was not a game piece.

Starfish immediately recognized it.

Made of the same dark blue stones as the game pieces, the figurine was a carving of the same creature she had noticed throughout the castle, hidden secretly carved into the walls.

"Grab the bucket and the rope."

The Wizard rose snatching the small figurine off the Board quicker than Starfish had ever seen him move.

"It is time we <u>both</u> visit the Water Square. An old night ends, so a new day made dawn.

"Sometimes the only way to always win the game is to be able to call on another army. Learn the rules, and then learn when to break them!"

The Wizard moved quickly, and they encountered no one on their journey to the Water Square, and on their way the stones were silent. Starfish imagined throughout the Castle by the Sea no one slept but stayed awake, and huddled around hearth and family, drawing what last warmth could be given from fire and friend, sharing it with one another.

One last time.

The Water Square was silent and empty. Even the pipes that gurgled constantly remained silent. The tension in the castle had frozen more than people it would seem. The normal echo of waves from below sounded muffled to Starfish's ears. It was as if a large room filled with loud beings lowered its volume, so as not to miss what was to come next, what was to be said next.

The Wizard stood at the stone rail. In one hand, Starfish could see he held the figurine of the creature, and in the other...a dagger. Starfish felt like running, but her legs refused to respond. Even after so much time spent with the Wizard, she still had enough self-preservation to fear him, but with her old fear she also had respect for the Wizard.

Starfish decided. Her life was in the Wizard's hands, for she had had no life till he gave her one.

The Wizard called her to the rail.

"Are you ready?"

Starfish without hesitation, "Yes."

"Good. Put forth your hand"

She complied.

The edge of the dagger was very sharp, and for a moment Starfish felt nothing as he drew the blade across the palm of her hand, but then a rush of blood began to flow, and searing pain washed up her wrist.   Next, the Wizard placed the figurine on the stone floor before him, and taking the dagger slashed his palm. The blood quickly began to run from the Wizard's palm. Clenching his fist, he rose to stand over the figurine so that his blood dripped upon it. With his eyes, he commanded Starfish to do the same, and she joined him, her fist clenched pouring drops of red onto the figurine.

The Wizard stopped and drew some pieces of fabric from his garb and handed Starfish one. Following the Wizard's example, she used the piece of cloth to wrap and cover the wound on her palm.

Then, the Wizard threw the strange figurine down to the water below.

...and then, they both waited.

...and the stones of the Water Square waited too.

Then the Wizard spoke his last words to Starfish.

"Do not forget. The Bishop represents the Divine, the Spirit, the realms of Magic; so, he, or <u>she</u>, can fill the gaps the Tower creates in its defending. The Tower is solid; the Bishop is like the water which fills the seams of our World."

Starfish did not believe she would like to be the "water" that filled the seams of the world!

The Wizard heard her thought and smiled!

"Well, if not this world" he gestured around them. "...how about another one?!"

The Wizard then began to speak, but what issued from his mouth were not human words, and a normal human could not have understood. But Starfish did.

The Wizard was speaking the language of stones. He was Stone Speaking!

He said one word repeatedly, and the stones began to echo his speech, and they grew louder and louder. Starfish could feel the very foundations of the Castle by the Sea reply in sympathy to the word and vibrate in response. All over the village and the castle, people fell to their knees in prayer, and fell to their knees in fear for the vibration of the stones demanded it to be so.

And still the stone spoken word grew louder and louder. Saying only one thing: "Come!"

Repeatedly "Come", and at the bottom of the Water Square, deep below the raging spoiled waters, something replied...and then...

All the stones went silent.

The figurine fell quickly past the exposed rocks of the Water Square before hitting the water. The normally oil slicked and fouled waters were clearer, having for the first time in decades been given a reprieve from the constant deluge of filth and excrement from the populace above. Still a layer of fine foulness skimmed the surface, but the magic of the figurine and the Wizard pushed the scum from the water just at the point of the figurines entrance to the watery world below.

The figurine drifted in slow motion as it continued its journey downward, passing with each second deeper, headed toward a band of black water, unnourished by the Sun, and, moments before it reached this darker zone water, a scaled and clawed hand attached to a scaled arm reached from the dark water to snatch and grab the falling figurine, pulling it down into the darker depths below.

Starfish and the Wizard waited, for what Starfish did not know, but they did not wait for long.

From the Water Square and the water far down below a sound like a mighty roar heard through a colossal horn charged its way upward to fill the silent spaces encompassing the Water Square. Starfish tried to block out the sound by covering her ears, but the sound was too great.

The foundations of the Castle by the Sea once again trembled in sympathy to a sound its stones remembered.

The golden light of a new dawn arrived...and, down below....an ancient monster followed!

Its roar was deafening.

Starfish didn't know what "It" was before and even after its arrival, but it came, nonetheless. A great wash of air rose from the bottom of the Water Square pushing Starfish back. The Wizard was not moved, neither by the sound nor the force of air.

The creature's full arrival was marked by a mist of seawater which exploded upward into the Water Square. Water poured and streamed off its massive body in ribbons and rivers.

The beast from below. The creature etched in stone walls. The figurine made flesh.

If shadow blocked the sky far above as it scanned the open air with its two mammoth eyes, disks of jet black, rimmed in gold, they missed nothing.

It saw the Wizard.

It saw the little serving girl Starfish.

And, it roared again. Its great sleek black sides expanding hugely and contracting strongly. It roared... but not in hatred or hunger, but in recognition.

Slowly it closed its maw, an opening to an unseen world of fluids and acids, once more concealing rows and countless rows of barbed spear length fangs. Sadly, the oldest and the weakest at heart, in the village and the Castle by the Sea, died at hearing the great cry. A few others, not old or weak, also died, their minds already brimming full, sick with dread...the roar broke both the container and the person.

Silence tried to return, but before the great beasts echoing roar would allow it, a new sound rose from the background, and from the back of the great beast...the sound of chanting from alien throats and the pounding of many weapons.

Starfish saw them. Hundreds of them! Clinging to the back of the creature like pebbles clinging to the back of a warm blooded sea beast basking in the sun on the shore.

Water People!

Starfish knew now another story had been proven true. Proven by her own eyes!

On the back of the great creature the Water People's small eyes shone like stars in the night sky, and even in the shadow Starfish could see the iridescence of their green and blue, yellow and red scales; and, the gleaming glare of their shell armor and their coral-edged weapons. The sound they made stunned her. Their mouths open, weapons and armor rattling, they sounded like a surge of waves pushed by a storm against rocks and sand. A surge that changed coastlines. The Castle by the Sea was in the path of this wave.

...and, this wizard!

The Wizard stood steadfast, triumphant, his arms raised as if to embrace the great beast and the army of Water People which clung to it.

Starfish did the only thing she could think to do, encouraged by her own little newborn power, and emboldened by the small cup of magic she held... she ran home!

No cries of terror. No screams for help. No wide-eyed panic for her. She simply ran, determined to not be there anymore.

By which route Starfish traveled, what or who she may have seen or may have passed in her journey, she could not recall later.

She just, ran.

She opened her eyes. She felt warm and the straw beneath her felt softer than she remembered. She was awake. She lay still looking up at the stones above her head, which seemed much... much farther away today.

"You're awake."

A face hovered unfamiliar, into view before her opened eyes, lit by a bright beam of sunlight... sunlight?...

Then she recognized him. His eyes.

The Wizard!

She could never forget those eyes... though his eyes today... oddly, seemed clearer... Clearer?

"I was dreaming." She had not been commanded to speak, yet she spoke.

"Really? And what did you dream?" he was smiling. "Dreams are very important!"

It took time to form her thoughts, but then she began to speak.

"We were at the Water Square, and a great beast with an army of Water People had risen from below..."

The Wizard looked at her puzzled, as a strand of his gray black hair fell over his right eye.

"I see," the Wizard replied.

Then he began to laugh standing to his full height. For a second, she was afraid he would hit his head on the ceiling of her home but could see that this would not happen. The ceiling was still far away... too far!

She sat bolt upright, throwing off the covers which had wrapped her in warmth.

This was not her home!

This was not her room! Though she recognized it.

The kitten, which had been napping quiet peacefully at the edge of the bed, raised up its head to look at her questioningly. She was in the private bedroom of the eldest princess.

She was in the private bed of the eldest princess!

She turned to the Wizard and her eyes grew huge. Fogged by sleep, lulled by the comfort of a warm bed, she had not marked the alienness of her surroundings, or the physical transformation the Wizard had undergone. This was a much younger Wizard.

Gone was the white hair and most of the wrinkling. Gone was the old body and bent back. The Wizard stood tall and young; the edges of his being only slightly licked by age.

All she could do was stare, and the Wizard seeing this laughed harder.

Then he told her a tale.

The tale was about betrayal and deceit; about a jealous family member and a hungry group of lords and ladies; of an army paid for and a kingdom won by trickery; of the murder of a king and queen, beloved by their humble kingdom; of a little baby princess, lost... and of a baby girl found in the rocks; of a serving girl named Starfish, secretly beloved by a few who remembered; and, of the luck of an Uncle, a great and powerful wizard, at finding his princess..." even though she was in a den of thieves and had not only lost hope, but had never known it."

...when the Wizard finished his tale... She sat quietly for a long time.

Then...she began to cry.

Finally, the tears subsided and when the Wizard felt her strength return, he continued.

"This," the Wizard gestured to the walls surrounding them. "...is our family's legacy. Built by our ancestors thousands of years before. Built with the blessings of the Water People as long as we protected the Water Square and the waters below. This was the contract. The Water Square's light, fed by a distant sun, is the star the Water People live by. For the last decade or more... it has been a very dark time for them."

"But..." she stopped.

"Yes?"

"Magic is evil."

"Ah," the Wizard nodded sagely. "Only when used by evil people for evil goals."

"But..."

"Yes?" The Wizard was very patient.

Finally, she said it, "The blood?"

"Oh," the Wizard said with raised eyebrows. "Blood in the water is not like blood on the ground. At least not in the Water People's eyes. Carried on the wind the blood scent may travel a mile or more. In the water it can travel much, much farther. To the Water People blood is the most sacred thing. Therefore, for tens of thousands of years they have signed all their contracts in it.

"With our blood in the water we just simply identified ourselves and renewed the contract. Not only that, with our magic blessed blood our connection is now greater to them. They are highly honored.

"With one action you say: I am not afraid to put my blood in the waters with yours. Let us live or die together!"

Work immediately began to bring the Water Square back to its former beauty. The sewage and waste pipes were removed, and the walls were repaired and their glorious multicolored murals, which had all but vanished under the rulership of the usurpers, were brought back to vivid life. The great pumps were repaired, so once again seawater filled the great pit. When visitors, and children, and families, and young couples in love visited the Square, they found beyond the railing, a green crystalline pool, lit at night by the glowing corals that once again flourished on the walls holding the great column of water. Corals once again cared for by the tender hands of the Water People.

The Water Square was lovely.

On rare occasions Water People frolicked in the pool, and on festival days, both human and Water People musicians would make music together, and all would dance. The Water People in their water. Humans, mostly, on the dry land of the Water Square's concourse. Some of the braver, or perhaps inebriated, human dancers began or ended a dance by plunging into the pool. The Water People found this to be funny and welcomed all.

Greatest of all days was a ceremony where the hidden wealth of the Castle by the Sea returned. It rose glistening into the sunlight from the great waters below, secretly given to the Water People in the kingdom's time of woe and protected until this time. Carried by the King of the Water People's royal guard they returned to the sunlight ten massive sea chests made from blue stone. Chests filled with giant blue pearls with liquid wet surfaces that when touched felt dry; large ropes of gold and silver wrought in the depths below; ancient silken tapestries unfaded by age, and treasured manuscripts from the great library long thought destroyed and gone forever; armor and swords crafted by Masters from steel forged from the iron found in the dark blue stones found only here; these and many more things appeared from the great chests, but the most important of all, a pair of crowns. Simple, unadorned objects with a pure simplicity which could have only been achieved by a master craftsperson. Their surfaces had no flaws.

Etched with an intricate pattern of finely engraved lines that were hard to see in daylight, at night they would reveal themselves like a spiderweb of light. Glowing coral had been powdered and enameled into the grooves of these crowns of gold and platinum.

The Castle by the Sea changed, not overnight, but still rather quickly. With attention and love and care, which had been missing all these years, the grand castle began to regain her beauty. With the help of masons to fix the stones, metal workers to repair the old furnaces, furors and weavers once again to carpet the floors, a dedicated group of loyal followers to scrub and clear away the dirt and the dust, and lanterns, many, many, bright and illuminating lanterns- the Castle by the Sea was made whole.

Some of the old serving staff stayed on, and in time they were forgiven, though most could not forgive themselves. The false lords and ladies vanished over the following weeks, finding no place in this new kingdom... also finding no supporters to their claims to royalty.

A Queen lives in the Castle by the Sea.

They say the people there are incredibly happy for she is very compassionate and thoughtful. The Water People say her name means cherished.

She used to be afraid but is rarely afraid anymore.

Her uncle, a great wizard, taught her the Game and the ways of magic, and, on the day she was crowned Queen, her uncle asked her this question:

"What is a pawn?"

And, with hardly a second thought and with a smile she had mastered, she said:

"I am!"

Ole Mary Margaret

Mary Margaret loved her cats.

Nice and sleek... juicy and fat!

For the Dark Days were here and there were no more rats!

All eaten,
Like the birds
Like the chickens
The cows...the herds.

And even the swine was now divine!
...For the starving there are no laws!

Oh! But when the Change swept the Earth
And the living saw the birth
Of things that walked in shadow,
And rare fine dirt spit forth seeds of no worth
The picky soon changed the tune of their prattle.

Meat....meat!
The hungry they did seek.
Beat....beat
The marching of their feet.

First the stores.
Soon empty floors.
Then the doors.
Kicking, screaming, roars!
Then the wars.
Skirmishes for apple cores!

Oh, the lucky?...
The poor!
Needing soldiers, they had more!

Angry youth
All claw and tooth.
Ghetto troops
With gats to shoot!

Hungry?...yes!!!
But for them...nothing new!
Raised on less and making do.

A recipe for an empty stew!

Everyone knew, Mary Margaret.

The old cat lady.

Her big house smelled foul
Sharp scented ammonia it did prowl
And day or night
Her pride was quite loud.

Sitting in her windowpanes,
Watching when the children spilled
From the school up the hill.
Watching as the people made
Their weary ways throughout the day.

Her cats would watch.
All whiskers and eyes!

But now...
...it was we who looked inside!

And it wasn't long before the question was asked:
Have you ever tasted....cat?

Big Kay was the toughest,

The roughest, the meanest man about,
And smart, so smart
He made survival an art.

He understood
That a cat could be food,
But it wouldn't be good
If they ate them all through.

So...with some persuasion,
Big Kay clawed a deal.
Mary Margaret would do the raisin'.
Big Kay would bring strays in.

And with the flesh of those he killed
Her kitties could have a meal,
For the dark days were not yet so bad
That cannibalism had become a fade.

This new system...with cats as victims
Over time began to work.
Enough meat was had,
Both the good and the bad,
And both new partners proved their worth.

Ole Mary Margaret had a new life.
A butcher and not a butcher's wife,
For that she had been long ago...
Before the accident that took her love Home.

She was quick with blade after she suffocated the strays
And the ones next to eat.

But a special few
Of her feline crew
Would never know slicing,
Or watery stews.

And one among them

Was the most cherished of all...
Pixie, a tabby,
A mother of Fall.

Born in October, under a crumbling grey wall.

She was prodigious of litter
Fertile her sweet paws.

And lovely of fur
Like a bright silken shawl.
Warm to the touch
And lovely to brush.
Her claws never touched skin.
Gentle her rub
As she nuzzled your thumbs
With small little kisses
With her nose and her tongue.

Ole Mary Margaret truly....truly...only loved her.

Pixie....her angel.

Then one night...the night did crack
Like the whip of the spine,
The smack of a bat!
And somewhere...
Something, broke loose
And the birds would have flown
If any had still sat in their roosts.

Then....silence....

The morning was grey and quiet.
The pressure felt before a riot
Or before something goes horribly wrong.

The cats were particularly silent
And all that morning and into the day
Mary Margaret questioned what was at play.

But only at twilight
Did she notice the tom.
A black as night cat
She stumbled upon.
Curled in a corner
In a home it had made
Of an old empty box
From a window display.

It looked at her...
It looked at her!
Without any fear
Eyes reaching in
Under her skin.

The air grew cold
As Mary Margaret stumbled away
And just for one moment
She thought...
She heard words pray!

"What did they say?!"

The moment it passed,
And with a little nervous small laugh
Mary Margaret...
Walked away.

For the next two weeks
She avoided that corner
And the jet-black tom
Her unwanted border.

For it was unwanted!
An alien intrusion.

Bringing fear, and dreams,
Nightly confusion
Into Mary Margaret's
Poor widowed heart.

Where had he come from?!
Had he arrived in the night?...
Or was he a stray,
Big Kay
Had grabbed on first sight?!

She didn't know.

But this she did
Of its presence she would like to be rid...

Then!.....it was gone.

Like the last heard remnants
Of a dwindling song,
That had tortured the ears
And had lasted too long!

Ole Mary Margaret sighed her relief
And in just a few days was back selling meat.

"Normalcy" returned
To her large crumbling abode
But things began to change for the worse
As the Winter grew cold.

Pixie was...
            ....pregnant.

Of course, Pixie being pregnant was not a new thing
Just a cog in the wheels
Of the feline butcher machine.

Yet, this time things were different....
Things were not normal.

For Mary Margaret could sense
The approaching of turmoil!

Pixie once warm,
Once so loving,
Acted very odd
As the litter was coming.

For now, she shied from all human touch
And cried when brushed...
And her little wet kisses
Came not as often
Not nearly as much.

On his monthly visit,
Big Kay could feel something was ill.
Mary Margaret was rather generous
With this week's part of the deal.
Her eyes kept shifting
To something in back,
To some cluttered room
Where her possessions were stacked.
But Big Kay was not known for his heart
So, he held in his questions
Before compassion could start,
And walked out her door
To get back to his art.

Two months passed
And in the house of Ole Mary Margaret sadness it sat...
And fear and pain
And unwanted tears,
For Pixie was late
And no litter appeared.

Her most precious cat
Lay sallow and fat.
Unable to move.
A knot

Caught in the loom.

Each day a debate
"What should I do?
Open her up?!
No!
That will not do!
I am no vet.
No doctor it's true,
But I must do something
Or my Pixie, my heart, will be through!"

Sadly...Mary Margaret
Could not decide
As she watched her precious love
Slowly grow fatter,
Destined to die.

"Why?!!!!"
Mary Margaret, she wailed, and she cried.

It was that tom!
That alien thing!!
That foreign intruder
Who brought her this pain.
Some messenger of doom
That had sat in a box
In the corner of a room...
She knew she kept locked!

Now she remembered!
That was the room.
She had sealed a tomb.
A reminder of her life
Before her days
Turned to stark gloom.

Was it a trick that Big Kay had played?
Taking advantage at some vulnerable moment
Introducing that stray.

But Mary Margaret saw no wisdom in that,
For her partner to risk
The road they had mapped.

Then...

In the deepest day of Winter,
Amongst the frost, and the splinters
Of old fallen trees
With futures of cinders.

Ole Mary Margaret was a shadow of self.
Her steps dragging
A weak picture of health.
Wheezing and winded
She moved through that day...
From room to room
A ghost she portrayed.

Her cats....her cats
Gave her wide birth.
She the matron of felines
Who gave them their worth...

....and the corner
Where Pixie fat sat,
A weak weary picture
Beginning to crack...

...A shape most unrecognizable as cat!

Now a tumorous mass
That writhed in wet pain,
And under its body
A growing foul stain!

Mary Margaret finally...decided!

"Tomorrow, tomorrow...
I will send Pixie, Home...
Tomorrow, tomorrow...
I also shall go..."

In the next room that night
Ole Mary Margaret kept watch
In an old beaten chair
By a weary old clock...

...she would not sleep!

...she would not!

....but....

She was Ole Mary Margaret
Not the Younger or Spry
So, it was with good intentions
That she still closed her eyes......

....Mary Margaret awoke suddenly!

No!

The air was cold!
Too cold she felt on her skin.
The house was quiet.
Too quiet,
Of any cat din.

Slowly she turned her poor tortured gaze....
To the room where her sweet Pixie had last laid.

A pool of shadows
Greeted her eyes.
Signs of movement
Her eyes did not spy.

"...Pixie..."

....silence...

She called again.

"...Pixie?..."

But still no sound from her friend...

She should rise.
She should run!
Quick to see what had become
Of her dear...
But something froze her...
Something other than fear!
Some encroaching force
Held her quick to that chair.

Behind her...a noise.
A creeping clicking implored
"Turn, turn."
She suddenly yearned.

Creeping and clicking.
Now, a gurgling breath.
Hissing and pulsing
Something it crept.
Ole Mary Margaret
Frozen in dread,
Hands digging and clawing
At the stitches and threads.
A movement she caught
In the corner of eye.
A stirring of air as it moved to her side.

Her eyes snapped shut
As if fleeing a dream.
Her lips pressed tight
Holding back screams.

Then...
A tentative touch
Of a small little paw...
And the piercing of flesh
From the sharpest of claws!

Her body shook as the claws clawed up her leg.
One at a time,
Slowly it came.
A cold heavy weight
On her heat she could feel that it fed.
Clicking and creeping.
Mary Margaret was weeping.
Gone the thinking of anymore sleeping
And choking on fear
To silence she fled.

It sat on her legs.
It sat on her chest.
Each little claw
Leaving small dots of red.

A long hairless tail she could feel
Encircled her legs.
Tight as a snake,
Yet slimy and wet.

And in her face
A fetid breath breathed.
Kissing her lips
And making her see!

Ole Mary Margaret opened her eyes
Forced to return to the dream and it's churning dark tide
She gazed upon It!
And that left her no choice.
She screamed a mad scream
Giving dread to her voice!

...bang-bang-bang!...

...bang-Bang-Bang!...

...Bang-Bang-BANG!

"Someone is going to die!!!"
Was what Big Kay thought
As he opened his eyes.

It was late in the night
And someone was brave,
Waking him up.
Banging his gate!

After explanations
And humble decrees
He found himself out
In the Night's sullen peace.
To Ole Mary Margaret's
He slowly was led
And he knew by the silence
Some blood had been shed.

Guided he was
Through the broken front door
His goons had breached
When they heard a dread note.

"Her scream...Her scream!"
They all kept repeating,
Like it was a prayer
To some God they entreated.

In a room...

A room
Off the first floor,
Big Kay entered
To discover true horror.

Ole Mary Margaret
Was now Mary Margaret the Dead!
Eyes wide open
Lamps to some dread.
The scream on her face
Frozen to bone...
A prey to something...
Something unknown.

Covered all over
In red running dots,
Like a balloon
Repeatedly popped!
By a fine little needle
That never knew thread...
Just old lady skin...
And old lady flesh!

In the patterns of dust,
That lay on the floor,
Lay many small prints
Of many small paws...
But instead of four or five digits
Were the scratch of three claws
Which gave Big Kay reason...
A reason to pause!

Tricking the eye
One could see the tracks of the many
But one...just one
Created this frenzy.

Small footsteps of brown
That turned into red
As Mary Margaret's favorite, Pixie,

Was found dead.

It was like she had been skinned
From inside to out
All that remained
Was some fur and her snout.

Big Kay recoiled
This scene it disturbed,
Every inch of his being,
Even down to his nerves.

Still reeling and rolling
From what he had seen,
Big Kay finally noticed
A missing part of the scene.

The cats!

Not a trace, not a sound,
Not even a glance.
Not even their eyes that shine in the game
Of stop and advance.

Once there were many!

Purring and moving,
Watching and waiting,
Under the foot,
Quicker to scoot,
Preening and pressing,
touching and testing.
Now there was none
Use to be tons!

...A chilling stronger hand
...All in his mind,
Touched Big Kay,
His skin and his spine.

Big Kay the artist knew.

It was time to retire
Striking a match...

...he fed her house to the fire!
To all that had been there.
To all that transpired!

Ole Mary Margaret loved her cats.

Nice and sleek... juicy and fat!

For the Dark Days are here!
Where are the rats?!

Eaten all
By a great...
Black...
Cat!

https://youtu.be/zXl8moqqoBY

Ms. Maybelline

Cats have tiny heads!
I mean their skulls when compared to ours is really small.

I reload the BB gun.

There were more tonight than usual, but what's usual about
that!

My neighbor Gerry. Taking out his trash. Gives me a funny
look.

What?!
Can't a lady sit on her back porch with a BB gun at night!

He thinks I'm crazy. He won't listen. Nobody would. But
thankfully I'm not completely alone. There have been others
stocking up at the store. All of us pushing and pulling carts
filled with cans and dry food. I cleared all the best of the
canned. One whole shelf.

I can't let Gerry distract me.
Moon's on my side.
Full, and beautiful...and cold.
How many more tonight?!
I can't give up! My babies are counting on me.

Felix and Coral.
After the divorce they're all I have left.
Charles...
I've been paying attention. Watching for signs. They were
right there.

Poison!
Ha!
Poison my ass.

They didn't catch me sleeping. The homeless ones clued me in.
Of course, they would be the first to show signs of the Death to
come.

None of the food I leave out at night gets eaten anymore.
Making my nightly rounds at first, I just thought they weren't
that hungry... but all of them at the same time! It didn't make
sense.

There!
(pap! pap!...pap!)
No, you don't! Not tonight! Not ever!

The FDA says blame the Chinese.
Blame the Chinese!
Last time I checked the labels, all the ingredients were in
English!
It's in the food!
I know it!

When you add it all up and looked to point a finger, point it at
your local officials, your mayors and your governors,
Washington and the Administration! The whole thing!

Right there!
"Administration."
Administration of what?!
Just asked the Tuskegee airmen... you can't! That's the point!
I see you!
(pap! pap!)
I just fed you a week ago!
Not another one...
Why?!
Whatever did I do to deserve this?

I must remember to restock the cooler and rebait the traps. Though I've yet to catch any that way. They liked meat, just not the meat I have to offer.

It broke my heart to kill Paintbrush.

He was the first.
A mangy old tom, all black except for a wash of white at the end of his tail. Like he stuck it in a bucket of white paint.

Paintbrush.

He lasted a long time, I guess. One of last ones to eat something I had to offered.
Mangy...but I could touch him.
It's different when they trust you. Says something about your character.
Everything you do and have done feels validated.

I didn't think the streets could be so silent without them. None of them was eating anymore... I still put out fresh food. They needed me... in a way they still do.

There's a small auto garage a few blocks from here and they have two junkers sitting on blocks on the sidewalk. I would complain but the little ones that live around that area liked to use the cars as cover. That is why, each night, I place one bowl of food and one bowl of water under each car's back bumper. One week ago... I went to refresh everything, and... there was Paintbrush... but he'd been hurt. Hurt real bad.

Some of the others must've finally cornered him. Paintbrush had survived everything till then... but not this... there must have been too many.

I heard him before I saw him. He didn't make a sound, no crying, no purrs... but I could hear his claws grazing the concrete as he crawled beneath the cars sitting on blocks.

I stepped back to see if I could catch sight of him, but even squatting I could only make his shadow out underneath the middle of one of the cars bathed in street light.
I tried to call him, but he wouldn't budge.
I knew something was wrong.
I always bring a flashlight-
(pap! pap!...pap! pap!...pap!)
You would think a modern city would have nicely lit streets, but no, so I carry a flashlight.
I turned it on... And I saw him!

He was pretty torn up. All he could do was crawl. It took him about 30 minutes to crawl out from under the car...
I just ran home.
What could I do?! I didn't know what to do!
I still couldn't get to sleep when two hours before morning I went back and found Paintbrush and put him out of his misery.

...A human head is different.
Now is different. I can do something!

...*Paintbrush*...

Why are there so many?!
(pap! pap! pap!...pap! pap!)
"Mrs. Johnson! You can't keep doing that!"
"Shut up Gerry!"
It's Ms. Johnson. Ms. Maybelline to my friends.
Charles is gone.

Gerry's going to call the cops. Last night he had said so.
Enough was enough. But he has nothing to protect... not anymore. Their kitty vanished 10 days ago.
Gerry also said not to talk to his kids anymore.
But didn't they deserve to know! Didn't everyone!
Gerry wears a tie every day, and a frown for me.
"The Cat Lady."
That's what he calls me.
I call him a jackass!

At the end of the day, <u>Gerry</u>, your life will have meant nothing.

No one wants to hear.
By the time they figure it out it'll be too late.
...If <u>they</u> only believed!
They'd just shrug it off again.

"Blame China!"

Everybody else just call it punishment for nine lives and laugh!

The writing is on the community message board: missing cat ads cover the whole thing!
This is the End!
(pap!...pap!...pap! pap! pap! pap! pap!)

They look and smell terrible. Why can't people see this?! I know they sure can smell it!

I already have too much on my plate.
Coral almost didn't survive the FDA fiasco, but I know my babies and could see how the "poison" immediately affected her.

My vet is the best!

Coral made it, and her and Felix will survive this. They have a human on their side, and I got plenty of the BBs!.. Though my aim is not getting better!

Coral has problems with her kidneys now, but with proper diet and medicine... I must get more!

Before this nightmare, Coral's death was many years away.
Reload!... Just in time!
They keep coming!
(pap! pap!...pap!)

They know Felix and Coral are inside. How, I don't know! I've washed down the sides of the house with water and bleach at least four times now, but they keep coming. Felix and Coral miss being outside, but they can't go out...not <u>now</u>... Probably not ever again. I can't risk losing them!

Sirens?

... No... I'm not afraid of jail. Anyway, never heard of a law where shooting already dead cats is a crime.
Bring in the forensics!

I'm tired...I'll sleep later.

More?! Dammit!
(pap!)
God!
(pap)
Damn!
(pap!...pap! pap!)
It!!
Hmmm?... Maybe I am becoming a better shot.
I don't feel proud.
I feel sick...
Angry!
(...wreowrr...wreOWRR!)
No!
That was close!
One more lost. One more I have to watch for!
I must be strong. I have to be stronger!
I am all that stands-
(CRASH! tinkle-tinkle-THUMP! wrEOWRRR!)
No!!!
That's inside the house!
I need more BBs!
Why is the doorknob so cold?
Run!
I can feel my bad joints explode.
No time!
Not that sound.

Always the same- first a cry of warning then a plaintive one followed by the sound of pain and then... a cry! A shriek like a tortured baby!
(CRASH!)

The bedroom!
No! No! No! No! No!
"Coral! No!"
Her beautiful eyes! Replaced by those cold things! Why? Why? Why?...

Felix! There's so much blood... but Felix... he can't have this much blood?! He's too small!
No! I don't accept it!
My face is wet.
I taste the salt.

Are those sirens?
Charles?!...No.
Gerry called the cops!
No cat could ever love you, Gerry...
... My babies!...

They're supposed to protect us... all of us!
It's all their fault and I blame THEM!
They have the power, so they are the cause.

I feel cold.
You think it would be simple.
Just a... classic movie scenario repeated:
shoot them in the head?!
But it ain't that easy...
Because cats... have tiny heads!

THE BARD

Tomorrow Laughs

Tomorrow laughs
full bellied and bold
clutching Today
lifeless and cold.
Its shadow a victor
no eye may behold.

It kicks Yesterday
into a corner of shame
and covers its presence
in moments unclaimed.
Tomorrow then sups up
whatever remains.

Tomorrow laughs
with swollen wide fingers
that beat a staccato
on bells and their ringers,
and the Future she smiles
say those who have seen her.

Standing full height
Tomorrow touches the sky
Sunrise's reflection
it's pale mighty eye
awake on the waters
of the oncoming tide.

Tomorrow laughs
that's its echo you hear
in the engulfing broad silences
of the Night's
layered tiers
of something approaching
that waits to appear.

Tomorrow laughs
and laughs
and laughs
and laughs
then laughs even more:
over weeping word widows
and motherless brides;
over lid welded warriors
and rich men's asides;
over swollen bellied babies unbundled
and covered in flies;
over writers and written;
over lovers and sighs.

Over everything
seen, held, coddled, and clutched
Tomorrow laughs
with a grin
finger to lips, hush.

Tomorrow laughs,
as sure as leaves descend
in the Fall.
Ashes
or boxes
Tomorrow laughs at us all.

Story of the Skull in the Desert

Ever seen a corpse in the blazing sun
the blood congeals and doesn't run.
Over the body the flies do spread
like rotten butter on moldy bread.
The skin is blue, the eyes are red.
The body huge, and air-filled bed.
The tongue sticks out all swollen and black,
a frozen smile, the teeth can't clack.
The legs are limp, the arms are slack,
a fallen in house without a tack.
The chest doesn't move for lack of breath,
no future goals or dreams are left.
A broken book you cannot heft
but if you could
the last page says:
Death.

The 1st Riddle

Silence sat sitting
in a house within the sound
of Echo's hall hallowed
to embrace the shallow ground.

Red umber hues the breeze
dark cliffs that face the sea
grasp skies of darks and grey
as wind whips waves to quay.

No life bestirs the plain
nor rains that wash away
the dust off mortal panes
lying bleached beneath the Stain.

The stones that use to speak
underneath the mortal's feet
have begun their subtle leak
back to ancient shapes.

The decay of every page
lays near and dear to dust
both fruits of all things lost
lacking hands to keep and trust.

The Ageless Armor sits
to its side the Sword of Lore
their color red with rage
for the lords who are no more.

Twice Sung

the tale is done
the story sung
the clock clicks no more
the gamble made
the stakes displayed
the Gambler's game Amour
twice the Singer
sung the tale
as dark night did fade
and twice the chill
that sweep the room
tossed quiet sleepers shapes

his hollow cheeks
his darken caste
his crippled countenance
his painful tones
his dread-filled poem
his haunted fountain pen

surely, no man may must
allow the heart to rust

but upon hearing such a tale
would rather run away
to cast out the vulnerable flaw
into the Ocean's gaping maw
so, to avoid that hungry touch
that kills the heart you clutch

and horror, and horror
to have heard the tale twice told
and sorrow, and sorrow
for love once warm now cold

The 2nd Riddle

The house of distant shadows
hidden in the vale
grows deeper in its weeping
ribbed in bones of pale.

The clockwork constellations still
their frozen fingers pinned
threaded deep was the strike
that let the Other in.

The day was night, the moment bare
of breath and living thrust
the sleeper's dream washed distant shore
as their spirit doors were brushed.

One flaw, one crack, was all the need
as the Other breached the seal
one step, one theft of every soul
was the sickening of the deal.

For the making of a place
to wear lament condemn
the Other strips away
the breath which holds us in.

To fill a place with silence
devoid of sound and life
to create a place of shadows
where houses weep in fright.

The Other lays its mark,
dead gray its symbol fine,
creating fields of lost
in the corners of the mind.

The harvest fat and sweet
the taste of pain and why
the ending clear complete
the Other's way - comply.

Leave what's hidden in the vale
for it is of the nevermore
the house shadows there lay weeping
for the Other is at the door.

The Carving Lantern

Hello Jack!
why do you run?

Hello Scratch!
cause of what I've done.

What is that
I'm questioning?

I stole from them
everything!

Life, where will you go
once it's done?

I'll go and play
with everyone.

But they will never
let you in,
because of all
your mortal sins.

So, what is it
I can do,
walk the earth
until I'm thru?

Take this piece
of burning stone,
then the Night
is not so long.

But what shall I
keep it in?

Your hollowed head

with a dead man's grin,
will be your lantern
to light your way,
at least that's what
the Deadmen say!

Howard Portman was an artist, and he loved many things. He loved the sight and smell of fresh vivid paints growing on a once blank canvas. He loved the precision of the Renaissance masters, and the childlike simplicity of the Impressionists. He loved his brushes with their many shapes, and how happy they felt when they were in his hand. He loved his studio and the numerous magazines which talked about him, showed his genius, in limited format. He even loved the critics, especially when they got it oh-so-wrong, showing a patience at their lack of imagination in the face of his true creativity: his shining brilliance. Howard Portman was an artist and his master's degree behind its sheet of glass said it was so, predominately on his living room wall.

He should have been happy, but he wasn't.

He hated.

He hated so deeply that he was sick with it. Everything he touched, everything he tasted, everything he encountered was washed thoroughly in his hatred. It wasn't a big hate, meaning an emotion for some large social injustice aimed at one group, one state, or one people. No. Howard Portman's ire was for one man, and one man alone. Howard Portman hated Mr. Lee.

If he had been a violent man, Howard, would have killed Mr. Lee a long time ago, but Howard was an artist, and artists don't destroy; they create!

He hadn't always hated the kind and considerate Mr. Lee, as the old man was viewed by most anyone. His hatred had grown. A small seed at first, it had spread its feelers and grown, swelling and ripening, drawing nourishment from his unacknowledged weaknesses, till it sat fat and swollen, a black gourd upon the vine.

The seed of his hatred had been planted several years ago, when he had first moved to the small town of Derrick, California.

Seven years ago, coming off a successful gallery show and a profitable ad campaign he had designed for an up-and-coming Silicon Valley company, Howard's management felt it was time for him to relocate. That he was at that moment of a pre-zeitgeist where removal from most distractions would benefit him the most. Howard at that point in his career, lived in a 24 hour-a-day city, a polished steel and shimmering glass undulating creature built on the back of an older one made of black iron and red brick and large dead trees. San Francisco. His management loved the idea of setting up shop in a small town. Small towns meant to them smaller prices, and even smaller excesses...or at least the avenues too them. At first, Howard didn't like the idea. Moving away from the hub of energy and influence which he'd grown so used to. This feeling soon changed.

Howard had begun to feel the claustrophobia from the constant jockeying for position and the constant and unavoidable sharing of the spotlight, which he had to do endure with the other artists in the city. This was far beneath the caliber of the artist he was becoming. Besides, often is the tale of the artist paramour setting up shop away from the common and trite, the hollow and vapid, to fine their truest voices that would cement their legacy for eras yet to come. A sanctuary with that artist and his or he art the deity of devotion, creating a place of pilgrimage for the devoted and adoring fans and the ever present ingenues, innocent of eye and malleable, to congregate and swarm. After a quick search Derrick, California, a quaint rural community located amongst the evergreen pines and the towering sequoias of Northern California, provided itself. A small house just on the outskirts would be the base from which they felt Howard's international career could, and naturally <u>should</u>, spring forth from. A small and old, but more than adequate, house it was far enough away from the heart of the small town and its small population to be intruded upon regularly, yet still close enough to be restocked with supplies with ease. Howard thought the house and the town were great ideas, and location "perfect" for his particular brand of inspiration. Howard could see himself one day being a point of pride in the hearts and minds of the townspeople, who would be able to say one day with great pride and large open smiles to the many visiting tourists:

"Yes, Howard Portman lives here! The Howard Portman Museum and Gallery is just down the street!"

It was only a month after moving to the small town of Derrick, California when Howard woke up to find the yet unfamiliar streets and houses decorated with a familiar image and shape. Orange and round, it was the great harbinger of approaching Fall. When the verdant green of nature's youth fell before mature rich slashes of reds, the deep aches of yellows, and the full glow of orange. Autumn displaying her colors, a warm last embrace of a dying world.

Pumpkins.

It would seem the small town of Derrick had some notoriety already, pre-Howard Portman. Every year, for the past 70 years, Derrick County has held their Annual Derrick

County Pumpkin Festival, which was known county and statewide. People, and those other things called "tourists", would come from hundreds of miles around to fill their bellies full with warm and spicy slices of pumpkin bread, and cooled wedges of pumpkin pie heaped high with dollops of sugary pure white whipping cream; to drink cool pumpkin juice, a foreign, yet familiar thing to most in taste, if not in texture; to stand in the shadows of the large and fat mammoth mutant pumpkins grown in the rural backfields for size rather than taste; and, the highlight of it ALL, to gaze at the entries for that year's Derrick Pumpkin Carving Contest, the event which every year drew the biggest crowds.

And, for the lucky and talented few, it was an opportunity to enter a carved pumpkin, and to possibly win a prize and bragging rights.

Howard Portman, artist, decided to enter the pumpkin carving contest that first year as a new resident. Decided to use this small local event in this small town, as a small stage, to announce his arrival to the citizens of Derrick, California. With a phone call Howard had several ripe and ready pumpkins delivered to his home and studio, specifying clearly over the phone he wanted pumpkins:

"Good for carving."

"Going to give old Mr. Lee a run for his money this year, I bet..." the man, Nick, commented.

The man, who had in one handshake: announced his successful delivery of Howard's pumpkins; his long-standing success as a handyman-at-large; and his preference to be called Nick rather than Nicholas, which his mother still called him to his utter annoyance and humiliation, looked expectantly, head tilted to the side eyes squinting in the glare of the sun. The corners of his mouth chewing on a grin.

"...Talented guy like you!... but still, Mr. Lee is _damn_ good!" Nick awed and simian head scratched his opinion.

The impressed look on Nicholas', preferred Nick's, face amused Howard for the briefest of moments, but only for a moment.

This was the first time he had heard mentioned of a, "Mr. Lee".

Mr. Lee, an expat from China, had for the previous 17 years won first place in every pumpkin carving contest held in Derrick. Other similar events in other counties didn't count. 17 wins, well, 16. There was one year where Mister Lee won, but in a crowd winning gesture gave it to his biggest competitor, Mrs. Rexle. Mrs. Rexle, whom everyone knew that year had been diagnosed with terminal cancer and was not likely to see another pumpkin contest again after this one. She didn't.

At first mention of Mr. Lee and his previous victories, Howard initially believed perhaps one of the great craftsmen from China was here, in this small town, but soon found out otherwise. In the major art circles he roamed, Howard had never heard mention of a "Lee" anything in this area, and he wouldn't have. Mr. Lee <u>wasn't</u> an artist. Mr. Lee was a retired 81-year-old Professor of Archaeology and Anthropology from China, small and apple wrinkled, who had spent his adult life mostly with his face: dirty from some currently uncovered ruin, or pressed into the dusty pages of some old book, or earnest, lecturing before numb to eager faces in a university lecture hall. Howard could only smile and shake his head in feigned sadness at the thought his entry would mean Mr. Lee's 17 years of uncontended victories would come to an end. It was a small price to pay, Howard thought, him being the only notable artist for miles around and farther.

The Pumpkin Festival that year went off without a single hitch or hiccup for anyone and everyone involved. All except for one person. Lucky visitors from miles around, and farther, left with bellies and senses full, small swelled satellites, rich and filled with the vibrancy and the meat of dying pumpkins. Happy and smiling, all returned to their near or distant homes, hands grasping bags filled with pumpkin bread and pumpkin pies; arms locked round knocked ripe balls of orange, fat pumpkins yet to be carved for Halloween, less than a week away; and hands storing away other items bought or won to commemorate their experiences, all more than prepared to return again next year for more of the same. Many were those who went home with tales of that year's Pumpkin Carving Contest's entries, and of the 18th win for the still-as-then undefeated and very old Chinese man, Mr. Lee.

Mr. Lee when he climbed up on the stage to receive his award, took a second to thank the people, and his competitors, giving special mention to Howard's work. Howard Portman had won two awards: Second Place, and Honorable Mention. Going up onto the stage, Howard had thanked the judges, the crowd and the townspeople, but gave no words, congratulatory or otherwise, to his competitors. He couldn't, for inside he was seething.

Howard Portman was an artist, a particularly good artist. A great artist! He could never lose to just *anyone*, never!... and in his mind, he didn't lose that first year! Howard's carved pumpkin for the contest was beautiful. Its lines were clean and well executed. The theme reflecting the changing season, the falling leaves. Howard had created something he would feel sad to see rot and vanish, as he knew it would. It wasn't his finest work. His finest work is not meant for the mundane, a pedestrian event such as "pumpkin contest". A flaw here or there. A few mistakes where the carving blade knife dived too deep into the rind, or a cut's sweep was a little "rough". Still...it <u>was</u> beautiful.

Mr. Lee's pumpkin for the contest, on the other hand, transcended his, soaring high above Howard's mortal, common work which left Howard's mouth bitter and dry. For every well-articulated line of Howard's pumpkin, Mr. Lee's threw back a greater line in laughter and mockery. Mr. Lee's pumpkin was a scalpel, carving into Howard's, saying with each cut:

"This is what you could be!"

It wasn't possible! Mr. Lee wasn't an artist! Howard would've heard of him. Mr. Lee, that old and slightly bent Chinese man, was not better than him!

Thus...a foul seed was planted in Howard Portman, artist.

The next year, as the Annual Derrick County Pumpkin Festival drew near, Howard Portman, still stinging from last year's embarrassment, decided he would not enter the carving contest. A high caliber artist's work was well beyond this local competition, he kept telling himself, but everywhere he went in the town, people...would not let him rest!

"You going to enter this year?" Kevin Kurin, the towns local DJ, asked as Howard stepped onto the sidewalk, both arms holding two equally full brown paper bags of groceries.

"Great job you did last year! Sad you didn't win though" Teresa, the cute barista had commented smiling as she handed Howard his extra-large iced coffee. Her forearms were covered in a swirl of vibrant tattooed stories and memories. "Mr. Lee is really good!"

"What?! That'd be a real shame. You really should enter again." Nicholas, preferred Nick, said, his head under the kitchen sink in Howard's home. Nick had proven his word from their first meeting at being the town's handyman. What Nick had failed to mention at the time, which naturally he wouldn't, was his inability to finish projects in a timely manner and his inability to be flexible around the schedule of his clients, and so-called friends. Howard had finally in frustration given him a set of keys to his home, to avoid the consequential frustration of being a victim to Nick's tardy behavior.

With two weeks away from the annual festival, Howard found himself on the phone ordering a few pumpkins for carving. Pumpkins for the approaching contest. They arrived at night and he immediately went to work. He worked slowly and diligently taking his time in sketching his designs onto the pumpkin to guide the carving he would do a day or two before the festival. He had learned this the hard way the year before, when one of his first entries perished way before the contest, followed by two more. The art achieved by carving pumpkins is a temporary thing and not meant to last long into the future, so the professional pumpkin carver sketched and sketched again refining a map to the piece which would be eventually revealed in the final carving.

It was only natural living in a town that dedicated itself to pumpkins for a good part of every year, that Howard, merely by osmosis, learned some basic facts and a few not so basic facts about pumpkins.

Those first Europeans who set foot on the soil, of the then unnamed Americas, found many things native to this new land: those of flesh and blood, the Native Americans and the hooved and horned buffaloes; and those of wood and sap, corn, tomatoes, and of course the pumpkin. Over time, the natives of wood and sap found welcome on the tables of the first colonist and their progeny. The natives of flesh and blood not so much

In the pumpkin lore there is really only one story to be told, and it is the story of "Jack of the Lantern".

The story goes one day there was this man named Jack, who being a criminal by nature, was being chased by some angry villagers he'd stolen from. During his escape who did the unlucky Jack come upon? Why no other person than the Devil! What follows next no one is exactly sure, but everyone can agree that somehow Jack convinces the Devil to help him; and in the bargain, somehow, Jack ends up cheating the Devil. This comes back to haunt Jack later, when, as a dead spirit, he is denied access to both Heaven and Hell! Now here's the bizarre part. The Devil, in what could only be called pity, gives to the forever-to-wander Jack, for he was not welcome in Hell also, a glowing ember picked from the fires of hell that will never extinguish, never go out, so at least as the cursed thief wander the road would not be too dark. Jack, thinking quickly, took a turnip and carved out its center, placing the burning ember within it, and from there after he wandered the dark. Eventually, over time and retelling, the turnip became a pumpkin, and Jack of the Lantern became Jack-o'-Lantern. This *of course* led to the Halloween tradition of carved and lit pumpkins on every street in America. Why wouldn't it?

Howard Portman, artist, gourd carver.

Howard's chose for his second carving popular and well accepted themes, and for him, this contest, was to be no contest at all. The year before had been a mere fluke he postulated, and as he worked, he put all thoughts of Mr. Lee and his "victory" to the side. He would let the art speak, and speak it does, earning him one award: Second Place. That year's Honorable Mention award going to a 3rd grade class, who had carved a large pumpkin for a class project on the pilgrims and the first Thanksgiving. Their work was childish and lacked any skill as far Howard was concerned. It didn't help matters any, when Howard looked across the stage at the awards ceremony, to see Mr. Lee laughing and joking with the said mentioned 3rd grade class. Be small and cute and you will always get the sympathy vote, Howard thought with gritted teeth. He did not share in their feelings of victory. His plate was full, and on it, lay something dark, and bitter.

The years go by for Howard, and the seasons change accordingly. Each year, Fall, and the Annual Pumpkin Festival rolled into town, swollen and bright. Each year the pumpkin carving contest is held, and each year, Howard Portman enters and loses. Always achieving second place victories, he never wins first.

First place seemed reserved for one person and one person only...Mr. Lee. At first, Howard blamed a local favoritism for the old professor. He only lies to himself, for each year Mr. Lee's entries are better than his, and he could not deny it.

Howard lost each time, and Mr. Lee won, and the seed planted that first year in Howard, grew. The seed had split, sending out tendrils, deep barbed roots, sharp and stinging. Howard's resolve had vanished over the years in a growing flame of murderous intent, unrequited. An unfamiliar passion for Howard. He was not a murderous man. He was an artist.

Howard Portman's art and his craft and his career, which should have been growing, faltered. All had dwindled under the heat of an undenied and inadmissible obsession. How could Howard live happily out <u>there</u> in the light of adoration, in the arenas of the art elite, when there was someone better than him, that *shouldn't* be better than him? Someone who hadn't worked as hard as him. Someone who didn't take the time to develop their natural gift. Someone who seemed to fall into it easily, like a child falling back into a pile of leaves. An artist, not an archaeologist?!!

It was after his fifth loss Howard came up with his plan.

There was no way an old Chinese retired archaeologist was better than him. There had to be some trick, some reason for the old man's remarkable skills. Someone was helping him, giving him the edge to win those victories thus far, and by their assistance they had unintentionally added to Howard's torment. He chose to do something.

Howard became a student again. A student of only one subject, with one sharp and clear point of study and focus... an old unthreatening Chinese man called Mr. Lee. He began to learn everything he could about the old retiree. He learned his schedule. When he traveled into town from his farm. Where he went to get his hair cut, and when. How often did he get his car filled up? How often did he have his car tuned up? Did he come into town for groceries, or did he have them delivered out to his farm?

Mr. Lee was, naturally, also a farmer, and each year a part of his farm was devoted, of course, to pumpkins. Growing your own pumpkins couldn't hurt one's chances at victory and guaranteed a standard of quality needed to get the best carvers. The old man had other hobbies but besides the farmed pumpkins they held no curiosity for Howard and his research.

Howard made long calls to far distant places in China. He sent many letters, veiling his true intentions, to the Chinese Embassy and to universities both big and small in China. In these communications he asked after Mr. Lee's family, his upbringing, his birth, his education and his tenure as a professor. When he was questioned, he spoke vaguely of a book being written on the man or archaeology or whatever worked to get the information he was after.

Howard Portman asked many questions and more during this time, and when he felt he had enough information, the second part of his plan began.

It only took Howard Portman two months of diligent and patient work to befriend Mr. Lee. He changed the pattern of his life to revolve around that of the old Chinese man. Mr. Lee became the Sun which Howard circled. Primarily, what most would call a "night person", Howard, moved his world and activities into the sunward hours, so as to move in the same world Mr. Lee and most of the common folk of Derrick moved in. He timed his every move, so as Mr. Lee was walking through a door, he was coincidently walking out it, allowing for brief and "friendly" exchanges, which in themselves helped to plant the seeds for longer conversations and greater opportunities for "bonding". Howard Portman's hands, held predominantly in reserve for the higher calling called art, for the wooden and carved shafts topped with fine haired bristles, became hands of assistance, hands of service, providing the retired archaeologist with a spontaneously appearing "bag boy" to help carry extra bags to the car, or a prompt doorman to hold doors open so Mr. Lee can enter or exit. Howard plied his foe with dinner invitations to his home, and it was after three of these successful accepted dinner invitations to Howard's home, that Howard was finally invited to Mr. Lee's home for dinner by the man himself.

Howard arrived on that warm August evening at Mr. Lee's house 20 minutes early on purpose, secretly wishing to jar the old man off his center. What secrets Mr. Lee held would have to be probed for, picked at, and revealed by cunning and by patience. Mr. Lee's secret would not come from a direct assault by Howard on a stable enemy. No, for his guaranteed success Howard needed an unbalanced Mr. Lee.

The evening didn't begin well for Howard, as the "gift" he bought solely for the occasion was declined. The bottle of wine had not been cheap and had been picked out for its clear taste which masked its high alcohol content. In Howard's study of Mr. Lee, he had learned Mr. Lee did not drink alcohol often, but Howard felt it was worth the trouble to buy the bottle, if somehow Mr. Lee could be convinced to drink it. Many the lynch pin is revealed and freed when one is inebriated. For the unaccustomed, a glass or two of wine can become a verbal lubricant, a sharpened spike to let the truth come bleeding out.

The evening progressed, and sadly, for Howard, he learned little more about the mysterious and too-talented Mr. Lee. He had been an "archaeologist" back in his homeland China, where he had specialized in the study of the rare and dwindling tribes of the high northern mountains. Most of these tribes had been forced to the edge of extinction by the Chinese government, who looked upon their ways and practices as antiquated, as primitive, as perversions. It was long believed in Chinese culture that some of these tribes worshiped "foreign gods" and practiced ritual cannibalism and sacrifice. It was Dr. Lee's, he preferred "Mr." in his retirement, studies which proposed that half of China's greatest knowledge, and most of its language came from these tribes, and that these northern tribes were the last remnants of a once great and powerful civilization dating to a the time before the pyramids of Egypt even began their upward climbs. Long forgotten by modern China, these ancient civilizations existed now only in stories and tales, myths and legends, broken artifacts and relics, passed down through the millennia. For 30 years, after his graduation, Mr. Lee diligently studied these tribes, and it was towards the end of this 30 year period of discovery that he discovered the art of carving.

When Howard pressed him about his art teachers, their histories, their pedigrees, and the length of Mr. Lee's tutelage, Mr. Lee only provided vague answers. His teacher, only one, he said was an incredibly old man in a very remote tribe near the Himalayan border, and at the time of his instruction was one of the last remaining wise elders versed fully in the old ways. When he talked of his teacher's craft and skill, of his master's artwork, Mr. Lee spoke with wonder, becoming a child again. He even looked younger!...for a moment. It was a sign that it was still possible in the world to still see something amazing, truly magical, springing from the hands of Man. His time of study with this master was less than a year, and as to the method and focus of this year of study Mr. Lee gave only cryptic replies.

"My teacher said '...to free the thing from within the material one must have the proper eye, and the proper lighting!' " the old Asian man had chuckled.

Regarding his own work, Mr. Lee spoke humbly, but to Howard's ears he bragged.

"Oh, it's all the same to me really," Mr. Lee commented casually. "The first thing I created, was pure, and sadly has tainted everything else to follow.

"So much so, that all the sculptures," he laughed. "'Pumpkins', which have come after, to me, are just mere echoes...shadows... of that first piece. Yes."

After a single year of training under the tutelage of this master, Mr. Lee finished his academic studies in the high mountains and returned to the city, where after completing his reports and submitting his papers, he turned his hand to art, to the skill he'd acquired at the foot of his master. His first piece of art was a joy to him. A joy like no other, but when he showed it to a colleague it was "not well received", and it was after this initial artistic failure Mr. Lee decided to give his resignation, and there, shortly after, he immigrated to the United States. He had paid a price and lost a friend, but he would not go into further detail. Mr. Lee's time in China was done, and if a future existed for him it wasn't to be had in the land of his birth. It wasn't until many years later, Mr. Lee, now a citizen of the United States, turned his hand again to the skill he had acquired in the high mountains.

As the evening drew to a close their conversation inevitably turned to pumpkins. Here, Howard perked up, hopeful that finally, some hint of Mr. Lee's key to success would be revealed, but for all his attention and eagerness, he learned truly little. To Howard there was no doubt Mr. Lee had been in the presence of a master, his carved, award-winning pumpkins, proved it.

Mr. Lee didn't attempt to carve again for years, not until he came to America, not until his first Halloween, and his first entry into the annual Pumpkin Carving contest held in his new American hometown. He was inspired.

"...Here in America we have Halloween," Mr. Lee was saying proudly. "When I first moved here, I found it strange when I first saw some of your rituals and festivities. American holidays."

He laughed.

"Really, for most, we Chinese have some puzzling things we celebrate too. Halloween is similar to some. A day marking the changing of the seasons, the transition from the days of sunlight to the days of darkness, harvest time, with costumes and, of course, pumpkins. A time when it was natural to fear the growing dark days, and to imagine the worst contained within it. Demons. Ghosts. That kind of thing."

Lacking, what he believed at the time were sufficient skills for galleries and the like, Mr. Lee felt the Halloween crowds could appreciate his crude talent. Mr. Lee had been surprised by the overwhelming response to his first carving. For the first time he felt really welcomed. At home. Ever since then, he had entered the contest every year, and each year, he had won. Each year as the Derrick County Pumpkin Festival drew near Mr. Lee took the month leading up to it to sequester himself in his barn at night, and then, to practice, to sketch, and carve into the late hours of the night.

The old Chinese scholar spoke like an artist, but what did he know?! What had he ever suffered?! What had he sacrificed?!

Howard Portman could not accept Mr. Lee. He did not belong in art's pristine world, but Howard didn't say this to the old Chinese man, neither did he show it that evening. There had to be more to Mr. Lee, to his "talent", and where it truly descended from. For his skill was not of this, common, Earth.

In Mr. Lee's home that night, Howard was shown the one existing example Mr. Lee possessed of his great teacher's work. At its viewing it took all of Howard's composure to not buckled to the floor, right there and then, and weep. The sculpture he viewed was beyond all mortal skill, and its crafter....assuredly had to be a living <u>God</u>! It was an extremely large piece, contained within an equally large display case. It was a carving of some creature which could have been a cross between a large mammoth fish and a partially transformed tadpole, it's front fins small with grasping appendages like fingers. Made of some exotic honey hued wood, every line sang. Every curve was a shape of barely restrained power. Every inch of the carved art piece held more images within images: the bodies of lovers made from the bodies of lovers, minute, precise, sublime, and decadent; grand arching castles and temples, which within themselves contained even more elaborate castles and temples; in one place, a delicate hanging curve told in one sweeping arc of a lone fisherman's life and the wondrous fish he one day caught; in one section, a wave of large crabs imitated scales on the big fish, and at their center their pincered claws reached to hold aloft a strange and complexly etched stone, like the whorls of a tortoise's shell; and on, and on, and on the art piece had opened itself to Howard's scrutiny, and he was humbled. Earlier, Howard had asked after what had become of Mr. Lee's Master, if he still lived. Mr. Lee had reported simply, that shortly after his departure, the great Master passed, and so, as Howard gazed at the master's work, within himself, an unexpected sadness pooled in an ever-widening circle. Sadness at a teacher he would never know or learn from.

He was jealous.

Howard thanked Mr. Lee as the evening ended, shaking hands with him at the door. He kept the desire to crush Mr. Lee's hand in his own deeply in check, fearing some momentary lapse in control might have made his hand clench down tight in an involuntary betrayal of his hidden inner turmoil and rage. Howard drove home, fingers white knuckled and twisting the gnarled plastic of his steering wheel, and as he drove his thoughts spun around Mr. Lee and the knowledge he had obtained that evening.

In his mind he could no longer doubt Mr. Lee had been in the presence of a true and wondrous Master, someone who could have easily ruled the art world and affected the many generations of artists to come, and beyond. He could not doubt Mr. Lee possessed skill, but such skill could not be gained in a single year alone!

A "good" artist in the hands of a Grand Master, with a few years of tutelage and guidance, can partially pierce the thin, but ever resilient veil, between being "good" and being "great", but a novice, an unskilled peasant, an archaeologist, would need years upon years just to reach good! Mr. Lee's skill could easily be classified as "great". It was wrong, Howard could feel it in his refined and trained bones. It was all a trick, and he was going to figure it out. He would show to everyone that Mr. Lee deserved no adoration, for he was a fraud. Howard was an artist, and it was his duty to his craft to unmask a charlatan.

Howard had everything he needed. It was time for the final part of his plan. The annual Derrick County Pumpkin Festival was fast approaching, and Howard knew, soon, Mr. Lee would retire to his barn to sketch and to carve, but this year would be different from those others years before, for this year, as Mr. Lee worked, someone would be watching!

It only took Howard a couple of days to set everything up, so that as Mr. Lee entered his barn for his evening's round of pumpkin sketching, someone was watching from a discreet distance away through a pair of newly purchased high-powered binoculars. Howard had purchased the binoculars online for a decent price and had them shipped overnight for expediency's sake.

Crouched in the bushes, twenty meters away from Mr. Lee's barn, Howard had the binoculars trained on the back of the old man's house as the back door opened and Mr. Lee walked out. Stepping out, Mr. Lee stood a moment admiring the night sky, which was full and open, every star stitched together with the warm and deep blue background of the surrounding night. Howard watched Mr. Lee's every movement, looking for any sign of the betrayal he knew to exist inside the old Asian man to glimmer forth, but nothing does. With a shrug of shoulders Mr. Lee turned his sight from the heavens above and flicked on the flashlight he held in his right hand. Mr. Lee was old, but still had no trouble navigating the night to the doors of his barn with light in hand without incident. Giving not a second glance to the surrounding night, or to any potential watchers, Mr. Lee opened the barn doors, walked in, and shut them behind him.

Howard needed to get closer but was novice to the world of stealth. Howard was an artist, and was still bound by common fears of recognition and recrimination, and it was with these thoughts running through his mind, that the small piece of man-made light, which represented Mr. Lee's flashlight, within the barn, clicked off. Immediately, those small cracks in the boards of the barn, which had provided points of definition in the night, vanished, sending the barn to join the enclosing tree silhouettes and the deeper shadows surrounding. Howard expected within a few breaths a switch within the barn would be thrown, and the darkness held within, which must have blinded and covered Mr. Lee completely, would be replaced with a constant and reassuring electric light, much brighter than a handheld flashlight...but, it did not.

Howard waited. After a time he began to wonder if this was the secret to Mr. Lee's talent, to work in the dark, when a strange light began to flower within the confines of the barn. It was like no illumination Howard had ever seen before. It grew slowly at first, but soon possessed the barn completely, pushing out at the embedded night through the cracks.

Something was not right, but Howard couldn't place the source of this feeling. The night, an unknowing victim, was made silent and still in the strange light that leaked out into it. Murderous, a quick and sickeningly sharp blade drawn across its throat, the night was silenced

Surprise slapped Howard full in his senses, as his foot pitched into a hole in the ground, and it took all his returning senses to keep himself from falling completely forward into the dirt. He'd been walking, walking toward the barn and the strange light, but he didn't remember starting to move forward. He remembered the hiding, the waiting, the watching Mr. Lee and his entrance into the barn...then the strange light, but the leaving of the hiding place, the <u>walking</u> towards it, he did not remember! In the grip of some unknown compulsion he had succumbed to his inward desire to know and had left his place of hiding. Howard realized something right then and there. The light had called to him clearer than any verbal summons, and the hole in the ground had been the only thing which saved him from himself. If he'd made any noise, a now aware Howard was uncertain, but out of fear of discovery he left determined to return another night soon to discover the source of the strange illumination.

Patiently Howard waited, letting a few days pass, returning to his normal routine to allay any imagined, or real, suspicions before returning to continue his nightly surveillance of Mr. Lee and his nightly activities. Now, with a new resolve, Howard was determined to get closer, much closer to the barn and to the inevitable identity of Mr. Lee's nightly source of illumination, for Howard now believed completely this light must be the key to Mr. Lee's quickly acquired and miraculous skills. How a light could make an anthropologist into a master artist Howard could not explain, but all his being screamed it was so.

The light was the key.

Returning to his surveillance, it still took Howard four days to work up the courage to hide himself next to the tall wooden slats of the barn, his body pressed between a rusty red shape, a wheat thresher which would thresh no more, and a long blue tarped shape, which possibly covered the leftover timber from an older structure which had existed years before on the property, according to Mr. Lee. On this night, Howard's hate had excitement for company, for he would have answers tonight and it was his courage and determination which had brought him to the achievement of this victory.

Howard was just beginning to relax in his well won hiding place when the familiar back door of the old man's house opened, to reveal the even more familiar form of Mr. Lee. Howard gripped his resolve and will to keep himself held in check, to keep a laugh of glee from escaping from his lips. He would win and Mr. Lee, would lose! With each paced step Mr. Lee took towards the barn, Howard felt more and more contempt for him. A greater man would not be so easily spied upon. A true artist would do more with their talent than just carve pumpkins in an old rustic barn. Only a true artist could deserve the gift Mr. Lee had received...had stolen! Stolen from true and worthy artists. To Howard only an artist like himself could understand and complement such a gift. After all his training he deserved it, he had earned it!

Mr. Lee entered the barn, and Howard tracked his movements as he entered, peeping through a chink in the armor of the wooden slats of the aged barn. There in the center of the barn on a low large table, illuminated in the common glow of Mr. Lee's flashlight, sat a fat large pumpkin, it's sides already covered in sketch lines, the beginning work rough, just beginning to hint at the potential piece to come. Mr. Lee shut the door and walked toward the pumpkin. He slowly circled the pumpkin, his art piece, his eyes taking in the progress thus far completed, and Howard watched. To Howard, Mr. Lee's behavior was something remarkably familiar. Howard had done the same thing himself many times before. Each work of art deserving a moment of appreciation and admiration, of inspection and calculation, the artist basking in the raw unfinished divinity of the art piece before once again setting to work. Noticing the things that worked, and maybe, some of the things that did not. Even a small similarity between himself and Mr. Lee, enraged Howard further.

Howard's left eye, peeping through the hole, was locked on to Mr. Lee's bent form, when Mr. Lee clicked off the flashlight. Immediately Howard's view of the barn's interior filled with darkness. So abrupt was this change from light to dark Howard blinked reflexively, drawing his head away from the gap in the planks. Placing his eye back to the gap, Howard stared back into the complete dark the barn's interior had become. The seconds passed agonizingly slow for Howard as the darkness persisted. Had he inadvertently moved to much when the flashlight was turned off? *Wait.* Did he dare adjust his position to counteract some subconscious movement his body he had made? *Wait.* What if he'd been discovered, and even now, Mr. Lee was sneaking around to confront him? *Wait.* Again and again, Howard told himself: *Wait.* He would be patient, for his reward would be great, his victory sweet and earned.

Howard was proud of himself when his patience paid off, for again as nights before, slowly, the inner dark confines of the barn filled with illumination, but for once, the source was now revealed to the well hid Howard. Mr. Lee stood in an ever-growing pool of light, his left arm raised holding the heavy metal ring of a long thin and strange lantern.

This was the source! The origin of the eldritch and alien light that invaded the normal world each night for the enigmatic and mysterious Mr. Lee stood revealed. It was like no lantern Howard had ever seen before. Made of seven long thin slats of old yellowed glass, the lantern had no standard base to rest on, being something that was either hung from a rafter or a post, possibly off of a hook or a long chain, or held aloft in hand. Lacking a base, the lanterns ends were molded caps of some yellow metal, too plain to be gold but lacking the red hue of copper or the warm shininess of brass. They were intricately carved obviously by ancient masters from some forgotten era, from some forgotten and ancient people.

Here was Mr. Lee's secret. This was the true gift, the true source of his talent, secured from an ancient source, from some lost city, a defiled tomb. In its light, all was revealed. There had been no Master, nor any year of training, only the luck and good fortune to find a relic of a forgotten and powerful people. In the all-revealing light of the lantern, Howard could truly see the pumpkin in Mr. Lee's barn, could see the hidden sculpture that swam and writhed underneath the hard orange rind. In the lantern's light, Howard saw every cut and every carve Mr. Lee's blades would follow, as if they were roads he'd walk down countless times, in countless lives; roads he had been the architect of; roads he had built with his own hands, so familiar were the stones. In its light Howard could see the potential for hundreds, thousands, of other sculptures, each one magnificent, each one a new and unique masterpiece. Inadvertently, as often the case of those unused to hiding in shadows, Howard's hand moved, hitting a loose board which leaned against the barn's side. The board tipped over, sliding against the barn like a falling clock's hand, moments away from chiming "You are being watched!" to the unaware Mr. Lee.

Howard swiftly caught the board, ceasing its fall, stopping the alarm which it was just beginning to raise. Returning his eye quickly to the hole, Howard was afraid of what he'd find, a missing Mr. Lee, now made aware by a small sound of a hidden observer...but all was fine. The strange lantern was now hanging from a chain from one of the barn's rafters, and Mr. Lee sat on a stool, his back to Howard, pen in hand, his hand flying across the face of the pumpkin, marking deftly the lines to the carving still hidden within.

Howard knew what he had to do.

Later as he made his way through the woods, leaving Mr. Lee to his carving, he accepted fully the task which had been thrust upon him. He would have to free the lantern from the unworthy hands of this grave robber from China, and then, and only then, could Howard's life, Howard's career, and Howard's subsequent adoration by millions, begin!

Howard Portman was an artist, he was not a thief, but he had to become one. He could not afford to immediately attempt to steal the lantern. He determined it would be best to wait, to bide his time.

Until the following year.

Mr. Lee took home another First-Place trophy at that years Pumpkin Festival, Second Place going to, for a change, someone other than Howard. Mrs. Schumacher, the 72-year-old widow of Mr. Henry Schumacher, following the inspirational example set year by year by the equally elderly Mr. Lee, had entered and won second place with her pumpkin art piece entitled "The Rose of Derrick County". A banal and oversimplification of a single rose carved out of a single pumpkin. Howard accepted his third-place trophy unfeelingly from a place of stone.

His lips smiled. His hands shook other hands. Accepting his trophy, Howard spoke at length about art, ending by giving thanks to the crowd, the judges, and even his fellow contestants, but "he" was truly elsewhere.

The call of the lantern was strong. As he interacted with those people that mingled around him at the awards ceremony, his mind screamed about it. Filled with a dark passion and a fierce glee, Howard's thoughts wrapped and coiled around the Lantern, and how to get it, and the indescribable joy he would know at possessing it. The months following the Pumpkin Festival passed slowly for Howard, but again he was proud at his patience, for he was going to win the next pumpkin carving contest, and much more! With the summer months, fading into those of autumn, the town of Derrick began to change under the waning light. It was not too long after the familiar shapes of pumpkins began to dot the farmlands of Derrick, orange spheres rising from deep green rows of viny dark tangles, which themselves had finished their welcomed and farmer-invited invasions.

Mr. Lee was a devout Buddhist, and once a month, he would make a 75-mile journey to worship at a temple which had grown up around a small Chinese community to the south. Howard Portman had to wait a week and a half into the month of September, before the familiar shape of Mr. Lee's small pickup truck headed out of town, the old man at the wheel and a bag of fresh vibrant oranges in the passenger seat, offerings for the shiny brass Buddha waiting at the temple. Howard would have about five to six hours before Mr. Lee would return to Derrick, and he planned to use this time to its fullest.

Thirty minutes after the departure of Mr. Lee, the crouched shape of Howard Portman ran from the forest surrounding Mr. Lee's home to the back of the senior citizen's home. The back door clicked as Howard turned the handle, and the door swung open freely. The community of Derrick still existed in an age where the farmer's daughters were always cute; where apple, and of course pumpkin pies, frequently could be found cooling on open windowsills; and, where people didn't lock their doors, because no one was that hungry or that desperate or that malicous. This didn't stop people from stealing. Occasionally a few teenagers would get a little rambunctious, "out-of-control", and go on a small, but thankfully, short lived crime spree of vandalism and minor thefts. Usually this was something which was discovered quickly and handled even more quicklier.

Howard had to be thorough. He would not lose this opportunity to find the lantern, but it was with much consternation, and a growing sense of trepidation, Howard found himself four hours into his search of Mr. Lee's home with still no lantern and no inclination whatsoever as to its location. He even searched the barn from rafter top to hay bottom. Nothing. He realized sadly he would have to abandon his search, and that Mr. Lee had hidden the lantern too well for him or anyone to find with ease.

Howard did find something. Something unexpected!

In the old Chinese man's bedroom, he had found a cabinet red lacquered with brass fittings, and opening its double doors with metal loops of brass that worked as pulls, he revealed a series of drawers, all of differing size. Opening a few he found only toiletries, and memorabilia, physical memories of a life and world the old man have left behind. Overall, nothing exciting or helpful to Howard's goals. One drawer had remained unexplored. The largest. In it he found an object wrapped in burlap, and, beneath the burlap, silk. Drawing the smooth red fabric aside Howard almost dropped what he discovered, for within was a wooden sculpture carved with the most horrific images. On its surface was a scene of murder, vicious and cruel: one man was attacking a much older and smaller man with hands like talons that dug into his throat. Intricately carved blood spiraled and spurted as the older man was repeatedly strangled in image after image carved into the wood's surface, till a final image had him lying in a growing pool of blood. Worst of all, layered in the background, warped and deformed figures cavorted. Hideous in their dimensions, their faces drooling and ghastly, these figures peered out at him from the wooden surface with eyes filled with such madness, that even carved in wood Howard felt ill and contaminated by this facsimile of creatures that could not exist. Howard could not hold back the shiver that passed through his frame. The only thing that stopped Howard from dropping the alarming piece of art was that for all its horror it was perfectly crafted. Every line and shape, perfection. Howard knew many collectors would pay great sums to display it in their collections of the macabre, but beyond their circles it would find more looks of distaste and unease among the general public. Carefully Howard had returned the item to its shroud of fabrics. Howard returned to his search for the lantern, but the object he had found had left him unbalanced.

No luck.

It was hard for Howard to leave the home of Mr. Lee's empty-handed, and for a moment, he was tempted to take the art piece of Mr. Lee's late master from the glass fronted showcase it rested in, and abscond with it, but he couldn't do it. He resisted the urge. He had been prepared for the abduction of the lantern, but not the overly large art piece. Howard knew, the theft of one was not equal to the theft of the other. The lantern was a well-kept secret. The art of Mr. Lee's master was displayed for all visitors to see and would not be lost easily. Though it loosely equaled in Howard's mind the gift of the lantern's illuminance and its otherworldly effect upon the artiste, it was not the prize he sought and needed. Mr. Lee had held all knowledge of the lantern, and its existence, and its ability, all to himself. If the Master's art piece were stolen Mr. Lee would call the police, but if the lantern were stolen, Howard strongly believed Mr. Lee would not report its lose, but would rather try to solve its loss on his own, so as to keep the lantern's existence a secret. The lantern's greatest gift for Mr. Lee lay in the fact no one knew he possessed it, that it contained and emitted an otherworldy power, or that it even existed!

Mr. Lee would not part with his pilfered gift easily. Howard acknowledged, bitterly, that searching Mr. Lee's house had been a waste, and would not gain him what he sought. He left knowing he would have to find another way. Somewhere, somehow, at some point, the lantern would be accessible to him. He just had to be in the right place at the right time. Unfortunately for Howard, he had no clue to the place, nor the time were such a thing could be achieved.

October arrived and the town of Derrick blossomed again in preparation for the Autumn's festivities, and Howard Portman, artist, had figured something out.

The previous year, Howard had spent a good deal of his time observing Mr. Lee, and his activities, especially those which occurred at night and involved pumpkins and the carving of their orange hides. In the Fall, as the annual contest drew near, each night Mr. Lee would exit from the back of his home with flashlight in hand making his way to his barn, there again to shutter himself for that evenings round of sketching or carving. Sometimes he would bring a thermos with him, probably filled with tea, hot and ready to go; on other nights, really cold crisp nights, Mr. Lee would bring a second thermos filled with a warm and filling soup; and on rare occasions, a sandwich or two held in a small paper bag, but never a lantern. Not once during last year's observations had Howard ever seen Mr. Lee leave his home carrying anything the size and shape of the lantern, yet during the weeks prior to the annual pumpkin contest, each night the lantern's light, faithfully and obediently, breached the folds of the deepening dark within the barn's sanctity. Howard may not have known the lantern's location the rest of the year, but during the days and nights of October, he knew it dwelled and waited in the barn for Mr. Lee's nightly visitations. Howard knew he had to get into that barn, that he had to find the lantern, and that the lantern had to be there!

Howard would have to find the lantern quickly. He could not rely on luck, or even keen observation, to provide him with a large window of opportunity. Howard Portman, artist, would have to move amazingly fast. Those were Howard's thoughts as he sat crouched in the shadows one lazy afternoon, just out of direct line of sight from Mr. Lee's house. Howard was waiting for Mr. Lee to leave.

Howard's legs were beginning to cramp, and he was beginning to feel the minor plan which he'd put into motion to get the elderly Lee to leave his home wasn't going to work, when Mr. Lee appeared on his porch. Mr. Lee made his way gingerly down the steps, taking care with a body of brittle bones and a deteriorating sense of balance. Walking a short distance to his pickup truck, Mr. Lee got in, started up the engine, and drove off.

Mr. Lee was heading into town to pick up a package, recently lost, which had conveniently just turned up.

Howard only waited a minute or two after Mr. Lee's departure before dashing across the old man's property to the closed doors of the barn.

Howard had been paying keen attention to the postman: his routes, and his habits, those both good, and bad. Howard was shocked to find the local postman, Arnold Draper, had a naughty habit, which made an appearance at least twice a week or more, in the hours of the early afternoon. When the habit appeared the postal vehicle Arnold Draper drove would find itself parked in the back streets behind the home of one Mrs. Carlene Kelly, wife of Norton Kelly, an American truck driver who often spent weeks away from his home, and his lonely wife. Arnold Draper, postman, was making extra deliveries, and it was during one of these "deliveries" a package intended for the hands of Mr. Lee wound up in the grasp of Howard Portman. It was a federal crime to steal from the United States Postal Service, but Howard Portman was an artist, and an artist couldn't be expected to follow all the rules. Arnold Draper surely wasn't! Arnold Draper, postman, later in the day, realized a package had gone missing...again! Arnold decided to keep it to himself and crossed his fingers. Things were lost all the time.

The barn doors swung open, heavy on their hinges, and briefly the interior was lit with a ragged wedge of orangish Fall sunlight, as Howard Portman quickly slipped in and closed them behind him. Even with the barn doors closed some light still penetrated through its wooden slats, allowing Howard some visibility. The hush of the barn, a held breath of shifting timbers and dust heavy motes of light, greeted the intruder Howard had once again become. The inside of Mr. Lee's barn consisted of eight horse stalls, four on each side, minus horses. Mr. Lee in his younger days, may have played with the idea of riding horses, but now left those types of pleasures to younger folk, and any heavy lifting on the farm was done by the sole tractor the old Asian man owned. The horse stalls had become storage areas for the tools of a pumpkin farmer. Plows, shovels, wheelbarrows, large sacks of pumpkin seed and even larger sacks of fertilizer, irrigation tubing and deep high coils of water hose lay scattered and organized throughout the barn. Dead center, sitting on a low table, sat a large pumpkin, its face, already covered with preliminary sketch lines for the carving to come. Next to the low table and the quiet pumpkin, a tray of carving tool rested, waiting for their time to sing and dance across the pumpkin's curved and ridged surface.

Howard went to work.

With a small flashlight Howard pulled from the inside pocket of his coat, he moved from stall to stall searching methodically. He let logic be his guide. Knowing it only took Mr. Lee less than a minute or more upon first entering the barn for the lantern's illumination to appear, Howard surmised the lantern could not be buried deep or secreted in some such location that an old man would have trouble getting to.

Howard had high hopes he would find it quickly, the reward for his dedication and determination, but it was not to be so. His frustration only grew as the minutes ticked by, and still the lantern remained unfound, and it was with horror and dread Howard's senses picked up the distinctive sound of Mr. Lee's pickup truck returning. If he was going to find the lantern, Howard would have to find it now. His eyes flew around the barn, visually ripping and discarding any shape that was obviously not the lantern he sought.

No. No. That's not it! No! Howard's searching eyes pleaded yet were denied any shape close to the size and dimensions of the lantern. The lantern was nowhere to be seen. Howard's last desperate attempt at finding the lantern was brought to a halt, as the sound of Mr. Lee's pickups tires screeched and slid on the gravel drive, shortly followed by the sound of the opening and closing of a metal framed car door.

Howard Portman was an artist, and there, in Mr. Lee's barn, as an intruder, he also became silence. He killed all his movements, and he waited, still and silent, the sounds of his searching from only moments before gone. Now, he listened. On the edge of his hearing, Howard heard the steady footsteps of Mr. Lee, and then the all to recognizable sound of Mr. Lee's footsteps growing louder, as he approached the barn, and the hidden Howard Portman. Then the footsteps stopped, well before the barn entrance, and Howard, waited. The seconds passed, thin razors against Howard's eroding stillness, yet the silence that had become Mr. Lee did not break. Finally, unable to take it anymore, Howard began to move, and slowly, made his way to one of the walls adjacent to the driveway. Tilting his head to the side, and again, as before, Howard placed an eye to a gap in the planked wall of Mr. Lee's barn. The shock Howard received at what he saw through the crack in the planks forced a small and defeated sound from his lips, as his heart fluttered into an atavistic fear.

Mr. Lee stood in the afternoon sunlight, staring directly at the barn, his arms wrapped around a square shaped cardboard box, its edges showing clear signs of a long journey made. Frozen, Howard could only stare back through the gap in the barn's wall. He didn't know how, but Howard sensed Mr. Lee knew he was in there and was looking directly at him right then and there, and in his mind, was deciding how best to deal with this intruder. Howard knew he should run, if he were quick enough in his escape attempt, he could remain unidentifiable, but his body refused to respond. He could not move locked in Mr. Lee's scrutinizing gaze. Mr. Lee was similarly held, for as Howard watched he seemed torn between going to the barn and not going. Howard now realized the folly of his initial response at the still and standing form of Mr. Lee. Howard himself, on many occasions, upon returning home, would feel torn between finishing the day, and the day's remaining menial tasks and common needs, or returning to an art piece left unfinished, which called for completion. The wrinkled Chinese man, Howard surmised, now stood at the edge: go sit in the joy of your art or go be common. Howard prayed commonality would win, and thankfully for Howard, it did. Moments later, Mr. Lee with box in hand, turned with a slight smirk and headed to his house. Once beyond the corner of the house Howard lost sight of him, but shortly after Howard heard a front door opening and closing.

Throwing off his stillness, Howard moved quickly and rushed to the close barn doors. Allowing for caution, Howard put his eye to the seam of the barn doors for a brief instance, before opening them. Howard Portman looked back once, his heart heavy with loss, his throat thick with sorrow, to the empty barn and the last of his hopes he was leaving there...and there, hanging in a worn burlap sack labeled with some faded design, at the meeting point between a post and a beam, hung an object. Even though the lantern was covered with a sack, its shape to Howard was unmistakable. Howard knew he was out of time, but he threw caution into the furnace of his desire. He ran across the barn, reached high, and with the tips of his fingers pulled the sack, with the lantern hidden within, down. It tumbled for a second before Howard caught it. The lantern's weight pressed into his arms and in that glorious instant Howard knew a joy unlike any joy he'd ever felt before.

The Lantern was his!

Embracing his prize, Howard bolted for the barn's entrance and his exit. As he exited the concealing confines of the barn, he gave only the briefest of glances to the waiting house nestled in the woods that sheltered within it the old and hated Chinese scholar. The house lay silent and still, its windows covered. With a backward hand, Howard closed the barn door, and with an eye still on the house, raced into the woods. With each step he drew further away from Mr. Lee's house, and the crime he had just committed, and with each step the grand vision of Howard's life to come blossomed in his mind. Howard Portman was an artist! Howard Portman was a winner!

The drive home was dangerous and several times Howard Portman forced himself to slow down, such was his excitement. He couldn't afford to be pulled over by the police or to be involved in an accident, not with the lantern now in his possession. Even so, Howard still arrived back at home in record time, though for a handful of seconds he didn't even realize it. His body was vibrating. Adrenaline screamed and ran inside him, and something dormant for several years awaken with a roar within him. Pleasure...unfiltered and unforgiving cascaded over him in gorgeous waves. Finally, acknowledging his arrival home, Howard released his death grip from the steering wheel, and then sat stock still for a moment under control, and without moving his body, peered into the rearview mirror, and the two side mirrors, and in each saw nothing. Still Howard waited, and finally after a reasonable amount of time, he shut the car's engine off and relaxed.

He had done it!

Howard exited his car and looked down the road that led to his house. Still nothing. Seeing no one, no lights approaching, Howard went to the trunk of his car and opened it. His hands reached in and moved aside the things he'd used to cover the lantern in its burlap sack, and there it sat exposed. He gazed at his prize breathless, before he snatched it up, sack and all, and clutched it to his chest. His heart thumped against the strange shape concealed within. The whole world suddenly grew still and calm, and the only sound which existed was his own heart beating, his own breath retreating and returning.

Howard came to his senses and rushed into his house; the lantern held tightly in his arms. He spared a few precious seconds and locked the door, before taking his acquisition to his carving room.

In anticipation of his acquisition, Howard had stripped bare a small room devoid of windows, at the center of his home. A room that lived free of potentially prying eyes, to be his place of carving. Months prior, Howard had Nicholas, preferred Nick, the local handyman, install a high-powered air-conditioning unit, which piped air directly into the small room. When Nick questioned Howard about the room, Howard simply explained he suffered from a mild case of agoraphobia

"Why that's no big deal!" Nick commented. "Lots of folks don't like scary films. A special room does seem a little too much though."

After patiently explaining to the local handyman what agoraphobia was and that whenever he was in a bad way, he could find comfort in retreating to the small enclosed room to work, sometimes to sleep, Nick's appeared satisfied. Howard added that over the last couple of years he had put up with the stuffiness of the enclosed room, but no more. Howard had finally had enough... with the stuffiness. Jokingly, Howard had said:

"What's the point of creating a zone of healing and rest, if you're going to roast in it!"

"I hear ya!" Nick stated from the top of the ladder. It had taken two and a half months, but Nick had finally returned to finish the job, and the screwing on of the faceplate to the air duct was the final touch. "Still, if you think this is stuffy, you should check out my place on laundry night. Talk about sweltering. Whew!"

Nick was always there to reassure you that things were always worse on his side of the map, but Nick hadn't had to deal with the pressures of planning a heist of a priceless object, that belonged to a beloved member of the community in his golden years, did he? At least Howard didn't think so. Nick didn't need to know Howard's more than common problems, nor was he needed, ever, to know about the true purpose of the small room.

Howard Portman passed the threshold and entered his carving room, lantern in burlap in hand. Two floorboards lay loose, ready to be pulled away. Howard had learned the art of floorboard removal from Nick. A few months ago, Howard had been faced with a coincidental accident, when one of the floorboards in his home cracked and caved in. One call and a few days later Nick had arrived to repair the broken floorboard pieces, and it was while Howard was watching Nick work, he hatched the idea to hide the lantern, once procured, under the floor.

Howard knelt and removed the loose floorboards, revealing a satin lined foam cushioned cavity he had created for his prize. He was no carpenter, he was an artist, and though he had successfully succeeded in prying the floorboards loose, the satin lined nest he had created for the lantern was nothing to be proud of, but for Howard's purposes it would do just fine. For an instant longer Howard held onto the lantern, his prize, still wrapped in its burlap sack, before placing it, sack and all, in the hidey hole he had created for it, and sealing it up with the two removed floorboards. Picking up the hammer he had left out for this purpose, Howard began the task of hammering the nails back into the floorboards.

The lantern would not be taken from him as easily as it had been taken from Mr. Lee.

Howard Portman, artist, had committed a crime, but he wasn't a criminal, or at least that is what he told himself. He would forget about the Lantern for now. He would forget about the place underneath the floorboards. He would view all his actions as if they were perpetrated by someone else, somewhere else. An interesting dream no more. Howard Portman was an artist, and why would he have need to steal anything from anyone?!

It wasn't until the beginning of the next year, well after the theft of the lantern, well after Derrick County's Pumpkin Festival and its famous pumpkin carving contest, where a shocked Mr. Lee still won First Place even with an unfinished pumpkin, that Howard Portman dared to allow himself the gift of freeing the lantern from its hiding place beneath the floorboards. A post-holiday gift to himself, Howard entered his carving room and shut the door, his hands quickly completing actions, actions practiced mentally over the past few months, to free the floorboards and reveal the lantern still in its burlap sack.

Howard was overjoyed, he had been very patient, as his hands reach down into the satin nest to bring forth the lantern secreted there, and under the artificial electric illumination of his small and secure carving room drew the ornate and ancient lantern from its common and plain brown container of cloth.

Howard had never been so disappointed in his entire life. Gone was the golden skinned and glowing thing from Mr. Lee's barn, instead there sat nestled in Howard's hands a crude thing of soot covered yellowish glass plates. The metal of its construction a dark and rotted iron, black and gray with an under hint of sickly green, it's carving, and craftsmanship was crude and childlike. This couldn't be the same lantern, and for several days after, this is what Howard believed and thought, but ultimately, he knew he was mistaken in thinking thus. Seen through the splinter of a crack in the side of an old barn one could be easily mistaken about the colors and crafting of anything seen within. By touch alone, minus sight, Howard Portman knew he had secured the thing that he had sought.

The lantern consisted of seven long yellowish glass panes. Molted and fluid once, the glass still flowed, their surfaces rippled with soft ridges and waves of age. The lantern's caps were sculpted to resemble rough looking roots, or maybe tentacles, which reached to clutch and hold the ancient panes. At the top of the lantern a single large ring of the same dark metal was formed to suspended it from a hook or spike. Its overall length was roughly 2 1/2 feet, and more than 8 inches round, and in Howard's unaccustomed hands had to weigh at least 10 pounds or more. He believed possibly the metal was some form of lead, forged and formed imperfect and impure in some long-ago time past.

The lantern was a puzzle, for as smart and as brilliant as Howard Portman was, it still took him a month or more to figure out how to light it.

At first, he tried to remove the bottom of the lantern, to expose the wick. That didn't work. Next, he tried to remove the top of the Lantern, but both methods proved pointless. Eventually, by luck and persistence, amidst an area of the rough carved metal roots on the lantern, Howard found a small opening, located near the base of the lantern, smaller than the circumference of the average human pinky. This had to be the key to lighting the lantern but try as he might Howard's attempts to get a lit match, even the long and narrow kind used for lighting fireplaces, up into the opening and to the wick ended in failure. The small opening did provide access to the wick, but unfortunately the innards of the lantern were a maze of twists and turns. No straight path would work. Finally, Howard pieced together a solution, for if Mr. Lee could do it, Howard Portman, artist, surely could!

The solution came in the form of a foot or more of armature wire, a metallic silver wire used by the sculptors of soft mediums like clay, that came in many gauges, thicknesses, and for Howard's uses, different stiffnesses, from hard to bend to extremely easy. Slowly, over the course of three hours, Howard used a length of this easily bent wire to guide a lit match to the wick. Slowly, the Lantern's light had filled the small confines of Howard's carving room, and immediately Howard knew something was <u>wrong</u>, as a bizarre tension suddenly seized him. With a gasp, following some instinctive reflex, Howard slammed off the electric overhead light, and the sense of wrong and tension left the small and enclosed space.

It was as if the two sources of illumination, one ancient, the other modern, could not exist in the same realm together. Immediately, Howard felt as if some pressure had been released as the electric light died, and the warm blanket of the lantern's light filled and possessed the small room completely, and Howard with it.

And...Howard Portman, artist...wept for joy for the first time in his life.

The next several months for Howard Portman passed in bliss. For the first time in Howard's adult life he was content...well almost content. After his initial success in lighting the lantern that first time, Howard lit it twice more after, and each of those times he had to fight the urge to produce art, to create under its luminance, but he would not. No, for Howard, that divine pleasure would have to wait. It would have to wait as the days changed and the seasons with them, Spring succumbing to Summer, Summer bowing to Fall.

It would have to wait for the streets of Derrick to change, as Howard knew they inevitably would, putting on their annual colors of orange and green. For the trees to steal the color of sunset and hold it in each dying leaf. The lantern and its gift would have to wait for the Pumpkin Festival, and for the unaware, for the ignorant, and for the old, Mr. Lee. Howard's first piece of artwork using the lantern's illuminance would not be for any gallery, nor would it be for those periodicals which catered to the rich and the talented, such as Howard. No, the first piece of art was for Mr. Lee, and Mr. Lee alone. That first piece would be a pumpkin!

In the passing weeks of September, Derrick began to buzz as it prepared itself for the influx of people for its annual pumpkin festival. Windows were cleaned and draperies washed, lawns were tended and groomed, fences were mended, and paint brushes were filled, and a few miles out of town Howard Portman was preparing for his pumpkin coup d'état.

October arrived round, fat, and ready, and on its footsteps, kids to be costumed, and pumpkins and more pumpkins. Howard's pre-ordered pumpkins arrived bright and early on the morning of the 7th, and it was with excitement and joy Howard ushered his orange colored charges into his home, and the awaiting carving room. As the day ended, curtains were drawn, and doors were locked at his home. He wished not to be disturbed. He would not be disturbed, for he had been waiting for this day since his first loss to the kindly Mr. Lee, since his first glimpse of the lantern's illuminating magic. He would not suffer any potential sighting of the lantern and its miraculous light. Howard had learned from Mr. Lee's mistake.

The first night of sketching under the watchful illuminating light of the lantern, Howard returned to school. He learned new paths never dreamed of before in the creation of art under the lantern's gaze. Every sketched line became something more. Every mistake, seen in ignorance, was perfection in disguise. Howard Portman had called himself an artist, and like many before him, he'd been wrong. Now, he was truly an artist. That rare being drawing the divine, and the yet unimagined, into the mortal world with mortal hands.

Things were finally changing, and for once, everything seemed clear...until his third night of sketching.

As the hour of eleven drew close to midnight Howard was immersed deep in the sketching, when the hook, a twist of coat hanger wire he had cobbled together, holding the lantern flexed. In horror, Howard heard the metal give and turned in time to see the lantern, his prize, plunging to the floor. Reflexively, he jumped to its rescue, arms out, hands open, but in no way was he quick enough as the lantern slammed hard to the floor. On his knees, Howard gently picked up the lantern, cradling it in his arms, the flame inside flickering then rising steady and true. With eyes wide open, Howard turned the lantern in his hands looking for any breaks or cracks. The lantern, thankfully, had suffered no damage. Howard knew he'd been lucky, very lucky. He also learned something especially important. At that moment as he had watched the lantern falling to the floor, it was as if his world were falling to, everything he held dear careening towards dissolution. For Howard, the loss of the lantern was something which would surely destroy him. The lantern, and his life, were now one.

Howard had learned his lesson and first thing the next day, in the morning hours, he headed into town to find a hook worthy and strong enough to hold the weight and wonder of the lantern.

In the local hardware store Howard took his time in locating the right hook. Passing up the normal fare of your standard hooks, meant for common things, Howard finally settled on a large stainless-steel hook, coated in a red and shiny soft plastic. Plastic that would protect the Lantern's ring from abrasion. Placing the hook in his basket, Howard spent the next 20 minutes filling the basket with various odds and ends, to camouflage his true purpose at only wanting the hook. Returning to his reliable automobile, Howard was dismayed to find its reliability in question, as he turned the key only to be greeted with an engine refusing to turn over. Thankfully, for Howard, the town's always reliable mechanic was just down the street.

The mechanic, who may have been called Joe, the work coveralls he was wearing attested to the existence of a Joe either in past or present, informed Howard his car's battery, once vibrantly electric and alive, was now dead. Howard was given the option to either purchase a new battery, or to wait the few hours necessary to charge the old one enough to bring the car's engine back to life.

Howard Portman was an artist, more so now than ever, who was now unfortunately living on the boot string of a budget, his artistic career and finances having languished in the blinding glow of his obsession. He opted for the less expensive. Leaving his car in the capable hands of Joe the mechanic, who would drive the car out later, Howard proceeded to walk the few miles back to his home, and the awaiting lantern.

Walking home, Howard was encircled by a peace he hadn't known for a very long time. Had it really been seven years, that Howard had been at war with himself and a small old Asian man? Howard decided after the Pumpkin Contest he would never let himself again be sidetracked. Never would he let anyone, or anything stand in the way of his greatness, of his legacy to the world. For seven years he had let down his public, his peers, and most importantly, his kind and patient management, all of whom deserved all his time and focus. After his forthcoming victory he would never let them down again.

The peace which had descended on Howard Portman's world during his walk home was short lived, for as he made his way down the gentle slope to his home, he glimpsed between the trees a familiar, yet unexpected vehicle.

Nicholas', preferred Nick's truck sat parked at the front of Howard's home.

Nick was not expected at all that day. Howard's pace picked up tempo as concern and fear dashed away his peace from moments before, the bag from the hardware store swinging violently against his legs. Nearing the front of his house Howard could see the front door stood ajar. Quickly he headed up the steps and through the door. The whole world faded away, as his sole focus centered on the lantern and it's wellbeing. Did he leave the small carving room's door open? No. Did he return the lantern back to its hiding place? No!

Howard Portman was startled, for the carving room's door stood open, and there standing, hands cradling the lantern, stood an equally startled Nick.

"Hey! Look, I..." the words barely had a chance to escape the nervous lips of Nick, before Howard Portman, artist, charged the local handyman.

Later, Howard would question himself on how the newly purchased stainless steel plastic coated red hook materialized in his hands, and, in the proceeding moments following, found a thorny purchase in the bone and gray matter of Nicholas', preferred Nick's, skull.

With a sickening ease the sharpened end of the stainless-steel hook had pierced Nick's head. A strange switch was thrown as Nick's synapses misfired in miscommunication, his eyes going far too wide and his mouth stuttering on an incomplete thought, never to be completed. The living record, called Nicolas, preferred Nick, skipped, and was heard no more.

Howard Portman was an artist, and now...he was also a killer.

Standing there Howard felt no fear, no remorse, no regret. No, Howard felt only surprise, and, sitting under that surprise, a deep and complete satisfaction. Howard could do no wrong when it came to the lantern, and this infidel to his temple had deserved this punishment for his desecration.

Nick's body slumped slowly to the floor; the lantern still cradled in his arms. Momentarily, Howard thought maybe he might have overreacted, that perhaps he had misjudged Nick's intentions and surprise, but noticing a bag on the floor, he investigates and finds Nick had been up to no good. It seemed the whispered rumors about Nick being somewhat untrustworthy were founded in fact, for within the small bag Howard found valuable personal items belonging to him. Items that could be so easily sold at any pawn shop.

Arriving at Howard's home and finding him absent, Nick had chosen that time to steal. Perhaps, if Howard had driven home Nick would've have heard his approach, and then could have been afforded the time to cover his actions, but sadly, for him, he wasn't lucky in this regard at all. Nicholas, preferred Nick, was a thief, and as a thief he had only gotten what he deserved. Howard Portman was also a thief, but not a common thief like the one Nick had proven be. If anything, Howard was a rescuer. He had rescued the lantern from the grasp of the undeserving one called Mr. Lee...hadn't he?

Howard Portman was an artist, a successful thief with limited experience, and now a murderer who had not the luxury of premeditation. Now, he was faced with the challenge of disposing of a body and the vehicle the once living body had arrived in. Being a multifaceted artist, Howard's home was packed with all the supplies any artist would need: paints, brushes, clays, solvents and thinners, canvases and card stocks, and of course large drop cloths and tarps to protect the floors when things got messy. Things had gotten very, very messy for Howard.

Working quickly, Howard wrapped Nick's cooling body in several sheets of plastic, finally sealing everything with a paint spattered tarp and a complete roll of duct tape wound tight around it all. Dragging the body to the kitchen at the back of his home, Howard then ran to the front of his home to retrieve Nick's truck, only to realize once there he would need Nick's keys, which were now more than likely wrapped up tightly with the now deceased. On the off-chance Nick was planning to leave rather quickly after his theft, which was most likely the case, Howard checked the ignition, and fortunately, Nick's keys sat engaged in the ignition waiting for familiar fingers that would never come. Howard climbed into the truck and turned the key with his unfamiliar fingers, started the engine, and drove it to the back of his home. Returning to his kitchen, Howard proceeded to muscle the corpse of the newly departed Nicholas, preferred Nick, down the back steps and into the waiting bed of the truck.

Howard Portman's home was set amid five acres of untended forest backed by federal land, land never to be used for human habitation, and land so removed from hiking trails anyone could hide anything without fear of discovery. Getting behind the wheel of the truck, Howard spent the next 30 minutes navigating and weaving the truck through the trees, and into the backwoods. Many years ago, when Howard still held an interest in it, he had explored the property and the adjoining backwoods, noting those unique features of land and wood. One of those unique features now called to him, a small ravine, like a nick in the land. Howard laughed. Now, that nick in the land, would have a Nick in it!

Nicolas', preferred Nick's, burial was a small affair, there was no family or friends, no well-wishers, no mourners, just Howard Portman, artist, thief, killer. Within an hour Nick's truck, again navigated and weaved its way back through the woods with Howard behind the wheel. Howard had enough common sense not to leave the truck anywhere near the recent burial. He would leave it on the edge of his property, and somewhere in the darker recesses of the night he would drive it away. Northern California is a place of lows and highs, both economically and geographically, and it would be the geography which would assist Howard now. A few miles away from his home there existed a dangerous curve with an even more dangerous drop. Like a seaside siren this drop called to Howard, it would gladly take Nick's truck, gears, gas, and all, but this would have to be later. Leaving the truck, Howard headed back to his home.

Howard stepped from the woods, just as the sound of approaching vehicles greeted his ears. Howard was expecting no one, but the empty site of his familiar driveway, reminded him. Joe the Mechanic was making good on his word, returning Howard's car with its newly charged battery.

Howard Portman was an artist, and as such, spent most of his time on his ass. He was not an athlete by nature, yet even so, it was with a burst of energy that any athlete would have been proud of Howard bridged the distance between himself and his home, diving quickly into the concealment of his kitchen. He made it just in time, as Joe the Mechanic, with tow truck and assistant following behind, came to a sliding stop on the gravel of Howard's driveway. Howard only had a gathering of seconds to hide a garbage bag and its bloody contents before he heard the tap-tap of Joe the Mechanic at his door.

"Hey!" Joe the mechanic, proclaimed as Howard opened his door. "Brought your car back. It's got a partial charge now which will be good for a while. Ya should have no problems but when you get the chance you should really let me top it up."

"Thanks! Yeah, that sounds good," Howard agreed, words uttered a little too quickly. "How much do I owe you?"

"Hey, don't worry about it. This one's on the house, just remember, if you ever make it in the big time..."

Joe the mechanic's reply stopped short as a strange look came over his face to sit and stay.

"Is there a problem?" Howard stated a little nervously.

"Are you okay?" Joe the Mechanic questioned.

"Yeah!... why do you ask?"

"Well, either that's red paint or blood. Hope you are not in their killin' folks!"

Howard Portman's world was rocked to his core as Joe laughed at his own jest. What blood?! What had the mechanic seen?! Howard's mind raced as he is gripped tightly my fear. Panic began to rise in him.

"What are you talking about?!" Howard laughed, doing his best to hide his sudden discomfort and instinct to run.

Gesturing, Joe the Mechanic pointed to Howard's torso. Howard looked down at himself, and there on his shirt, in a patch of pure white fabric, sat a vivid stain of red. Most days, one could've found Howard working on his art, his clothes a kaleidoscope of spilled and smeared paints, where a vivid stain of red would have been lost in the riot of other colors...but not today. Howard Portman had started his day in his civilian attire, plain cloth canvases that would never know the spectrum of Howard's artistic palette. Cloth canvases that to well showed the vivid smear of Nick's blood, that had escaped the plastic shrouding and Howard's sight. Howard's mind clicked as possible answers dodged and darted through his thoughts.

"Oh, that!..." Howard smiled awkwardly. "...actually, it's neither paint nor blood! You would think a guy like me would know better that to buy a cheap pen but look! Ruined a perfectly good shirt."

His words came out sweet like humble pie shared with a trusted ally. Joe sniffed the air, a brief look of puzzlement moving across his face...a look which vanished to be replaced by a conspiratorial good ole boy smirk.

"Happens to me all the time in my line of business," Joe the Mechanic replied smiling, matter-of-factly. "Just when you're not dressed for it, something mucks you up. Too bad that is a nice shirt though."

"Right! Ah well."

"Well, you have a nice day Mr. Portman...Howard," Joe the Mechanic winked as he made his way down the front steps, and to his waiting assistant and the tow truck.

"You too!" Howard said, giving an enthusiastic wave bye with his right hand. Within seconds, the tow truck was heading away, but Howard waited on his porch until he couldn't see nor hear the tow truck, before going back into his home.

Working he cleaned up all traces of blood and violence, then he gathered the remaining scraps of plastic and the rags he had used to clean up and placed them into the large black garbage bag he had concealed when the mechanic had arrived. The garbage bag and its contents had a date with Howard's fireplace, where they would give up their secrets to the flames and heat and be consumed.

Howard knew he'd been lucky, and that if he had not been an artist his story may not have been accepted so easily, and looking down at his shirt, Howard knew the garbage bag and its contents would not be the only thing to be offered up to the waiting fireplace. Like a closing sale, everything must go!

The Pumpkin Festival was just three days away, and Howard Portman, artist, was on schedule. For most of the month of October, everything had been going Howard's way, even the incident with Nick was affecting nothing.

Nicholas, preferred Nick, had been missing for a few weeks, and no one seemed to care, or more to the point, his disappearance was seen by the general community of Derrick as standard Nick behavior. It would seem Nick's life as a wanderer did him no favor, either in life or death. Howard felt it would probably take more than a year for anyone to possibly grow suspicious enough to think perhaps something bad had happened to the irascible Nick. By then Howard would be gone, back to the big city, and the waiting arms of his future.

As the days peeled away to the festival, Howard spent more of his time sketching and preparing under the light of the lantern, and was inwardly savoring the final days of preparation, when the sketching would end, and the carving would begin. It had taken several years, but finally he was coming to the end of a dark tunnel, with the light of the lantern leading his way.

The day of the Pumpkin Festival arrived, and Howard was ready. He'd spent the final hours of the following night adding the final touches to his pumpkin, and stepping back, almost fainted on his feet. His pumpkin was the most beautiful thing he had ever seen, and for a moment, all thoughts of victory left him. There before him, his pumpkin sat, like a sunrise crafted just for him by him. A harvested sun proclaiming to the world the approaching reign of Howard Portman, *artiste*.

Howard woke bright and early for he had much to accomplish. First, Howard had to get his finished pumpkin into the back of the pickup truck he had rented, which proved to be no easy feat. Briefly, Howard lamented the loss of Nicholas, preferred Nick, who in life had had his worth, especially when it came to heavy lifting. Howard Portman was an artist. He was not a mover, but after about a half hour of struggle Howard successfully loaded his pumpkin into the truck without any damage. Next came the drive into town, and as Howard drove his eyes constantly shifted to the rearview mirror, and to the back of the truck, and to the tarped and covered pumpkin which rested there. He would not let any mishap mar this day for him. At the edge of town, the traffic increased, for the town of Derrick's was already beginning to swell with arriving festival goers. Navigating his way, Howard arrived safe and sound, pumpkin and all, to the judging area, where with motherly concern he guided the volunteers for the festival in the safe unloading of his magnificent pumpkin. Howard could see he was not the first to bring his pumpkin as evidenced by three other pumpkins already set on their bales of hay. Each of these pumpkins were just as covered and hidden as Howard's pumpkin was and would remain so until the earlier part of the evening, when the public judging would begin. Without seeing them, Howard already knew they didn't stand a chance at all against his work.

Howard Portman, artist, spent the remaining hours, till the time of judging, in or around the judging area. His pumpkin, his masterpiece, had become another treasure for him, like the lantern, and he would not suffer its loss or its destruction, at least not yet. Many would have been impatient, but not Howard. He'd waited for this, and he was savoring every moment as the judging grew nearer. Long had he sat at a table of bitterness, impotent and angry, while a little old man from China usurped him, but in just a few hours that would all end, and the table would turn.

The judging was still two hours away, when Howard spotted Mr. Lee through the crowds. It had been a long time since Howard had last seen Mr. Lee. In his mind, Howard played with the thought of pity for the old man, for had he not lost the lantern, a unique gift of wonder, power, and magic? He must be devastated. Briefly Howard envisioned the husk he himself would become if <u>he</u> were to lose the lantern. Briefly, he felt a kind of empathy, but then he looked again at Mr. Lee, and the moment passed. Mr. Lee was smiling. Mr. Lee was happy. He wasn't a husk, nor a shadow of his former self. No, for all intents and purposes, outwardly, Mr. Lee had not changed at all.

The minutes ticked by and Howard resisted the urge to confront the seemingly unchanged and un-depressed Mr. Lee, then unable to bear it any longer, he sought the old man out.

"Mr. Lee!"

Howard Portman's voice called over the several feet which separated the two from each other, the young from the old. Mr. Lee had his head bent over, looking over that year's selection of pumpkin pies and other treats just as sweet. Hearing his name called, Mr. Lee turned, and the small smile on his face grew bigger at the site of Howard.

"Howard, good to see you," Mr. Lee responded back, grasping Howard's hand in his in greeting. "I have not seen you for a while. I hope all is well?"

"You know how things are Mr. Lee," Howard replied, the smile on his face getting bigger as the thoughts of his approaching victory danced and swam around in his head. "The lifestyle of an artist demands what it demands and gives when it can."

"Yes, so true, so true!"

An awkward silence descended between the two as they simply shared smiles.

"So, it really should be a good contest this year," Howard stated. "I really think I've outdone myself this year."

"Good, good," Mr. Lee gave back. "I would expect no less from you."

"Well with a master like you around, Mr. Lee, one has to step up their game. As always, I can't wait to see your entry."

"I'm afraid you'll be disappointed," Mr. Lee mumbled, looking down at the ground.

"Why Mr. Lee?" Howard smiled, inwardly having fun at the old man's expense and discomfort. "I could never be disappointed in any of your pumpkins."

Finally, here was the sign Howard was looking for. Try as he might poor Mr. Lee was merely hiding his sorrow at the loss of the lantern. Mr. Lee already knew Howard would be "disappointed", for this year, without the beneficial magic of the lantern, Mr. Lee's pumpkin would look like crap, the garbage it truly was. The work of a child.

"Well," Mr. Lee said, looking up sheepishly. "You're going to have to wait till next year."

Next year! Without the lantern there would be no more years, no more victories for this old man!

"What do you mean?" Howard nervously asked. Something was not right, and suddenly, it seemed highly possible his plans were about to collapse around him, like the walls of a decaying pumpkin.

Then Mr. Lee laughed ever so slightly, and said:

"I didn't enter this year."

The shock of Mr. Lee's answer stabbed Howard to the core. No. No! It couldn't be! All that time, all the risks Howard had made, all the time Howard had squandered flashed and dashed across his mind. He was supposed to win tonight, but how could Howard claim victory, when the enemy had vanished, leaving the battlefield bare, the fight unfought.

Howard Portman, artist, suddenly did not feel so well, in fact he felt sick to his soul as the world he orbited was twisted and bent off its axis.

"... no inspiration this year," Mr. Lee was saying. "Besides, I'm pretty sure everyone was getting tired of seeing this old wrinkly Chinese face up there anyway. You know!"

"Right, right..." Howard said absently, his mind elsewhere, peering down over this new unexpected situation, and, in denial, grasping at the edges of his well-constructed plans, trying to hold it all together. Even as these same plans lumped and decayed into the dust.

"Well, there's always next year, yes?"

"Yeah...Yes. Of course!" Howard answered, momentarily regaining some of his composure.

"Good luck Howard. I will see you later," Mr. Lee said, excusing himself, and Howard watched as he left, his eyes on the back of Mr. Lee as he made his way into the crowds, and was soon lost to Howard's sight. Standing there in the crowd, Howard felt bereft, a lone mote suddenly set adrift. He didn't know how, but somehow and in some way, Mr. Lee had won again.

By the time of the pumpkin judging, Howard had regained most if not all his previous composure. So what if there was no pumpkin to gain pumpkin revenge against the elderly Mr. Lee, had he not won already by the very fact Mr. Lee had not entered, and more to the point, could not enter due to the loss of the lantern and its extraordinary gift?

The crowd began to swell and stir as one by one, each pumpkin was unveiled to the waiting judges. As was the practice, the order of unveiling was determined by your ranking in last year's contest, if you'd entered, and your relative newness to the event. Those professional carvers coming from outside state for the first time would not be in those groups first to be judged, like all talented in the craft they would have to wait their turn. For the past several years, the last two pumpkins to be judged, had always come down to Mr. Lee and Howard's pumpkins. Howard's pumpkin going first and Mr. Lee's coming last wrapping up the whole event. With no entry from Mr. Lee that year, for the first time, Howard's pumpkin was set to be the last one to be unveiled and judged, and Howard, proudly, knew this was only right. The best was always saved for last, and this year, Howard's pumpkin was the best by far. It was destiny.

The time came for Howard's pumpkin to be unveiled and the crowd, which had filled to bursting, buzzed with excitement, for this would be the final glorious orange tinged note on the Pumpkin Festival, and Howard Portman, artist, was ready. Young and old and the in-between gathered round like it was Christmas morn and the best gift was about to be revealed in all its glory. The crowd barely made a sound as two volunteers cut the strings holding the covering down on Howard's carved pumpkin, then under everyone's watchful eyes, the two lifted the covering.

"Oh my God!"

This was the first sound anyone made after Howard's pumpkin was unveiled, and then, what followed was chaos. Quickly parents turned children away lest their eyes see and not recover, while others rushed to the sides of those that had immediately become nauseous or had passed out on their feet. Small gasps and cries of horror came from the crowd, as more and more of the crowd made out the details of Howard's pumpkin.

Howard Portman, artist, thief, murderer, stood bewildered as confusion swept over him in unforgiving and unrelenting waves.

"What was wrong with everyone?!" Howard thought. His glorious moment of victory had somehow been eclipsed and turning to the eyes of the people in the crowd, he saw hate, and fear, and disgust, and he did not understand. Standing in his confusion, Howard did not notice the hands pointing at him or the approaching men in uniforms. He had only just begun to come back to himself when rough hands seized him and began to march him through the crowd, the crowd parting for him, not in honor but in loathing.

"What is the meaning of this?!" Howard yelled, as the crowd suddenly got louder, the hands holding him rougher.

"You know what you done! You sick bastard!" one of the owners of the rough hands snarled into his left ear.

"Disgusting!"

"How could you?!"

"You sick fuckin' bastard!"

The rough hands that had grabbed Howard quicken their speed, as the crowd's mood darkened further, their voices rising in anger. Fear locked down on Howard completely, and he knew, somehow, his world of possibilities and brighter futures had vanished. With a last glance at the crowd Howard Portman, artist, was put into the back of a waiting squad car and driven away.

And, in the back of the gathered and outraged crowd, a silent Mr. Lee watched.

The following week and a half passed in a daze, as Howard was shuffled from one jail cell to another, from one questioning room to another. Howard Portman, artist, was now a prisoner, his crimes discovered.

"We found the body. Wasn't hard to find...not with that big clue you gave us."

"We can't understand Howard...why?"

"Why did you do it?!"

They kept asking the same questions, but Howard had no answers. Somehow, his secret had been revealed and the body of Nicholas, preferred Nick, was discovered. Locked in his confusion, Howard couldn't answer how everything had gone so wrong. This was not supposed to happen. His artistic management assured Howard he had nothing to fear, and assuredly, the police had gotten the wrong man. He was relieved to hear that already lawyers were looking over his case and preparing a defense, yet the days went by and still no one came to his aid, legal or otherwise. Slowly, Howard realized no lawyers were coming to see him, and after several attempts to reach them, that his artistic management had let him go. Howard's life descended deeper into the dark.

Within days of his incarceration, Howard was notified in the following week he would be transferred down to San Francisco to be tried, and most likely convicted. The days passed, and Howard drifted into silence, his confusion succumbing to despair. Even his own body was against him, as the trauma of events set in, giving itself up to sudden chills, his skin breaking out in raw red rashes.

Howard Portman, artist, thief, murderer, criminal was one day away from his transfer when the elderly Mr. Lee came to visit him. Gone was the hate towards the old man that had so deeply and completely enveloped Howard. That prideful being, which had been Howard Portman, was nothing now, just a shell of confusion and absolute loss. Mr. Lee took the seat across from Howard, and both sat in silence.

"You had to do it, didn't you?"

For a moment, Mr. Lees comment was met with further silence.

"...what?" Howard asked in his confusion and numbness, for in the last several days he had lost all understanding of the world around him. All the confidence Howard had previously possessed was gone, leeched away by the gravity of current events, and now he relied on the world around him to inform him, to guide him like a decrepit war victim, made blind, dumb, and crippled by the circumstances of an unwinnable war.

"You could not leave well enough alone?" Mr. Lee continued, his voice rising slightly. "Was second-best so bad young man?"

Howard's mind spun, even more confused by the old man's statement. What was the elderly Lee talking about, Howard thought. Was this unexpected visit all about pumpkins?

"... I-I don't understand," Howard said after a time, and it was with this statement the elderly Mr. Lee looked deep into the eyes of Howard Portman, and Howard Portman, was forced to return the gaze and there he saw something that rocked him back in his seat. There, in depths of Mr. Lee's eyes, the purest glint of malice dwelled and thrived. The slight upturned smile on Mr. Lee's face, told Howard he was not mistaken. He had not been the only one to know and hide hate.

"The lantern," Mr. Lee finally offered.

The simple statement caused a cold chill to take Howard in his seat, his thoughts suddenly spinning into even greater confusion.

"What? I don't understand... I..." Howard's reply stuttered into silence as the smile on Mr. Lee's face grew larger, and the malicious glint in his eye grew darker.

"Did you honestly think you were the first to discover my secret? Did you think others hadn't tried before... and failed?" The elderly Lee smiled, brightly.

Then, the sweet and kind Mr. Lee began to explain.

The stories he told Howard about were all true, minus a few very important details. His skill had indeed come from the high mountains of China, but they had not come easily nor without cost. The Master who had possessed the lantern prior to Mr. Lee, was determined it should never leave the high mountains, and also believed its gift could never be understood by a modern world, nor should it, but Mr. Lee, like poor naive Howard, had also been inexplicably drawn to it, called to it. Mr. Lee knew he could not, he would not, leave the mountains without it, so, like Howard, he devised a plan, and one fateful night, went to visit the Master in the high mountain cave he dwelled in. Under cover of night he entered the cave and approached the sleeping Master. The master always kept the lantern close to him, and that night like any other found the Lantern hanging suspended above the dream held master's head. Quietly, the young Mr. Lee had stolen across the floor of the cave to the waiting lantern, and the unsuspecting and still slumbering Master. Mr. Lee was surprised when just as his fingers brushed the surface of the lantern the master's eyes opened, awake and clear, in full understanding of the obvious intentions of this city bred scholar. The then young Mr. Lee only had seconds before the Master raised any alarm.

Mr. Lee much later, back within the comfortable confines of his familiar university, reflected on how easy it was to silence the old Master once his hands found his throat. With ease his thumbs had pressed into the soft flesh of the master's throat. As frail and as old as the Master was it still took the young Mr. Lee a few minutes to squeeze the life from him, sending him down into the unfathomable abyss, perchance to join the strange gods he had worshipped in life. Mr. Lee had stood over the dead body of the master, and like a future Howard, felt only a profound satisfaction, and having no further obstructions made away with the lantern in the early morning hours. Describing his crime Mr. Lee maintains eye contact with Howard and his smile grows when he sees Howard's eyes grow wide with comprehension.

That carving! The one he had found in the cabinet in Mr. Lee's bedroom. The carving that depicted what Howard now realized was a younger Mr. Lee strangling a much older smaller man. The Master!

Mr. Lee wagged a single finger at him looking a little disappointed, as if a favored student had made a mistake with unforeseen repercussions.

"Ahhhhhh! You are not a good thief Howard, but you are a smart man. I know you searched by home and found it... Did you like it?"

Returning to the university Mr. Lee hid his discovery and his crime and waited. He waited for some word to descend from the high mountains to implicate him, to send him down to a lone prison cell to become lost and forgotten. The days turned into weeks, weeks into months, but no word of his crime came down from the mountains, and when he felt the time was right, he turned to the lantern and the gifts it would bestow upon him.

"It took me some time to figure out how the lantern could be lit, I'm sure you faced the same dilemma. But you and I figured it out? When I saw your pumpkin, I knew you had!" Mr. Lee said proudly. "But the lighting is the easy part. No, the other demands of the lantern are much more difficult. Cost more than time."

Mr. Lee continued to explain, and as he did so, Howard began to understand how his world had unraveled, and how his crime was accidently revealed. Mr. Lee had won the lantern's gift through murder, and later through the loss of one friend. Once he had figured out how to light the Lantern, Mr. Lee began to carve, and with that first carved piece he had known an indescribable delight. This delight lasted only briefly, when with pride Mr. Lee showed his first carving to a dear friend and colleague. This was a mistake. His dear friend and colleague had recoiled in horror and disgust. Mr. Lee was surprised, and then frighten by his friend's response, for he realized his friend did not see a work of beauty, a work of divine craftsmanship. He questioned his friend and demanded answers to his reaction, and so his friend told him. He did not see any beauty. No, what his friend saw was a depiction, in supreme detail, of his childhood friend grinning like a demon, surrounded by monstrous malformed shapes, as he brutally strangled an old man to death.

This stunned Mr. Lee. Mr. Lee saw only beauty and divine shapes. His colleague and friend had seen only the truth of his crime. The look of horror upon the face of his friend told Mr. Lee he must leave the country, for if word passed around about his artwork it could lead to awkward questions, and potentially some type of investigation. Assuring his friend that it was only a joke (Mr. Lee knew his friend didn't believe him), and a sick one at that, Mr. Lee resigned and began the process of emigrating to America.

"This was the true gift, the true power of the lantern," Mr. Lee stated. "Carve an angel and all around you will only see a devil. A lovely dove...becomes a plague filled rat. A loving mother and child...a starving mother feasting on her own child still steaming and fresh from the womb. That is the magic! Seeking to create beauty, we only show the authentic horror of our own being unshielded for all eyes to <u>see</u>."

Understanding awakened within Howard.

"But how? You-" Howard mumbled. "Each year your pumpkins have been fantastic! Only images that appeal to those ignorant people. Not one demon. Not one offensive image... how?"

"It took me a little time." Mr. Lee responded drawing himself up in his chair proudly. "But after a few years here in America, I <u>had</u> to figure it out. Who would know where I'd be right now if I hadn't solved it? It's quite simple, really."

Howard Portman, artist, thief, murderer, criminal waited as silence nestled between them.

"Isn't it obvious?" Mr. Lee began happily, his face wrinkling in delight. "Craft beauty and all will see monsters! Craft monsters....."

He waited for Howard to fill in the blank, but Howard was lost. That once bright beacon that had been Howard Portman, artist, was dimming and dwindling out on the horizon. Shaking his head sadly Mr. Lee finished.

"...and all will see beauty!"

The little light alone on the horizon grew a little brighter and Howard realized his fatal mistake. Under the false light of the lantern he had carved beauty, but the whole time, he had been carving his crime in undeniable clarity. Clearly his pumpkin had depicted in perfect detail the murder and burial of Nicholas, preferred Nick.

The old teacher continued.

"All these years I have carved the same image over and over and over again...an image of violence...an image of my <u>birth</u> into the extraordinary!

"The death of the Master under my pressing hands!"

[179]

A horrific enlightenment shone sickly upon Howard, as the old Chinese man called Mr. Lee began to chuckle. Howard's light grew brighter, filled with the desire to kill the man who sat across from him, but before he could even act his body was seized with an intense and blinding pain, his skin screamed under thousands of invisible pinpricks that dug and racked across the flesh of his world. His body tried to fight it immediately drenching him in sweat attempting vainly to cool the rapid and uncontrolled rise in his temperature.

"Oh! That's not good! What's wrong?" The laughing Mr. Lee asked eyes wide falsely concern. Looking into his eyes, Howard knew the old man knew the answer already. He only asked to torture Howard. "Oh yes. That's right. Did you think the lantern was only affecting the carvings?

"Do you know how old the lantern is? Can you even imagine from where and when, and from whom the lantern has descended from?! It is so old that the ones who crafted it did not have human hands! Great was their craft, their magic, their skill that to touch any of their relics means to have one's self forever changed! I'm afraid your changes have begun, and sadly without the lantern, and it's calming effects, you will continue to change until you are no more!"

Howard Portman, artist, thief, murderer, prisoner, wracked with pain, looked up at the now standing, grinning Mr. Lee, and was horrified as the elderly man from China licked his lips with a tongue grown incredibly long and sinuous, with a hue and tone resembling pale death, lifeless and cold. Equally so did the fingers of Mr. Lee change and twine together. Fingers thin and worm-like and numerous. Howard could now easily imagine this was the how the old man had lit the lantern, by these wriggling appendages. And for a moment the years sloth off of the old Asian man and Mr. Lee stands before him younger and stronger, but the moment passed. In the pause that gripped Howard by shock and revulsion, Mr. Lee's tongue receded back into his mouth regaining its normal proportions and color. His fingers followed suit, once again taking on the resemblance of normal human ones.

"Do you like?!" Mr. Lee grinned. "At first, like you, I was horrified, ah, but then I learned. Here was a gift given by the ancient ones...but long before its arrival, I too felt the pain, the discomfort of being...transformed. Gratefully, I learned that it is through the lantern's grace and its presence the transformations are not as profound, nor as deadly."

"You can't get away with this!" Howard grunted over his agony. The pain coiling inside him, slid over the parts of himself that were still human.

"Oh, but I have Howard. Who will they believe, you or me? The crazy man who killed or the kind old man from China?! It doesn't matter Howard, without the lantern your changes will continue, and rather sooner than you would hope, you will end."

"Damn you!"

"Yes, of course!" The demented Mr. Lee happily proclaimed. "But I've known that for a long time now. Now I must be going. Oh yes. And I must thank you. News of your exploits have traveled wide and far, and has brought the larger world to Derrick, where I have been recently discovered. Invitations have poured in, and it seems the artistic world is ready to embrace this old Chinese professor."

"Ah!" Howard smiled maliciously over the pain. "...but without the lantern, you will go nowhere! You'll never find it!"

"But my poor Howard...I already have."

The light on the horizon once more dimmed and fought to even be seen amongst the dimmest stars that line the sky.

"With the police's investigation, your home was searched, and my property was reclaimed. After this it was quite easy to get the lantern returned to me.

"Now, once again it rests in its container...the hollowed-out belly of the late master's carved beast that you so admired, Howard."

The Master's carving?! The one displayed so prominently in Mr. Lee's home in its glass case!

The last threads of hope, of any victory, slipped smoothly from Howard's hands and out through the cracks in the floor. He'd been so close to the lantern's hidden location and missed it.

Mr. Lee had won.

Howard Portman, artist, thief, murderer, prisoner, fool sat in pain and agony, as Mr. Lee, with a backward glance and grin, was escorted out.

If only he had stolen the master's art piece when he had the chance, but how could he have guessed the art piece of the Master was only a container for a greater prize!

But clever, had never been a title...Howard, artist...had ever worn!

The 3rd Riddle

And in that place forgotten deep
grows the Tower, a darkened keep,
and there the ones that sleep
fill the halls with frightened screams.

To play their game makes one their slave,
makes one's pallor a haunting shade,
for the stones they cast
are the bones that laugh
well beyond the grave.

You're sealed away till one dark day
you also play their tune.
You'll pray for life, you'll pray for light,
seen: two eyes, twin baleful moons.

A maiden's madness mingles
with fears of fickle youths,
who shine for a time with wayward minds
till teller tells times are through.

The vast bell wrings
and cobwebs swing
with petty mortal forms.
The coil it snaps,
the Beast it taps,
the door closes on their tomb.

"Heard no more,
heard no more"
the solemn make their cry,
for the stones they cast
are the bones that laugh
beyond the mortal sky.

The Hottest Hot Sauce

Beginning.

Begin.

I was a man of the road
Not hampered my goal
To get clear to there and back again my kin.
I traveled the road all gritty and grime.
I traveled with goal in mine.
See I was part Irish, part Chinese, part Cherokee, part African,
Chicano
And I'd lived a fire blood life
That left me all cold and Hollow.
So, jabs and jobs I take
To carry this load ta that,
Always ready with pitchfork, gun, Remington, or baseball bat
To set any attacker or cracker who knew to step the fuck back
Cuz I was about the road, the school of ain't looking back.
But like I said I had it a goal
To travel up and down every road
Delivering cargo for the man,
Till fate walked crept stole in.

I'd stopped on the road to lighten my load
And cool my poor tired feets
And they're sat a diner
Like a woman's vagina
Already for a hungry man to eat.
I set my heel and started to spill my way through the diner door
And when I winked in wasn't it a sin
The waitress was as clean as the men's room floor after gangster fights and Rodeo boys.
So, with that hunger killed
I followed my will and ordered myself a three taco meal:
With beef and pork, huevos rancheros;
A slice of that pie and a piece of a mango;
And dos cervezas shaped like osas
To toast my friends who live on the coastas.
It all was prepared.
I gathered myself and everything else looking for vacant seat or chair.
A table.
A window.
A picture of God... a pitcher of God?
Nothing else.
Empty seats and dinner treats
My food and myself.
I was the only one
Just me and the setting Sun given the night a cool run.
I chose a seat which ain't no feet just by the door at the window looking out
Someone touch my baby, my rig, I can get up quick and give shout.
I bowed my head and thank the Lord
For giving me all I got:
A good ass woman;
A house to share;
And all the best indica pot.
My rig of course I'm gratefully praising
Happy, satisfied, and truthfully thankful.
Now with the Lord in check I set to wreck

My meal of utter abundance.
I grabbed my fork and stole a knife
Ready to give that food a fight
Skinning it to the bones in sight
Leavin' nothing but a plate in fright.
I took my first bite.
I start to chew.
I took my second bite...
Hey something wasn't quite right!
Something was missing from my sight!
Immediately I knew what was wrong
But looking at my table an essential decoration was gone,
Or absent I'd say.
A dear secret friend that brings taste buds to life'
Makes you howl at the Moon and jump like a kite.
A treasure of Earth.
A warming desire.
Liquid heat,
Magical fire!
Hot sauce...hot sauce.
You see
When I was a child about only yay high,
I lived on the corner of Treat,
And there on that corner
Past prostitute and porn wars
Was Mademoiselle's Taqueria Suite.
It was a lively mix of Cajun, Creole, Chinese Szechuan, and El
Salvadorian scrap food,
And every single meal you got
Was extremely hot and good.
And what made it hot?
And what made it good? Pause.
Was everything was covered deep in Mama's Cajun hot sauce!
Ever since then,
My dear close friends,
Every meal I ate
Whether on napkin or plate
Wasn't a meal without hot sauce.
I sat there thinking

Eyes steadily blinking
Looking for a little hot fire,
But on every table I looked at
All I saw was empty desires.
But they're,
Just there!
Way deep in the back!
I could see alone bottle
Deep in a crack.
All red and dusty.
The top of the bottle all crusty
With crystals all charcoaled and black.
It was a bottle of the hot
Waiting to be got,
And use that moment right on the spot...
But I hesitated a second and gathered myself
Cuz this bottle had a red-hot glow.
It glowed with a light you couldn't deny!
It looked. Yes looked!
At me as if it twere alive!
Saying
"I'm delicious, surely nutritious."
But something told me actually quite vicious
And definitely malicious in intent,
But I was set, my food growing cold
And I never met a bottle I couldn't control!
I kicked back my chair and hitched up my belt
Ready for a hot war and a bottle to get,
But an army of tables stood before
With chairs is as infantry ready for war
Creating a defensive wall between that bottle and me.
I lashed out hard,
Kicked down chairs like cards
Set on tables of molten steel,
For today would be my victory
Cuz I was hard to reel.
And there it stood all hot and red,
Asking the question
"Howdja like ta be dead?"
I replied simply fine,

Grabbed it real unkind and held it too the night.

"I dare you..."

"What?"

"I dare you."

It was the bottle ah speakin'
Though my mind might be tweaking,
But I heard it twice and once more.

"I dare you."

Ha!
I grabbed its head like I was ripping some bread
And pulled the top clean off.
Tilted my head back deep
And gave my poor mouth a shot.
Nothing.
Nothing!
Why it wasn't even hot at all
At least this is what I thought,
For down deep in the heart of me
I felt something rising a lot.

It was a heat.

It was the Heat!

The kind of heat you can't ignore.
The kind of heat you feel when the fire is right at your door.
For one second
I thought it would end in a drop,
But once again I played fool!
Cuz the heat kept ah comin'
And I was a feeling ah done in
For I had no moisture left to drool!
And then again something started to rise,

And to my utter surprise,
A scream rip that room and everything in sight.

It was me!

I screamed!
I yelled!
I almost fell
As I scrambled across the room.
All I could think to myself was
You are most probably doomed.
I got to my table as best as I was able,
Eyes blinded with tears.
Searching lurching frantically!

"Where the hell is my beer?!"

It may have been luck;
The dimmed viewed side of my truck;
A little of both and fate,
For fingers grasped bottles,
Felt tops that were hollow,
And that was just wonderfully great.
But I couldn't stop ah screamin'!
Entrenched with a demon
And didn't know what to do,
So, I tip my head back
And opened my red blistered crack,
And threw the beers in
One and two!

Beer...cool beer

I wiped my head free of some fear.

The Heat had gone.

Wait...
No...
No!

Again, I played fool!
For the heat had just left elementary
And jumped into graduate school!

The fire return and once again I burned
I stumbled like a buffoon,
And as the Heat coalesced and I began to regret
I lost all conscious view....

I woke I don't know when
On the side of the road.
My rig sitting simply,
Pretty alone.
The restaurant that I ate upon
Had vanished. No Trace, gone.
My tongue sat in my mouth all swollen and numb,
Like I'd just been to New Orleans and swallowed 2 tons of
rum.
So that is my story assuredly not gory
About a bottle I once met.
The first ever in my life
To cause me to break out in sweats.
Yes. And tears and screams and long forgotten dreams.
And a deep wish for my mother, Mommy.
The next time I see that bottle chum
I definitely won't be no dummy!
Pass the hot sauce.

End.

The ending.

The end.

To Sleep Hungry

He stands knee-deep in the verdant green grass, the land rolling away from him in long graceful slopes. Majestic trees dot the vista, their gentle branches swaying in a tiny breeze. The Sun is full and hot and wonderful as it drapes across his skin, lifting the smell of green grasses straight from the ground and into the air. He raises his face to the Sun, eyes held shut. His shopping cart stands a short distance away. It's insides full of his many bags which themselves hold his life: a ragged thing of traded for, bought, and found objects. In the distance masterless herds of shopping carts roam, their metal frames glinting under the hot blazing Sun. He knows he is only a temporary visitor to this paradise.

He is dreaming.

With a staccato flash of brilliant blinding white pain paradise vanishes. Her green fields, her abundance, all gone as a boot heel shadow, black on blue-black night, strikes the man lying tucked against the back building wall amidst the weeds, the moist and molding cardboard, and the homeless nesting debris of other discarded things like him. The night is still young.

"Wake the fuck up!!!"

The boot rises and descends again, striking the man a shoving blow against his rising right shoulder. The man had come awake fully at the guard's yell, the first blow the initial spark back to consciousness, the second blow an unnecessary wake-up call. He was awake. Now.

"I'm tired of you lazy ass muthafuckers comin' round here!" Yells the man dressed in the blue security guard uniform, his boots planted firmly on the ground, feet wide apart in a defiant stance. The homeless man is awake, eyes open, hands already moving automatically pulling personal possessions together, grumbles under his breath. He glances at the security guard:

"Leo."

At least that is what the name tag on his uniformed chest says.

Leo the security guard is an angry man. The homeless man averts his eyes from the security guard's hate, so use to this life of the dominated nomads: always forced to move and always moving.

"Get yo shit and take your nasty ass someplace else!"

The guard yells more, one hand on the baton handle in his belt. In his eyes, the homeless man can see the reflected wishes of the many, who find great offense at sharing a world with such people as him, a mar on an otherwise perfect world. The homeless man knows not to talk back. He can see this security guard, this man, was only looking for one thing: an excuse. With years of practice, he gathers his few belongings into his shopping cart and begins to move away. His eyes take in the guard one last time as he leaves.

"If you come back again, I warn you, it's your fuckin' ass! You piece of shit!!"

The guard's raged tainted words fly out into the night to hit the homeless man's dusty dirty mildew scented shoulders and his life, contained in a humble shopping cart full of colorful and once bright bags. The words and the rage find a place there, where they fit, vampire seeds in a foul and fertile soil. The homeless man doesn't notice.

The *Presence* in his head doesn't seem to care. A booted beating was nothing new, and the *Presence* would not speak any more about the subject.

He pushes his life across the concrete. It rattles and shakes, and catches at every crack and crevice, making a rhythmless music under streetlight. The fog has rolled in like a slow chilling wave of smoke, moist and heady with a note of salt dragged from off the ocean's surface miles away.

Where?

That eternal question flicked and feathered him at every moment and haunted him every day. Where could he find a place for just this night, for just a moment, to rest, to sleep, to be sheltered and unafraid?

Most of the good places were taken.

Luck lived and breathed when you can find an abandoned building or house, something still heated with intact windows, and all usually with somebody in them already laying claim. Usually punk kids prone to violence, or the products of pushers: drugs and the junkies who used them.

Don't let the drugs or the slurred speech fool you, junkies are always more dangerous...unless it's punk junkies with murderous minds. Then run.

As he pushes his cart, he finds peace, if not rest, in his meandering. Drifting on autopilot, he visits those places in times past which had provided temporary havens and shelters from the cold and the prowling predators. He finds himself in older yet familiar territory.

Months back, an old warehouse district was swept clean by the cops and now it had become a ghost town. Word on the street was the whole area was going to be demolished for a new industrial park. Yet one more place not meant for him and others like him, but for now, it still held the potential for a discarded-thing-person to find shelter.

Somewhere in the distance a car drove blasting music which pumped bass into the arteries of the otherwise quiet night. Late night wanderers enjoying themselves, carrying their tribal sounds as they went. Injecting the dark with sound, a heartbeat that pulsed and retreated somewhere in the unseen distance.

The building is old.

Built in a time of coal and brick, racism and ragtime, it is surrounded by vacant lots, barren slabs and cracked gray concrete beaten by the Sun, and dark asphalt black swatches, burned by it. At its front, a large parking area had become a display in the tenacity of the invasive and local vegetation. Weeds of varying species, popping up in patches of gregarious greens, dirty browns, and dry yellows, homeless in their own rights, warred and won against the crumbling stone. Long ago, this building had a purpose, but that time had passed. Shattered windows, missing teeth, smile out on the ever-emptying human world around it. To the homeless man the building looks like a hospital.

It is.

He doesn't like hospitals.

The whole building and lot are surrounded by new fencing, a geometric web of dull silver and black lines laid out on the night's face. The fencing wasn't here a few months back. Someone had been taking care of the place, but why would they go to the trouble of putting up a new fence if the whole area was going to be demolished the *Presence* asks.

He shrugs and mumbles.

The homeless man can only guess, and guessing was for those who still cared, for those who still had stakes in the game.

He had cashed out many...many years ago.

The building is empty. He can feel it. After years of experience, years of roaming the abandoned shells and unguarded manmade boxes, he knows all the signs necessary for lawless occupation.

The police sweep of a few months ago had been highly effective.

The homeless man walks casually around the fenced-in building. He finds no weakness in the new fencing, so he makes one. Taking a second to search in his cart he pulls out wire snips, blue handled and worn.

Excluding a job and a home, there are some things you can find for free, especially when you're a "bum" with time to scrounge, but certain things must be bought or traded for, or, for the brave, the foolish, or for those desiring the secure comfort of incarceration, stolen. The wire snips had cost him one pint of gin.

He moves to the support posts for the fencing. Patiently he snips through eight of the fence's links, focusing on the ones connected to the support post. It only takes him a few minutes to create a gap for himself and his cart. Peeling back the now free section of fence he pushes his cart through and follows after. Briefly turning back, he pulls a small pile of assorted wires and cords from his stained coat and taking a minute or more loosely reattaches the fencing to the fence post. His is not a sharing world of either resources or shelter, most reciprocation was forced with either you giving or you taking!

In seconds he is darting into the much deeper shadows which surround the waiting building. His shopping cart's wheels pitch sound back at him loud and sharp, as he approaches the cool red brick and mortar walls of the old building, like bat sounds signaling and proclaiming: Here, Here! Here, Here! Here, Here!

Leaving his cart in the shadows the homeless man circles the building looking for luck: an open window; an easily jimmied door. He will find neither here.

He finds better.

On reaching the back of the building he goes to the first promising door he can see. He raises his hand to test the doorknob. The doorknob turns and the door opens. His mind wanders to the possibility maybe his instincts are wrong in their initial determination that the building was unoccupied, but to his street honed senses, the building's breath is empty. Pulling, the door pushes against leaves and rubbish piled against it.

Nobody home, but he still will be cautious: prepared to run at the first sign of wrong. Darting back into the deep shadows that lean against the building, he returns seconds later with his cart. The door stands open waiting. Pushing his cart at the door it jams on the doorsill with an audible crash. The noise it makes rings out loud and clear through the night streets and the presently people vacant night realm around him. In a rush he moves to the front of the cart, lifts it front and drags it in. Returning to the door he glances out briefly to see if he has been observed. Seeing no one, he shuts the door.

Everything is still inside the building. All he can hear is the sound of his own harsh breathing and the soft settling of unsettled things in his beloved cart. He pats its handle as his eyes slowly adjust and his breathing settles. He can hear the silent stones shift, brick kissing brick, and the quiet echo of empty hallways and rooms.

He begins to explore, his cart before him faithfully leading the way.

An old gurney or two; a few chairs here and there; a wheelchair neither going back or forth; a desk overturned and broken. Other things. Shapes covered in dust. The deeper he goes the darker it gets, and after a time he realizes he can't see.

After years on the streets he has grown use to moving in the dark, hiding in the shadows, but inevitably one needs light. He rummages in his cart and comes out with another cherished and traded for item: a scarred and beaten flashlight, which at its best only illuminates a few feet ahead of him but would put up a good fight against the dark interior.

He has found this building, he has gained entrance, and now he is looking for something else. He now has the time.

Down a long dirty and white tiled hallway, he finds what he's looking for: a room with a solid door, that wasn't too far from the "entrance", but wasn't too close to it either. Defendable and escapable. His flashlight shines through the small window in the door revealing a long room with several wheeled beds pushed against the back wall. On a few, old and worn mattresses still lay, waiting for patients which long ago had departed: healed or dead and gone elsewhere, or still undecided, and at the time of the hospital's closure merely relocated, gently or pushed out on to the sidewalk in hospital gowns on wooden crutches to hobble off to somewhere else.

One bed would not have much longer to wait for a new occupant.

Nestling his flashlight in his bags he pushes the door, and it swings freely open, and stays that way, for a moment. It begins to close slowly. Grabbing the familiar handle of his shopping cart he pushes it into the room, all thoughts on the rest to come, when it jams on the door's sill. With a small grin on his face, and a side glance at the *Presence*, he goes to the front, lifts it gently, and pulls it over the threshold. It is just as he is noticing a strange smell, something dead and gone wrong, that his world whirls into confusion and disorientation.

He doesn't see the hole in the floor. The hole, gaping big and dark, which isn't supposed to be there! It only takes him a few backward steps, pulling the cart with him into the room before his feet reach and pass over the edge of the dark opening. His hands desperately hold onto his shopping cart reflexively, as for just a moment the carts weight slows his inertia, but only for a moment. He lets go. He falls. The smell, he had noticed, invades him completely as he falls, soaking into his skin. He doesn't fall for long, though the sensation of falling stretches for an eternity. He lands hard and wrong, the area of his landing something nonuniform and sharp, that gives, but not fully beneath him. The pain is inhuman and sweeps completely through him, leaving heat and nausea, and an encroaching darkness. He screams. The shopping cart's little front wheels spin and quake, losing their precious contact with the familiar ground they love dearly, and follows him down into the hole. Through the deepening darkness his cart, flashlight illuminating from within, draws closer. It looks spectral. It's metal struts strange silhouetted ribs in the weak flashlight's light. He is mostly unconscious when it lands on him.

He lies heavy in an inky black coat and somewhere close a baby is crying. It doesn't sound right. Something is wrong with it, but he doesn't know what it is.

Why won't anyone help?!

There is another sound. A pain sound. The sound of someone whimpering. The coat is lifted from him and his eyes open slowly.

The homeless man lies in a ragged heap. His shopping cart, the punctuation of his fall, lays across his chest and hips. He remembers nothing, at first. The dead and wrong smell envelopes him. The smell is a strange mix of death and a body left unnoticed, of a hospital room's wall-to-ceiling industrial grade cleaner scent and antiseptic liquid aroma. He knows both smells well. Was he in a hospital where the patients were left to rot? He had been dreaming of a baby, a poor and a hungry thing, and then something woke him. A sound. He tries to sit up. Pain flashes through his body and he screams again. In his attempt to rise, he feels his carts weight and sees it through the fog of his pain and confusion. The entire back of his body feels wrong. He passes out again.

The *Presence* is talking to him.

"They all want you to die!"

"But we show 'em, don't we?"

"This is nothin'!"

"Move the cart. Move the cart. Move the cart!"

His body has changed position. No longer prone he is sitting up. His thoughts are a broken painful haze, fevered. His body shudders and shakes in between the pain and numbness as he looks around. His cart sits off to the side loyal and confused. His flashlight has fallen out and lays casting its feeble circle of light up at a dark hole in the ceiling. He hasn't been that long in his gravity induced slumber. He sits in the depression created by his fall in a field of plastic bags. Varying in size and color. Some white, some blue, most black, some red, and all bulging and bursting, ripped, ripping, and rotting. Their contents tearing at them. Eating them away. Syringes with their still sharp points glinting in the flashlight's castings; bandages soaked with dark virulent substances; IV drip bags holding still small traces of once life preserving fluids, now turned milky and black; gauzes and swabs still rich and full from their last tasks before being discarded; and, mingled throughout these piles strange clear plastic bags, labels white, interiors skinned with condensation, with even stranger objects held within. Objects which look soft and lumpy, and which glisten even in the weak light.

The waste piled high in mounds surround him completely. An ocean of bad biology where he could not drown.

Looking upward, he can see the hole in the ceiling he fell through maybe some 10 to 12 feet up.

Now he remembers.

The security guard, the concrete, the building, the room, and the fall into darkness. Yet this darkness was not empty. It was full and ripe and sharp and vicious. In his fallen flashlight's dim light, he has discovered the truth of the world he has unwittingly descended into. He, the unwanted, had unwantedly found a place for the unwanted things medicine had created and discarded.

Hospital trash. Piles and piles of it.

These things were not supposed to be here. He was not supposed to be here either.

A sharp scalpel, its edge a curving gleaming white smile, grins at him from a pile of waste close at hand. Reaching out a suddenly curious hand to pick it up he notices something sticking out from the back of his forearm. Turning his arm over the true horror of his fall, and his landing sinks into him in more ways than one. The slender needle of a syringe is buried deep in his forearm...and it is not alone. A sibling to the syringe, another scalpel, rests its fine blade cleanly in the upper layers of his skin, so smoothly that it draws no blood on the back side of his left wrist. They are not alone.

Tears begin to stream down his face as, slowly and methodically, he begins the unwanted and necessary task of removing these sharp and vicious things from his tormented flesh.

Pulling out the syringe it leaves behind a line of pain. His head down he sees another syringe. This one sticking out from the fat which wraps around his midsection. He bites down on his lip in fear acknowledged.

If there were pointy dangers around him, they would also be under him. Fear makes him awkward as he clumsily turns, and there he sees the place of his landing is a topography of blade edges and needle points, valleys and peaks of harm. His tears turn into racking sobs and he sees more of his damaged body, punctured and penetrated. His back and legs have suffered far worse. Adjusting his position, he stands hunched over his legs sinking and ripping into the bags beneath him, and begins the process of freeing himself, drawing each needle, each blade from the flesh of his tortured body. As he works the *Presence* repeatedly inspires him:

"You can do it! You can do it! It's okay!"

A new day has dawned, but not for the forgotten man who lays curled in a fetal position amidst the forgotten waste of the modern medical industry. A strange bearded and flightless bird, he has created a clear space for himself on the floor. A nest. Freed from the metal barbs that had wounded him, moving slow with a keen eye and delicate touch he had attacked the mounds of horrific trash that had surrounded him. He had used the talents gained through years sifting through refuse, through other piles of unwanted things, to carve out a space for himself, free from further being violated by the many sharp implements lying sprinkled throughout the mounds.

He organized. He saw what was here and there. He saw how these things should be touched or not touched, how these things should be moved or not moved. The smell of death and old medicine clung to him as he worked and even for him nausea bent him over making him threw up what little solid matter still laid fermenting in his stomach.

In time he reached the floor, a hard surface covered in a miasma of decaying and co-mingling fluids. A short time after that he had enough floor to rest upon. Another traded for object covers this open space, doubled up for greater protection: a blue plastic tarp, one of three he possesses. Tarps, synthetic blue sheets: used as windbreaks, blankets, tents, table clothes, store fronts, and funerary shrouds. A truly precious item now, a thing bought and not traded for, it provided a barrier from the hard floor and its thick coating of rancid and rotting liquids. The stench of it all was so overpowering his only retreat was to push his face deep into the familiar mildew and sweat scented fabric of his own clothing.

His shopping cart now lays on its side, showing its vulnerable belly, in the cleared area. It forms a protective wall at his back. It dislikes this place.

A bottle of something mostly empty lies nestled in his arms as he fitfully sleeps. He is dreaming.

The Baby is hungry.

He knows this without a doubt, but everything is cloudy, muddy, fractures, shards, fading embers. He stands in an jet black perfect sphere. He hears crying, but he can't tell where it comes from surrounded by darkness. The scene changes. He is wandering down halls, long and empty. The Baby is still crying. The crying is so sad. He stumbles quickly along, growing more desperate in his search. He must find the Baby! He sends his voice racing ahead.

"Where are you?! Where are you?! It's okay. It's okay!"

His words are comforting. Words he thinks the *Presence* would say, but real. Words a person he was long ago would have used with his own little-

"No."

The *Presence* is firm. He must focus.

He turns down a new hallway. Down this hallway the Baby's cries echo. There is a door at the end. He runs. He slams into the door...then he is falling!

The dream fall slams him awake.

His mind fumbles and locks onto his moment of awakening forgetting all else. He knows he was dreaming but of what?!...

Crying.

He remembers. His thoughts spin to the Baby in his dreams. The Baby was so sad, so lonely, and so hungry.

Soon he felt he would be as hungry. No...he knew it.

He sits up slowly. The blue tarp has strange dark wet marks on it from where his body has lain. His wounds have leaked in his sleep. His waking thoughts all to quickly turn to hunger.

The lucky in life may know only one of the many hungers life has to offer: hunger for food; hunger for love; hunger for justice, peace; perhaps even hunger for knowledge. His hunger is two-faced, crooked and clawed, and has many hands.

Turning he begins to rummage through his cart.

He takes inventory. He has: a couple of slices of bread still in the plastic bag they came in; a unopened can of tuna; and half of a convenience store burrito, a meal quickly heated and consumed by those of desperate means and/or shallow pockets. He had found the burrito on top of a public trash can, discarded by someone who could afford to listen to their functioning taste buds. In weak moments folks often succumb to the opportunity and ease of access provided by late night microwave meals purchased after hours in questionable establishments, when better can't be had nor found. Many regret this decision, but they always hope that maybe this time things will be different and the cheap meal will taste better than good.

He would save the tuna and the bread. He eats the old burrito mechanically, his mind going somewhere else. Eat. Survive. Eat. Survive. This was a familiar mantra for him, used again and again over the years of sitting down to eat the unfinished meals of others. Unfinished meals that most often were either one step away from decay or many steps deep into it. Leaving his thoughts to wander, eventually, they swing to that other hunger which would demand satisfaction.

His life preservers, bottles filled with liquids both clear and dark, are mostly empty.

He had to get out.

He begins to explore the room with his weak flashlight. He is in a long rectangular room at one of its two ends. The tops of three of the walls can just barely be seen beyond the medical waste piles. These walls reveal no signs of a door or its framing. The one remaining wall at the other end of the room, he cannot see, for it is lost beyond the waste and the untouchable shadows beyond his weak flashlight. On all sides he is surrounded. These piles, these hills, at their peaks may have reached six or seven feet, and even higher at the corners and the middle of the room.

He sits, his thoughts floating, and one takes hold, gathering him in its current. Grabbing his cart, he repositions it flipping it on its top, belly up, its four wheels twitching back and forth awkwardly. He slowly climbs on top of it. The hole in the ceiling is no more than two or three feet away from his upward reaching hands, if only he can reach it.

For one hour he attempts escape, and fails, and just when he's about to give up, perched on his precious cart, a section of the cart's ribbing gives way. With a snap and twang of metal again he falls. He passes out only briefly, succumbing easily to the shadows that haunted his already injured body and his already clouded mind. Opening his eyes, moments later, blurry he sees a glint of light close to his face. His eyes come back into focus on the tip of the syringe needle just an inch or more from his right eye. He realizes his situation could become much worse if he is not more careful. Much worse.

He is not ready to face more pain again, more time spent pulling shrapnel from his already tormented body. Indecision has him curling on the floor in his man-made nest. Closing his eyes, he breathes a shuddering sigh, and tries to sleep.

The waking world intruded as it always did.

Not with honking car horns and squealing tires begging for purchase, or the rolling pressure waves of sirens sounding, always, somewhere; or, kids running loose and screaming, in pain or joy; or by adults in all octaves yelling at the screaming kids or each other; or by large objects colliding with other large objects in callous clangs and deep thuds; or by the shifting maelstrom of flapping pigeon wings as they were disturbed from their pigeon-ness and perches. This doesn't wake him.

No, the clarion call to his reemergence into the waking world is the same one that had greeted him since he was small and could remember.

"Marcus!"

He mother is a loud woman.

"Marcus get your lazy ass up!"

He does.

Forcing sleep off himself with the tossing back of covers, bed frame creaking under his weight, his feet hit the cool carpeted floor in the bedroom he shares with his little brother. Th-thud!

In the doorway she stands. Small, yet somehow larger than the doorway that frames her.

Marcus leans forward, elbows on knees. Stretching up, he scratches and paws at himself, reconfirming his flesh and blood still exists, heavy and soft.

"Marcus!"

"I'm up!" accidently irritation colors his reply.

"Take the bass outcha voice. Don't be thinking you are too old to get your ass beat."

He does, but saying so would only result in glaring eyes, flaring nostrils, and a smack to the head or some improvised projectile launched in his general direction.

Summer.

The beautiful pause between one school year and the next was here. A minor reprieve in the 4-year sentence called Mission High School.

One more year and an alluring freedom from the cage of convention to an adult life with adult things and if luck favored, Marcus would escape further with four wheels and four walls all his own, but for now-

"- you need to go pay the electric. There is a check on the kitchen counter. If you see Mr. Morales, you tell him our sink is still leaking and if he wants his rent on time he best get his idle ass up here and fix that shit!...Marcus!"

"Yes momma! Mr. Morales, sink. Electric. I got it!"

"You best got it."

Silence. Maybe she forgot.

"And don't think I forgot! If I hear you've been hanging out with your cousin, I will toss you and your shit to the curb...Marcus!"

"Yes momma!"

His cousin. Tony. Not a blood relative, he came into the family when Marcus's great uncle's brother's daughter married an older man who had done a favor for his father's side of the family.

Great Uncle Alfonz was a well-respected man. A "very" well respected man. Loved by many and feared by most. Small in stature, he was still a man of considerable prowess, and legend has it even in these latter years he was still beating men of the worst luck to death with hands crafted in the shipyards and docks. Hands and strength gained many years back when he was younger and not yet in the inner circle.

Marcus would love to follow his mother's wishes, to avoid hanging out with his sadistic cousin....but he can't.

Marcus is out the door the minute his mother leaves for work. He hits the sidewalk, feet and his new high tops leading him quickly the few blocks necessary to make his rendezvous.

Tony is there. Waiting.

Guys his age, most often, would be leaning against walls or perched on someone's stoop, but not Tony.

He stands defiant in the middle of the sidewalk, tense like a spring, jaw clenching and unclenching. Anyone that sees him circles wide, like water in a river moving around a stone that will not move. He gives off ripples of unfiltered raw aggression barely held in check.

Tony doesn't like waiting. Tony doesn't like much.

Marcus, in a way, looked up to the shorter Tony. Marcus was also afraid of him, as most were. Marcus had once seen him knock an old woman to ground and smash the man who came to her rescue. Tony's whole family were boxers, and out of the ring they honed their bare knuckles on each other's bodies and faces, and anyone life sent to "test" them.

Marcus is Tony's only friend.

"You're late faggot!"

That word.

For a moment Marcus tenses and his thoughts flee in every direction to find how he had let that happen, for he knows he left his house earlier than planned to avoid any altercation with is cousin.

"Yo Tony, I - I thought we said 10am. I can't be late, I-"

The coiled tension relaxes as Tony laughs full and loud.

"I'm fuckin' witcha!" he grins, his laughter dying down. "Let's go!"

Tony starts walking and Marcus quickly follows.

They make an odd pair, Marcus light brown of skin, his mixture of Black and White, large and overweight but strong.

Tony, fair pale skin with the undertones of olive speaking of coastal ancestors in faraway Italy. His body lean and doubly mean.

It is going to be a busy day.

They have plans.

The morning and early afternoon would be spent shifting from one hangout spot to the next. Beers and hard liquor and boisterous acquaintances would be the main attraction. Here the language of teen male conquests would be flowing. Tales of this girl and that, from beautiful and easy to not-so beautiful and so-so easy. Here Tony showed his masculinity with names and dates, locations and time frames. Nobody doubted him. No one could.

As always, he mentions their mutual cousin. Sarah. 15 and beautiful and naive and easy. With a mix of groans and appraising looks Tony would sing of her praises as an "easy lay". You couldn't marry your cousin, but you could fuck 'em. That was the consensus.

Marcus didn't like the girls in his neighborhood. They were all too loud with minds focused on trivial pursuits and beauty products. He couldn't see in them what attracted the other boys.

Later him and his cousin would visit family, those which accepted both. His brown skinned and Tony's trouble. Here were places where free food was always attainable.

They were killing time, and along the way some brain cells, for the real action was at night when the sun went down, and their "job" started.

The family worked best at night, all under great uncle Alfonz's leadership, and all hidden from the watchful eyes of the police. From the very beginning of Summer, Marcus and his cousin were put to work. Moving things. Watching places. Delivering packages to people, sometimes given packages back. They knew not to ask too many questions and never did. The big job started at the end of June.

Once a week they would meet a distant cousin, a good ten or more years older. Petey.

Petey drove. All kinds of vehicles but had the knack for vans and trucks. Each time he picked Tony and Marcus up he would be in a different truck. Nothing to small and nothing too big which could draw unwanted attention.

His nickname was "Stumbles". A wiz behind the wheel but standing on two feet, or walking, was a humorous activity. He just drove. It was up to Marcus and his cousin to do the grunt work.

Bags. Dark black, white, yellow, even red, and plastic. Piled at loading docks throughout the city waited for them every week. A guard or an orderly in blue or green scrubs was always there to watch them to make sure the job was taken care of to complete satisfaction. They didn't know what was in the bags, but they could guess for the loading docks always connected to the same type of facilities.

Medical.

They knew for sure when Tony jabbed his thumb one night 2 weeks ago. The needle almost invisible in the darkness against the black plastic bag it was in easily pierced his cousin's skin. In a rage Tony had tossed the bag, its contents spilled across the asphalt confirming their suspicions.

Tony's hand still hurt.

They both bought gloves. Thick ones made for work with sharp things.

For 2 to 3 hours they would shuttled from one place to the next till the truck they used was full or near to it.

At 10:53pm they met with Petey at the corner of 22nd and South Van Ness. This night he drives a 15 ft delivery truck, paint with a fading logo of some ancient delivery service.

Hopping into the cab Marcus took the middle as Tony and Petey didn't sit well together, literally and figuratively. Tony annoyed Petey as he did with most people that weren't afraid of him.

The night moved smoothly as they headed to pickups at various locations across the city, and at each the back of the truck got fuller and fuller. In a short period, they finished and headed to the last spot. The dump site.

The streets grew quieter and quieter as they moved into the less civilized and inhabited parts of the city. Making a left they can see the large old brick building surrounded by fencing, windblown trash, and patches of concrete destroying weeds.

Petey kills the lights as the truck moves the last half a block to the only way into the open area surrounding the building. A locked gate.

Without a word Tony grabs the keys sitting in the ashtray and jumps out. Even with his injured hand Tony swiftly has the gate open and swinging free, and Petey nudges the gas and the truck slowly gravel growls its way in.

He doesn't wait for Tony as he shut and locks the gate. Well-practiced Stumbles moves the truck up the slight slope to the front of the building and then around back to a loading dock they used to unload the trash. The dock was down a ramp in between a valley made from the building's back walls.

"Hurry up."

Petey never wanted to stay too long. Each minute there increased the chances of discovery. Not by the police per se. The police knew the family and generally kept clear of their extracurricular activities. No, what they feared was other operators, other criminals, who could take advantage of the situation and the fact they were in an area where they could get away with a strike at a rival family.

Marcus always hurries.

He dislikes the old building and how it made him feel.

Afraid...though he would never admit it to his Marcus.

Long ago it must have served a purpose, been a place where that neighborhood could turn to for help and healing. Now. It was a house of shadows. A dwelling for ghosts made of rust and rot and old crumbling stone. With gnarled boney fingers the building barely held its old memories.

"Get the cart."

Tony eyes Marcus as both put on their gloves. After the first two dump runs it was Marcus's idea to get a cart to help them move the bags of trash more efficiently, and it was Tony's idea where they could steal one. Marcus climbs up the stairs of the loading dock pulling a store stolen flashlight from his coat pocket. Searching around he located a key hidden in a crack between two bricks to unlock the padlock that held the double doors of the loading dock secure.

Years of dust and funk clouded the glass on the doors, blinding them like cataracts to those who may desire to look inside.

He lies sleeping, empty bottles stand around him accusing. He is covered in sweat, and behind his closed eyelids, his iris race about.

The Baby is there with him. He has finally found it, a tiny mewling thing. It is wrapped loosely in a blanket, a threadbare patch of grays held together by filth and foul. Its arms stretch into the air, pale, thin, sickly sticks waving in a weak wind.

Its face is thin, too thin!

Its eyes are bright and wet with fever, and too large for such a bone thin face. It cries. It wails. No one else can hear it. It is buried, but only just a few feet underground. His dreaming eyes peer with ease through the layers of deep brown dream dirt. He begins to dig. His hands scratch at the hard packed ground, nails splitting pulling away, fingers becoming red and bloody. His digging keeps time with his dream body's dream beating heart and his labored dream breathing. He hears only the baby and himself.

Other sounds enter.

Voices...but not the *Presence's* adder sweet one.

A grand dinner table long and dark, set with gleaming silver plates and glittering silver trays layered in food, and around the table eating, dinner guests. They all sit dressed in fine clothing, their backs turned from his plight and the surrounding room. Their voices are boisterous and loud, happy and carefree. He steps towards the grand table. He begins to plead. He begins to cry. He begins to scream. They don't hear him. He steps up to the table, eyes locked on plates, he reaches, but try as he might the food is always just beyond his reach. The chairs which the dinner guests sit upon seem to move of their own accord, cold hard velvet padded walls blocking his every attempt, and the more he tries, the louder the diners become. He screams again, but this time no sound comes from his throat. He does not exist.

The Baby is starving and still buried beneath the earth.

He wakes shaken, the voices of the dinner party drifting into his waking world to taunt and tease him. The dream was only a shade different from similar dreams he has already had many hungry times before this garbage prison. He can still faintly hear the voices from his dream. He props himself up becoming more awake, yet still, they remain, but now instead of many only two, two distinct voices remain. It takes a moment, but it begins to dawn on him he may not be dreaming when the hole in the ceiling lights up. The two voices are real, and their conversation spills down the hole to awaken the homeless man fully.

"...Uncle's men don't play! So cool we don't need to use those nasty ass stairs anymore."

The first voice is saying, youthful exuberance pitching the timbre of his tone an octave up and an octave down.

"I know, saves us the long haul."

The second voice, young, but harsh at the edges, a sharp knife getting rougher, agrees coolly. The homeless man can hear the rasp that only comes from lots of yelling to be heard, amongst others who are yelling louder.

The first voice is commenting.

"Fuck! I hated going down those stairs with all these bags, you know -"

"Help!!!"

The homeless man's cry immediately silences the two young voices.

"What the fuck?!!" The second voice, the rough blade, is agitated immediately.

Two bright lights shine down the hole illuminating the homeless man and the surrounding medical waste. The lights are amazingly bright to the homeless man's deprived eyes, now accustomed to the perpetual night of his prison. Lights that to him could have easily been mistaken for the bright embers of descending angels, if he had not heard the two youth's conversation first. Under the glaring lights he can't see their faces.

"How'd you get down there?!" The first voice asks, his young youth edges finally glint in his tone. Him and the blade were from the same forge after all.

The homeless man begins to explain his plight: the tragedy of the hole and his fall. He talks of his hunger. He talks of the Baby.

"What baby?!!" The two voices, yell in close unison.

"There's a baby down here," he pleads. "It's starvin' too!"

The sharp blade doesn't believe him.

"No way!!"

"Where is it?!" The first voice questions.

"Here!...under tha' floor!"

For a few passing breaths, the homeless man's answer brings only more silence from the two youths, then the sharp blade stabs. Laughter.

"He's fuckin' crazy!!"

The blade is amused but his companion makes no sound. The two lights draw away. The homeless man hears a quick and hushed conversation but is only able to catch snippets of it. He tries to force his ears to pierce the space separating him from the two youthful voices. Willing them to hear what was being exchanged. The blade is speaking.

"-not our problem."

"Not our problem?! Tony we-we can't..."

"Yes, we can!...Uncle would kill us both!" Tony, the blade, sounds afraid but sure.

"... but..." Tony's partner is more afraid and less sure.

"Hey!" Tony threatens, a fist of sound. His voice returns to whispers. "...he can't last much longer... nuthin' to eat..."

Tony's disposition seems to match his voice, sharp, a brightness going dark. The homeless man is right. Tony likes to yell, and really likes to yell at people. He had sadly met many men like Tony before. The ones like that thrive on not caring, and in this attitude their greatest pride dwells and hunts.

"...I know, still..." the first young man hovers undecided. The homeless can tell this boy had a heart that felt human things. He wasn't doomed just yet.

"Look!" Tony's voice rises, loud and clear, "Let's just get the job done! We are not paid to fuckin' think and we are not paid to rescue bums who know better than to fuckin' trespass on private property!"

Their conversation ends, and all the homeless man hears of them for the next few minutes is just the sound of them moving about on the floor above. The dance of their lights above him lighting briefly here and there the room above. Their cart's wheels cause the homeless man's cart to envy their freedom to tick and skip on the dust and refuse above.

The first bag of medical waste is a surprise as it slams completely into the homeless man's chest, knocking him almost off his feet. He only has a second or two to recover and move out of the way before another bag, and another, and another follow closely after the first. Many burst upon landing, their guts flying open.

These two were the ones that had made this room into a dump, and they were adding to it. With each bag thrown down the homeless man throws pleas for help back up. All go unanswered.

It takes the young men little less than half an hour to complete their task. They leave, but just as they leave the homeless man is sure he hears the unsharpened boy's voice drift down to him, in a hushed whisper...

"... sorry."

The homeless man doesn't think he could feel any worse, but with the chance of rescue, so briefly shown and so quickly taken away, his plight attains a new dimension of sorrow. Depressed, he begins to clear the floor of these newly arrived bags. As he works his flashlight starts to stutter and flicker, and he knows soon the batteries will be dead. Going to his cart he finds his last ones.

A short time later the room's darkness has retreated a little from the homeless man's nest, driven back by the warmth and light of a small fire. Black sooty smoke rises and rolls upward before exiting through the hole in the ceiling, finding the freedom the homeless man sought with competent ease. The rich, potent, and rotten smell of the room is slightly hidden behind the smell of burning. The homeless man sits before the fire and absentmindedly feeds it from a pile he has collected. In the pile lie bandages caked and dried with unknown but once human substances; clotted and dry gauzes; a few desiccated paper coffee cups with bottoms rimmed in dark brown almost black circles of dried coffee; old medical scrubs, matted bundles tossed away by skilled manicured hands. All were fuel for the fire. The smoke is heavy with the smell of cotton and plastic, charred fat and burnt meat.

Hunger gnaws at him.

Rummaging through the contents of his faithful cart he pulls out the tuna and places it onto the tarp in front of him. He continues to search.

His search grows frantic.

"Where's it at?! Where is it?!!"

He doesn't know.

Tucked into the back of his cart there was a bag, was, and in that bag had been a can opener, traded for and precious. No longer. He can't find it. He spends the next hour, moving through the shifting walls of his plastic bag prison, searching and hoping. His time is wasted, the can opener is lost.

Unseen by his eyes during his plummet, it had fallen deep into the mountains of waste. Never to return. His soul sinks deeper into depression. The Baby is starving, and now he is too. He tries for a bit to force a scalpel's blade into the hard metal but gives up quickly realizing he is asking for more trouble if the blade slips. With the tuna a lost cause, he turns to his last source of food, those few meager slices of bread still contained within their plastic wrapping.

All he finds is a shredded bag and crumbs....and a few dark droppings from the rats who had visited him.

Other things lived down here, and with the theft and consumption of his bread they had proven their existence and their dominance. In defeat he lays back and begins to dose, but abruptly sits up.

The wire snips!

He had not put them back in the cart when he had clipped his way through the building's defenses. Unconsciously he had placed them in the lower pockets of his abused coat. Hands scurrying in desperation he searches his coat and after a held breath or three produces the wire snips from the inner folds.

It takes him more time than he would have thought to work the wire snips around the edge of the tuna can, but he eventually succeeds in freeing the top from the squat tin cylinder. Tuna oil and saltwater drip and stream down his fingers. Drips run down the back edge of his hand to his wrist continue, riding along the dirt covered regions of his forearm, to finally slide down into the darkness of his sleeve.

With passion and great hunger, he devours the tuna hunched over, fingers in the salty flesh, the tin can directly under his waiting mouth. A baby bird feeding, finally.

Every oily salt rich bite shocks him, jolts him. Salivary glands activate and increase the joys of simply eating, but they soon mourn.

Too soon the can is empty.

Fingers with clogged dark ringed nails have scrapped it clean. A road rough ravaged tongue, mottled and pink, abused by ground groveling destitution, had swept through it, all cleansing, taking with it any further salty remains.

He is now even more hungry.

The tuna had only awakened his hunger to its own immensity.

Time passes more slowly. His eyes gaze deeply into the only comfort he has now. His foul fueled fire. He tries to turn his mind to many other courses, but it always returns to the hunger, staring and sitting, watching him.

Eyes bright!

Walking the vast tangles of long and bent streets, the hard stone halls and corridors, the cart-less majority with their glances and uncovered mumbles said the homeless man was talking to himself, but he wasn't. He was talking to the *Presence*, responding to it. Most times things were one-sided.

The *Presence* always started their conversations.

It had been born. It hadn't always existed. There had been a different man. Homeless, but still a clear-thinking man, one voiced. But that was before the night of dark boots, hard swung bats, and the suffocating violation of unconsciousness brought about by unprovoked brutality; before the waking to the light and pain, the sanitized hospital, the scent of piss and shit, of vomit and fear, industrial grade cleaners laced with artificial pine from an artificial world; before everything stopped. Still alive in his body, he was a mummified maze of tubes.

New words, from old: *brain trauma, severe.*

He was just another victim; his young attackers: in the city for a night of ramble rousing, then a stealthy and quick retreat to homes where unknowing parents slept secretly knowing.

From this time onward there had been only descent, there had only been things turning the wrong way, and it was when his life began that deep spiral downward the *Presence* had awoken. Guiding him, comforting him, giving him the will to survive. Even if for just one more day.

When the *Presence* had appeared, he knew it was something different, not him. A necessary survival tool. A by-product. A new sense flexing new muscles. The *Presence* was a mutation of a right-thinking mind gone wrong, but he didn't know that, or he did but didn't care.

The *Presence* is stronger than him.

It had gotten so over the years from more night and day beatings and abuse; from the necessary-to-the-public arrests which left him in healing hospital hands, where the pills flowed like wine and the side effects erased everything, leaving psychic chemical burns that always left scars.

Everything gone...almost.

Before, before. Homeless. A home. His home...their home. A job. Jobs. Babies. Kids. Bright. House and friends and schools and holidays and vacations and mistakes and bad luck and fighting and fighting and hitting and-

"Stop."

...the *Presence*.

It has always helped him.

His survival is its survival. His voice, but not his voice. It tries to help now.

"Other things live down here."

Silence. The homeless man is not too tired to answer and knows the *Presence* will persist until he does. After one drawn breath and a single barely breathed sigh he answers.

"So?!" The homeless man is terse and rough. He is tired. He has all the time but done of the patience for games.

" 'So?!!'..... *so, you can too!*" The *Presence* sounds so hopeful to the homeless man's depressed ears tears immediately come to his eyes.

"How?" His question is mumbled. He has no reason to hope.

"You know how!"

The homeless man thinks. He looks around. Bags, bags, and more bags. His "home": cart, fire and all.

"Tha' rats?"

His answer is unsure. He waits, head cocked to the side, as if the *Presence* is above him and him the one below.

"Well, yes," the *Presence* says after a time, consolingly. *"But they can be hard to catch. Sure, you can probably catch a few, but....isn't there and easier way? When there is a demand, use what's close at hand!"*

The *Presence* is clever. It sounds proud.

The bags.

It is not something he wishes to except. The implications of this one road of salvation rattles and runs through the homeless man. He knows what the *Presence* is asking...what it is proposing.

"...No..."

"*No!!!*" The *Presence* is laughing now, cold, calculating, and unsympathetic. "*So, now you give up?! So, now you're goin' to let 'em win?! Let 'em win!!! Is that it?!!!*"

For something unreal, the *Presence* can be very loud. It had to be a bully to keep him alive. That, was best for him.

Silence emanates from the homeless man. The laughing *Presence* 's admonishment is heavy and all encompassing.

"*Well?*"

"... no..."

"*I can't hear you!*" The *Presence* cheers.

"No."

"*No what?!*"

The *Presence* waits.

"....no....we ain't gonna let 'em win...ever."

"*Good! Have I ever been wrong? When they all went away, who was there, to support you? Give you courage?!*"

"You."

"*That's right! That's fuckin' right!!!*" The *Presence* is happy, it's twisted ebon core flickers and flashes. "*Fuck 'em all!*"

"Yeah...fuck 'em!"

Unsure, the homeless man still feels better.

It takes one more day before he full commits.

Slow and steady he goes to work, searching and gathering, making small piles out of bigger piles. Occasionally he revises his decisions, removing some things and adding others. It is hard to know what was safest to consume but he does his best. He doesn't stop until some part of himself, more blind animal than seeing man, turns his hand to the other necessary, preparations.

His cart holds his entire material world. Used clothes, string, lengths of rope, knickknacks and bric-a-bracs, twisted metal oddities and melted glass, and more.

Going through his belongings, he pulls out a small black frying pan that has seen better days, it's handle just a nub of its former self. He makes a wire stand from some twisted coat hangers he had discovered only last week, and places it over his small fire. He then places the frying pan upon it. Meticulously, as the pan begins to heat, one by one he begins to place his grisly collection into the pan. An immediate sizzle rises and greets the air. His eyes see and his hands move of their own accord. That dusty particle, the unsalted earth of his of humanity which recognized birth and death, that remembered name and history, had cautiously and quietly secreted itself away amongst rare, securely cradled, childhood memories, next to the empty tracks of past happiness.

"This ain't me. This ain't real."

Though most of him is locked away the animal in him still has senses. It whimpers at the lovely scent rising from the pan. The scent speaks to the animal that a hunger soon will be filled.

The first piece of many is ready. His hand reaches out and he plucks a sizzling piece from the pan. He places it in his mouth. Hot on the lips and hotter on the tongue. Immediately he begins to cool the piece letting it dance across his mouth as he blows cool breaths upon it. He chews. His mouth immediately begins to salivate, to sing, lubricating his meal, beginning the first necessary steps of digestion and satisfaction.

"Yes," the *Presence* cajoles *"Eat. Eat."*

... and he does.

The days pass and the homeless man loses all sense of time. He doesn't own a watch. You don't keep time when every clock reminds you of lost things: love, jobs, homes, life, time, time, time, time-

"No."

There is no day here, there is no night, just him in an undiscovered country for one. He creates his own microcosm. His own kingdom with a system of guides, structures to live by. In a bid for freedom he has begun the Herculean task of creating a path through the ton or more of waste to the hidden end of the room, and a door that should be there, a door which must be there. As he works his body is racked by seizures, strange chills, and feverish visions meant only for the soon to be inspired, or the soon to expire. He knows unshakably he is facing the latter.

His body is being poisoned and purified in a cauldron of side effects. Drunk sick from a lack of alcohol with veins and blood tainted from a cocktail of old meds forcefully ejected by his fall, he tries not to move. Digestive system rimmed with clumps and layers, puddles and pockets, of badly cooked never-meant-to-be-consumed "meat", he has become a shambling thing held up by something other than will. His will had never been a strength.

At least he isn't hungry.

He learns, from error and trial, what to eat and what not to eat, becoming a farmer with discerning eyes in this field of discarded things. He finds water. An old sink and faucet, which let out a steady trickle of red-brown tinged water. The rusty water had an old timey taste when men of his color were called boy and every major city was covered in a cloud of steam and soot. To his thirst, it tastes like an imperfect heaven.

His luck bobs and weaves as he catches one of his furry tailed neighbors. He skins and cleans the little four-legged tailed resident as best as he can. He cooks it slowly and smiles. Here was a salvation from the damning meals of days most recent.

He almost vomits at the taste of it, and almost vomits again when he realizes he preferred the other sustenance found in the bags around him.

He forced the rodent meat down.

At night, he dreams.

The Baby is still starving, and all his dream efforts are spent trying to find it, trying to free it, trying to feed it. Upon one occasion, waking from a particularly strong Baby filled dream, he wastes hours trying to find a way through the concrete floor he had previously uncovered. That other man, that existed before the beatings, the bad meds, and the *Presence*, before the stolen jobs and the divorce, had a baby too. Two babies-

"No."

...that was long ago when there was another man. The homeless man can't remember where the man lives, or where he has gone to. Sometimes, sometimes, it makes the homeless man want to weep.

A man.

On the skin of this world.

The surface.

Above. Far above, it.

Time had passed, only a blink, since the near above warmed with the presence of a human. A brief fragile crystal of time when compared to its long eon spanning existence. It was one of many that rested and hid like chrysalis in the meat of this planet. Dormant, in a state like sleep, but not sleep. They were still aware.

Humans. Naked of fur two leg walkers! Mere specters of their fear-filled knuckle dragging thick browed predecessors who scurried across the ancient earth. Predecessors, of these modern creatures, who had sifted through the muck, and who had fled to caves when dark possessed day, and huddled around infantile fires. They had flesh, young and old, and blood, hot blood no matter the maturity. Rich blood and flesh to snatch in the dark folds of the night...feeding those who prefer shadows. These primitive humans had road on the back of the ancient ones, barely noticed, yet even in servitude they did all they could to free themselves from their fear of the ancient and unforgiving gods from between the stars. In supplication they sacrificed their own and fed the remainders to a madness close to the language of gods...primordial, deep, and overwhelming.

Deep below. Above, a man. A dim light but living...weak. Weakened? Yes. He languishes in his suffering, the tasty waves of his pain dive deep, and these brief touches of warmth awaken some long-ignored need. It wasn't hungry, but it still craves. Life. Red and hot, ran through with pain. Their stay on this terrestrial world had changed them. They were all long absent from the pressured touch of space. A few were changed so dramatically the possibility existed that the great dark would not know them and would reject their return.

The Baby had changed the most for it had been fed the most. Early human herds had fed it as it lay in a vast swamp as great as the smallest seas. Screaming, mewling, writhing sacrifices were flung into its influence. It, like all its kind, accepted these offering without thanks or need, but the more it was fed the more it became tainted. This began its change. Its shape becoming a parody of the human one, and its belly swelled round and immense. A mind unchanging changed, and washed in a mimicry of sensations, faux emotions, and held in what could only be called *pleasure,* worldly common fingers wrapped around its consciousness and would not be removed.

The man.

Oh, the taste of him! The currents of his anguished sank fast and steady to touch the Baby's sleeping mind and immediately it reached out in response.

It had been too long....and now, too far from the surface, it could only feed on the man's mind and thoughts, sweet morsels which hinted at a rare and special feast this man's flesh could be.

Tonight, as the human world slept above, it reached out with its full might from below!

The Baby is starving. Still.

On the eighth day of his captivity the homeless man wakes from a black dream to the less black surrounding him, his fire a squat ember on the floor before him. It is dark on the outside too, the city covered in Night's star speckled hand, but he cannot see it.

Something is different. But what?

He begins to think it is nothing merely a play of his poisoned and hungry mind, yet still... something is different! The air is charged, under pressure. A calm moment before a storm breaks and the sky cracks with lightning and the rains scream down. A tense suspended moment before an earthquake caused the ground to ripple and rise.

There!

Sounds. Lost and searching.

A strange discordant series of tones, a melody warped and forgotten, trickles and leaks through the unspeaking room's silence. The homeless man's body vibrates suddenly at the touch of it, something alien, yet familiar, as it played at the edge of his hearing.

Then the room...dawns!

His mouth hangs open, and his eyes widen to feast on a pleasure they had been denied these past eight days, light. Slowly a cool luminance grows and creeps towards him over his limited horizon of plastic bags.

The Baby approaches.

Other lights dawn and move to follow the first light's procession towards him. Together they slowly fill the dark space, revealing the infant god. At first he believes, mistakenly, here is his rescue, unexpected but here, then the first source of light crests the mountain of madness and medical waste. His breath stops.

"This is not real!"

The Baby, its body blanketed in a nimbus of gelid bloodless light, climbs over the highest peak of trash. Its body is a thing he has only dreamed, and at first his instinct is to fear for it, as it scales down the needle and scalpel rich piles head first, moving slowly and carefully, passing over a terrain that would have left his homeless hands and knees ravaged. The other lights follow after, and with their arrival the homeless man sees clearly the strange and malformed shapes of their owners. Infantile forms that may have once been like the baby, but not now. Not now. Flesh constructs that may have once been hands and arms. Gatherings that may have once been legs and feet. Amalgams that may have once been torsos and the heads which had rested upon them. Confluences that had mingled and gone through some perverted metamorphosis of the flesh. Normal casings of skin and wads of red rich muscle are now collected into swollen, knotted, and discolored masses, ghostly translucent and sweating. The bone, hard calcium coated structures, reduced to flexible and sinuous devices. The ardent shapes move in a sick imitation controlled by parasitic animators, that had constructed decaying vessels of puissant life. In their unholy possession they had transformed and desecrated these fleshy remains into screams of desecration!

And, among these deformed, yet recognizable earthly shapes....other things moved! Configurations that cannot be recognized as springing from man, or any earth-bound species. They wore no puppets bodies, no makeshift mannequins. No decaying shells of manipulated human flesh, for here, only here, would their original forms suffice.

Original forms from a place an earthly human God had never visited.

Strange shapes and ropey coils skinned in a fabric made from non-terrestrial flesh, undulate and constrict on the edges of his vision, gangrenous motes of virulence. Somewhere, in the frozen halls of space, beyond all traces of life generating light, soulless cyclopean intelligences cloak themselves in the exact same cloth. Eyes, perfect vessels of perfected black, gaze out cognizant from their deep orifices.

They are forgotten creations, these "others," drawn from some vast and ancient nightmare Earth where after each sunset the jungle night was filled, from horizon to horizon, with the bloodless screams of apes.

Never experienced before, instinctually the homeless man knows to fear them, and to fear them with all his might. Here were no chances of victories, no enemy to defeat or defy, there was only running, running, and then more running. Escape.

He cannot.

He feels their corrupting touches, icy wreathed needles that stab at his warmth. His brain overflows with caustic thoughts and images alien to all he has known. Each thought, each image, another level of death and madness, opened for him briefly, then shut. He collapses to the floor.

Reaching out, the homeless man screams through flowing tears.

"Where are you?!!!"

The *Presence*, his only source of comfort, his brother in armless-ness, his longtime corrupting savior, is gone. After all these years he can find no trace of its presence within himself. He can feel the place where it had sat so comfortably as an onlooker, but the chair is empty. He knows it will stay that way from now till time's end.

The *Presence* is dead. Slain.

Truly small are the petty threads of madness which run within the common man's mind and, quickly do these threads break and run, when faced with the true archetypes of that foul and wretched kingdom.

"... Wha-what do you want?... What do you want?"

He mumbles this repeatedly to the floor, body locked rigid in dread. The Baby approaches. It stops mere inches from his cowering head. Its hand, grim hued, pale, a phantasm of blue-black veins, and matchstick bones, and paper-thin skin, rises to reach out to him.

The Baby's touch pitches him into a fathomless and hungry gloom. His scream dies in his throat as his conscious gives way.

"Marcus?!....Dinner is ready!...Marcus!"

His brother is already in the kitchen sitting in his seat. Feet dangling an inch or more above the floor. 12 years old and growing. Marcus's seat was across from him. It stays empty.

"I'm not hungry!"

Marcus couldn't eat. Everything he tasted tastes wrong. Bland. Lifeless and without sustenance.

He had left his appetite in a hole with a homeless man, and not only hunger but deep sleep as was his norm had also been missing over the last few days.

Marcus had known guilt. Lying guilt. The guilt of impatience. The guilt of greed stealing things from shops. Guilt of laziness putting off requests from his mom. Guilt of anger often focused on his little brother. All shades and hues of guilt he has known....but the guilt he was feeling now was making him soul sick. Troubled and in turmoil.

Has he condemned a man to die by his inaction? It would have been no trouble for him to return to the old hospital and the hole and the bum below. Quite simple to steal some rope or a ladder and make his way back. A small act of heroics was all it would take, yet he did nothing.

The days pass and, as he nears the next dump day, he runs through what if scenarios. What if cops found out they had left a man trapped; what would they do this time if the man was still there; what would he, Marcus, want if he was the one trapped. That answer was easy: freedom.

He tried to convince himself of unknowns concerning the homeless man: He was nobody. He would be fine. He would rescue himself. He wouldn't die from being stuck a day or more. He would be fine. He had to understand why they didn't help him. He would live. He would be fine....he would be fine!

"Marcus!"

He went to bed early, chasing sleep that ran too fast.

A new morning.

Today, another pickup and dumping, Tony met Marcus once more at their usual spot, and immediately he could see that Tony was not acting like his "normal" self.

"What the fuck is up with you?!" Tony lacks anything close to patience.

"I-...nothing. Nothing." Marcus is too afraid to bring up his fears, his doubts.

Guilt of omission.

"Don't be a faggot. We got shit to do."

That word. Tony knew Marcus hated that word, but Marcus says nothing. If only he had never befriended his cousin those many years ago. Vainly he wished he had listened when his mother intuitively had warned him to avoid the mean-spirited little boy. Now, he only can see years of living under the shadow of his abusive cousin.

"Yeah...yeah." Marcus submits, as he always has.

"Let's go."

After, Marcus notices his cousin is in a rare mood, and looking closely he can see the sheen of sickly sweat which clings to his face. His wounded hand hangs heavy at the end of his arm. Ignoring all, Tony had yet to see a doctor and if his immediate family had cared they would have noticed his illness, but they were not that kind of family. What most would call "caring".

Their usual routine wasn't usual as they wasted time before the day's late-night activities. Detouring from their regular stops Tony brought them to the roundabout where the cable cars reversed their journey next to the popular Montgomery Wards. Here they grabbed pizza slices and Cokes before spending an hour amongst the breakers, as they spun and twisted on sheets of linoleum to a blaring boombox's beat. Their music pump faked on the surrounding buildings feeding the office workers at their cubicles the latest sounds from the poorer sides of the city.

The homeless man sleeps again. Many hours have passed since the visitation from the Baby and its nightmare entourage. His body shakes and shivers on the floor. His skin is scarlet and fevered, glistening sickly. Beneath his fluttering eyelids his dilated eyes roll upward to hide in the cool shade of his skull. Somehow the voices above him penetrate his sleep.

He wakes to a light shining down through the hole in the ceiling, and for the briefest moment he thinks he is back under the boot of the security guard named "*Leo*", and the Baby and hospital were nothing but a flash of an imaginary realm, born from his wounded mind.

"He must be dead by now." The voice drops down the hole.

He recognizes it. The blade. Tony.

"Do you smell smoke?!"

The kind one. The not-Tony

He remembers. The angry security guard was several days ago, in his living past. The two young men who had visited days before and left him to his plight, the crafters of his unintentional prison, have returned. The not-Tony has noticed the scent of his last fire, now a low pile of ash with still smoldering embers, which had laid unfed for hours.

"Help... please," his voice, a raspy dry weak groan, pleads up as the lights appear above him.

"Shit!! He's still alive?!" Tony's voice rises hard and harsh and swoops down to strike the homeless man in his living nightmare.

"Help! Please..." His voice trembles with emotion. "... there's s-somethin' down here..."

"Fuck!! Come here!" Tony is not happy, and the man imagines he probably rarely is.

Their lights vanish and he can hear their footsteps draw away from the hole. Their conversation is heated, and quick, and partly heard.

"What's that guy talking about?! Something down there?..." he hears the kind youth's voice ask of his partner.

"Fuck him!... next week..."

"No way! I didn't-"

"Marcus none of that weak fag shit!"

Marcus. The not-Tony. His name is Marcus.

Tony continues.

"... it'll go quick... the whole building!"

He hears them, Tony and Marcus, as they move further away, and then he can no longer hear them. For a long time, the homeless man hears only silence, then footsteps returning and the sounds of wheels rolling across the rough and debris filled floor above. Then as days before, more bags cascade down from the hole above. The two young men finish quickly, and the man weakly continues to implore them for rescue as they work, but both say nothing. One last flash from the lights above and they are gone. Again.

The return to silence is crushing on his spirit, but then shuffling feet return.

"Here."

Marcus whispers from above and a smaller bag dressed in brown paper, much smaller than the bags surrounding the homeless man, lands on the floor before him. The man reaches out and draws it closer as he hears Marcus leave.

Trembling hands peel back the paper to reveal a cold slice of pizza, missing one bite.

The homeless man is left alone again.

Rescue is not coming. Not by those two, "Tony" and "Marcus", and not by anyone else. He is now certain of this!

He must get out of here. "Tony" had plans that would culminate next week. Death was coming for the homeless man, either by starvation or by what was planned for this building, and him with it, or from the continue assault of the infant that lay deep below him. Sick as he is, he feels better than he had before, and after this last visit from the two boys he is galvanized.

Provoked!

He rips into the pizza, devouring it.

It is delicious. He sobs a little at this sign he has not gone too far down the road of unwilling cannibal. Pizza can never lose its appeal he thinks as a few joyous tears streak down across his dirt cloaked cheeks.

He must escape. He would not die here. He needs no mutated inner voice to give him this conviction. The thought alone of dying in this room, this hospital, his human husk disintegrating, liquifying and draining through the earth to be greeted by the waiting greedy orifices of the Baby below is enough to motivate him.

The days pass quickly and he's sole desperate focus becomes the hidden other side of the room, and the moving of the bags blocking his escape.

He pays for his desperation.

He gains new wounds, mostly to the palms of his hands and his fingers. He is forced to wrap his hands in makeshift bandages to continue working. He takes more care in his efforts after this point.   There had to be easier ways to complete his task.

Using one of his valued tarps as a makeshift sled he can move much more material over a shorter amount of time. The back wall nearest to him is now a formidable towering wall made from bags, stable yet precarious, which he has moved and piled high to the ceiling. When he can, he flings bags up out of the hole. A few bags rip open in his attempts. Every day he draws closer to a door that must be there, on that far side. He works, and he eats.

He finds the can opener, but it is no longer needed.

He succeeds in catching another rat, another bread thief in this city of decay and stench. He cooks it. He eats it and refuses to think of what he would rather eat.

The Baby visits frequently...whether he is awake or not!

In his dreams it always travels alone, and when awake it sometimes comes with the others.   Their arrivals always signaled by the diseased light of their approach. The Baby's light is always the coldest, stealing the warmth from his body, his small fire, and his mind.

It never speaks.

In dreams, it cries, wails. In the waking world it watches and waits. It will not leave him alone and he knows why. Each hour, each minute, his fear grows more and more. The Baby is no fevered dream, and it is not starving...it was thriving! It had worn the mask of a human, an innocent infant, to lull him, to entreat him, but now all pretenses have dissolved. All disguises have been laid bare. It is not some planet bound infantile fragile product of Earth!

It is a god!

It is a "sleeper" slumbering.

Young, compared to those other sleepers, it is still ancient and old to the infant called humanity. It is a singularity of consciousness and flesh that holds memories of a once empty and lifeless earth. It recalls easily the infinite and empty darkness, devoid of warmth, called space. An impenetrable darkness before the nodes of light called the stars ever existed. It and these ancient others slept imprisoned...like him. All confined to a moment when select stars would align, and they all would awaken, shaking the earth from their great and monstrous forms to rise, to tread the great cosmos again.

The time of man would vanish, washed away by an unfathomable cold and unforgiving tide.

The homeless man knows this building, this ground, has long drawn misery and death to it, to the waiting mouths of the Baby.

In the time of dinosaurs, when all land was covered in a great forest, many great beasts came here, lost and lured into the great quagmire the Baby had called home. They came and died in rich numbers.

After them, it had called, and humanity answered unknowingly and unwittingly. In a far more recent history, this land had been a battlefield where young men, bled out and died.

Before its present, in its last living incarnation, this building had been a hospital, and the homeless man's current prison the hospital's morgue.

After all this time, the true banquet for the Baby was now, the true feast these mounds of medical waste, for here from the mingled liquids of these discarded things that seeped, the

Baby gathers nourishment of a new and wondrous kind. Here this forgotten patch of earth had found a satisfied tenant in the buried child. Its slumbering sentience somehow fermenting these mortal toxins into something dark and sweet.

The Baby sleeps, but it knows no hunger.

It is different from the others. They had grown emaciated and weak in their slumber. It, had grown fat and corpulent. Here, over the eons as it rested deep in the earth, the Baby had created a place where it would know no hunger. What should be weak, is now much stronger.

The homeless man knows it must never wake.

As the hours pass, his knowledge intuitively increases, a flood gate of instinctual information has opened and now he is caught in its current.

The Baby, this child of ancient horrors, wishes for him to stay, wishes for his demise and then his decay into liquids that would leak down to it. It would sup on his taste as it is filtered through the loam of the earth. The homeless man is a thing now uniquely made from his plight, his sufferings, and his solutions. The homeless man has eaten at the Baby's table, and in so doing he has inadvertently become an irresistible treat. A human delicacy like no other that had ever existed. Feeding on human flesh and filled with much suffering.

Slowly, what common modern mortal fears the homeless man possesses are stripped and sifted from him, leaving him hollow, filled with the empty echoes of something ancient and horrific. Echoes and shadows, distorted reflections last experienced thousands of years ago by primitive ancestors, who huddled together in caves, pointing their spears at the dark, and at the things that squatted on back bent legs in the dark and watched back with glowing pale eyes.

Marcus is filled with dread.

The next day, after the last delivery to the abandoned hospital, he spends hours trying to convince his cousin to help free the homeless man, but each time he is met with anger and resentment, and the epitaph his cousin used to torture him and keep him in agreement. That night he slept finally but is plagued and ravaged by nightmares...of guilt; imprisonment; and a dirty man carrying a dirty crying baby.

He wakes weary and determined to convince his cousin no matter the repercussions.

But his cousin is nowhere to be seen in the days following and the demands and tasks his mother give to him seemed to increase, so there was no time to search his cousin out. He would have attempted a phone call, but his cousin's family were known for their anti-social behaviors, and unwanted phone calls were never to be trusted. The week went by and the last day of the job assigned to them arrived.

Arriving at their usual meeting place the pacing predator that Tony always portrayed is nowhere to be seen. This surprises Marcus and for an hour he waits but his cousin doesn't appear. Not knowing what to do Marcus spins about in his indecision.

Though he hated doing it he headed to the only place he could think to go.

Tony's house.

Ringing the doorbell, he waits a few minutes for a response and resists the temptation to ring again. Tony's "family" didn't like visitors of any kind. Somewhere a map existed in some enclave of Jehovah Witnesses with a big red "X" right over the address. Marcus imagined above it, in old timey lettering, the warning read "Beware...here be dragons!".

Marcus waits and is rewarded with one of Tony's older brothers begrudgingly opening the door.

"What do you want nigger?"

This is expected, and Marcus is not bothered by it at all.

"Is Tony here?"

"Naw."

The door slams in his face to end the brief encounter.

It is only in the early afternoon that Marcus learns Tony's fate.

"He's in the hospital."

His other cousin. The 15-year-old female with the bad reputation told him on the front of his favorite aunt's porch.

For a moment Marcus is confused. What would Tony be doing at the dump site without him and how did she know but realized he has assumed wrong.

The night before, or so the story went, Tony had passed out. The injury in his hand had poisoned him. From his hand up to his elbow the swelling and inflammation had been wrecking havoc on his immune system. He was admitted to General just after midnight and word was, he was in bad shape. Whispers had begun he might not survive.

A strange sensation rose from the place Marcus's anxiety always grew from, the pit of his stomach. He knew its name but in the last few years it had been a less than frequent visitor.

Hope.

Marcus hopes.

Hoped Tony would die. Freeing him from the Faustian bargain he had made a little over 4 years ago, when Tony had discovered his secret.

Marcus didn't like any of the girls in his age group, or in his neighborhood. Marcus didn't like girls....anywhere! Tony had figured and found this out and had used this information to keep Marcus living under his shadow. He couldn't say no to his cousin and he couldn't reveal his true self to anyone without being ostracized and abandoned. Tolerance is a part of his community of color, but that tolerance only extended so far. Being gay, being a... "faggot" could be a death sentence...or worse. There <u>are</u> things worse than death: loving people who once did but now don't, is a pain Marcus could not imagine being able to live with.

The hours pass and night found him waiting for his older cousin Petey "Stumbles" on a lonely street corner in a yellow pool of street light. Marcus is only slightly surprised when a two-door dark blue compact pulled up next to him. The window rolls down and his cousin leans over from the driver's side.

"Get in."

Quick as you like Marcus hops in and his cousin pulls away from the curb and into the night. They drive in silence, then Petey begins to speak.

"The little fucker deserves it."

The little fucker...Tony. Marcus says nothing.

"I don't wish death on no one, but that punk is nothing but trouble."

Petey glances over briefly.

"My advice is you get as far from him as you can," Petey give Marcus a knowing look. "...but then that may not be possible."

Marcus holds his silence.

"Just my opinion."

They arrive quicker than Marcus hoped at the abandoned hospital. Uncharacteristically Petey parks, kills the lights, and shuts the engine down. He exits from the driver's side and Marcus wordlessly does the same from his side. They both gather at the back of the car. Petey pops the trunk and there amongst everything else were two matching red cans. Gasoline.

"Alright. Take those gas cans and here," he hands Marcus a book of matches from his top pocket. "You don't need to be thorough. Just poor the gas down, light it, and get the fuck out. Got it?"

"I-I can't...I can't."

He surprises himself with his answer, and in a few breathless sentences explains what he and his cousin had found in the hole. Petey isn't happy, but he does well to contain most of it.

"You stupid muthafuckers."

Grumbling Petey grabs both cans.

"If Tony doesn't die, I'm gonna kill him!"

The homeless man doesn't feel well. He no longer sleeps, or when he does try to, he merely feels himself sinking into an encapsulating darkness, being drawn inexplicably downward to something waiting that is not death.

The infant in its cradle of dirt.

Patient and hungry it calls to him. He fights back this dark, returning to his dying body, kick starting his failing heart and re-engaging his laboring breath.

Only two clear things exist for him solid and real, finer than any vision held before: he will not die here! He will not be food for this nightmare child that sleeps far beneath his feet!

He is close, so awfully close, and so very tired. He must keep going. He refuses to eat from his cornucopia of meant to be lost things. No more would he prepare a feast of himself for this other, this Sleeper. The turkey being stuffed. A Hansel and Gretel to a monstrosity.

He is close!

He can see the edge of a doorframe. He has moved mountains. He begins to laugh. His laughter comes free and strong and his strength begins to trinkle back to him. His laughter turns to tears as he places his face in his hands. He would survive. He is still crying and sobbing into his hands when the light begins to grow behind him.

It is the Baby...the one who slumbers has arrived!

It has cast aside all of its human illusion and now its true form shines malevolently forth. Even with his back turned, he can sense it completely, as it stands towering behind him.

Immense, a composition of ills, the Baby is not meant for mortal senses to perceive.

He dares not turn as he feels it draw closer, slowly closer. It's unnatural light growing brighter. He knows it is not real, it is only a vision of the Baby, of the Child That Sleeps Below. It should not be able to touch him, but he knows this is not true. The danger is real. The fear is realer.

"Wha-what the fuck??!!!"

The shout breaks the preternatural silence which had descended on the trash strewn room from the raw presence of the Child. With the vanishing of the silence, the Child vanishes also, it's known existence only to be gained and retained, briefly, by the doomed and the damned, by the forever to be lost. These intruders are not worthy.

The witnesses to the homeless man's imprisonment have returned.

"What the fuck are you talking about?!"

The homeless man does not recognize this voice. This voice is new.

"... just a second ago..." Marcus's voice trails into unsure silence.

"'Just a second ago' what?!" this new voice had an edge like the young blade, and his impatience rings out, bigger and sharper.

"...I-I don't know. Didn't you see it?! A strange....light! It was coming out of the hole!"

"What the fuck are you talking about?!" anger easily replaces impatience. "I knew this job would be too much for you and your dumb shit cousin!"

"Whatever!" Marcus surprises himself at his own vehemence, most often it is never let free to roam and cavort near bigger predators. It stretches its muscles and briefly is touched by a warming ray of sunlight. Light from a sun that most times glows hidden behind clouds. Marcus amazed, hides a smile on the side of his face that is turned away from his older cousin's gaze.

"Let's just get it done-"

"Please..." the homeless man's voice again rises to fall on new and uncaring ears.

"He's still alive!!" Surprise and relief ring out in Marcus's voice.

"Holy shit! You weren't lyin'."

Petey moves to the edge of the hole and peers down. There he sees a disheveled figure. Dark of skin, dirty, and starving. The man's eyes wide and crazed.

"Wow. You are a tough one, old man."

"We can't do this!" Marcus has had enough. He isn't going to walk down this road. He still has choices.

"We?" Petey is taken aback. He is about to say something harsh but pauses and sighs. Marcus was an alright kid compared to the psychopath his cousin was.

"Listen. This is on me. You, your fucked-up cousin and this," he points down at the hole and its discarded contents. "Are on me. My job. My problem."

He lifts one of the gas cans and starts to unscrew the cap.

"Go back to the car and wait for me. Keep a look out. This will only take a minute."

The cap frees and without hesitation he begins to pour it down the hole onto the piled high bags of trash. Working around the hole, he kicks the few bags the homeless man had flung out back into the hole.

NO!

Deep beneath the Child rages. It senses and sees all that takes place above it, and knows this new human, if not halted, would ruin everything.

Fire, the Consumer, was an old acquaintance and the Child had watched it in loathing as it breathed in the heart of stars and in the pathetic fires of the two leg walking apes.

And here it is again! It was an offense to the deep and the cold of space and the swimmers between stars!

If this new human accomplished its task the human morsel it had helped to cultivate will be turned to ash and cinders. This would not happen!

Under the dirt and stone, deep below....its vast. Eyes...open!

Marcus stands frozen.

Indecision holds him to the old tiled floor of the hospital. He does not leave nor does he try to stop Petey in his actions. Petey already had opened the second gas can and when he finished the blaze would be lit with ease. Marcus stares down at the homeless man. He watches as the old man dodges the splashing gasoline.

He is so close!

The freedom he has sought is just before him. The unseen door only feet from him, behind the last mounds of medical waste.

An amber stream of gasoline pours from above refracting the light. It is only luck which guides it away from the last embers of his floor fire.

The homeless man's time is now up.

Frenzied and possessed of monstrous will he attacks the last piles of waste that keep him from freedom. He is only action and purpose. He will not die here. He will not succumb. He would not be food. The Baby lays waiting under its blankets of earth and stone. He can feel it.

He doesn't see the spark as the world behind him ignites, only feels it's rising flames, the bright flash of heat as it starts to burn at his back several feet away. Eyes unhindered he peers back and up to see the new man standing lit by the growing conflagration.

The Child stirs!

The hospital is jolted suddenly by an earthquake.

The homeless man already on unsteady feet falls to his knees. He is lucky.

Petey is not.

As the ground pitches and the building shakes Petey "Stumbles" lives up to his nickname. Abruptly his balance is comprised and his eyes flash wide as he tries to correct himself...but it is too late.

Like the homeless man weeks before Stumbles falls into the hole, and into the waiting fire he had just created. Already the fire is expelling plumes of noxious black smoke from the burning plastics. Plastic already liquid, viscid. Plastic which immediately clings to the skin of Petey in flaming black tendrils.

His screams are also immediate.

Marcus runs, and the screams from the fire follow him, but these are not the things which freed him from his paralysis. The indecision that had held him as things degenerated below him.

It was as the fire licked up and down the body of his now dying cousin, he had seen....something:

A trick of the light.

A mirage made from the rippling waves of heated air.

His guilt manifest!

He could not say with certainty, for what his eyes had seen would surely forever stay with him in this world and perhaps would follow him into the next.

A thing!....swollen and hewn from some unusual material much different from what he could call skin and flesh had risen like a ghastly apparition from the floor of the burning room. Mostly translucent, bulbous and wet, with a mass that could only equate to a head, which sat atop the strange and horrid form's...body. It displayed two twin bulging and sickly pale blue orbs rimmed in black, a parody of common eyes, which rolled in lidless sockets. It had moved clumsily on six squat limbs ending in a tangle of writhing fleshy tendrils, dragging an engorged belly across the burning floor with it. It was when it touched Petey and Petey's screams scissor snipped and abruptly ended Marcus had regained control of his body and fled.

The fire rises and grows, illuminating everything, but he only feels it on his back, for his world, his vision, is locked on a door and the escape it must provide. Behind the homeless man the sudden vacuum of silence writes warnings of doom and fear across his fragile mind. He knows without looking the man who fell behind him is dead and the Child is approaching. His hands feel nothing as he scoops and hurls the last remaining bags of medical waste behind him into the path of the approaching, encroaching, nightmare. Flames and smoke fill the room, and his breathing begins to come in gasps in the now rarefied and toxic air. The bigger fire reignites the homeless man's floor bound fire, which he had allowed to die down to its embers.

The door is revealed, finally, at least its upper half, and in this upper half a faded and cracked window sits waiting. Without hesitation he grabs the handle of his now broken and dejected cart. Its wheels fearfully sway and rock as it is lifted suddenly. It had been his faithful companion through thin and thick, his lodestone in troubled waters, but the man who had died in this room had needed it. This new man needs only one thing: to survive. From some deep reserve of strength this new man lifts the mangled cart above his head and flings it at the door and the revealed window. In a trajectory made perfect by his will, the door's window smashes into a thousand glittering and flame lit shards.

For a moment, the ghost of the homeless man mourns his shopping cart's sacrifice. Then the new man runs and dives for the glass edged opening, just as the fire engulfs the room completely...

...and the Baby, which had been so close, lowers its out stretching hand and vanishes into flames.

An old building stands engulfed in fire, its shadows running to hide around the nearest unlit buildings. Thirty yards away a shape lies prone on the broken concrete, fingers of smoke rising off it. It is a man. His chest rises slowly and steadily. All is silence except for the roar of the growing conflagration spitting glass and other debris. The prone man's laughter is surprising as it echoes out clear and true, all him and no one else. No <u>one</u>. Slowly he rises. He can hear the sirens already approaching in the distance, yet they were still far away. They would be too late for the building, and for him. He has things to do. No pain, well a little, but over it is strength, reawakened and restless. The man is reforged, remade. He is something new and something ancient. He is free. Truly and utterly free. He knows now, there are things to be truly afraid of; he no longer fears the world with its common men and common concerns. The *Presence* is dead. The homeless man is gone. He is possessed with clarity, sharp and defined, crystalline and sane, and as purifying as death. He has things to do.

"...Marcus?...."

The looming intimidating figure, that his small mother always was, that next morning was gentle and awkward as she woke him.

He hadn't really been sleeping.

She had bad news.

The family mourned as the next day word passed around of the untimely death of Petey....and Tony.

There were questions for Marcus of course. He answered as best he could, leaving out all mention of the homeless man and the Child That Sleeps Below.

It was not hard for any to imagine Petey falling prey to his own lack of dexterity, and for many the death of Tony freed them from future fears of the man he would have become.

They said Tony died of "sepsis". The infection in his hand poisoning his blood till his whole body failed in the fight. Marcus didn't know what to feel. Yes, Tony had been holding him hostage, blackmailing him, but he was still the closest thing to a friend he had had. He couldn't help the guilt at the thoughts he had harbored previously about his now deceased cousin.

The following day things got worse. Somewhere in the night his great uncle Alfonz had been murdered.

There were many questions and no answers. The men who guarded and worked closest to his great uncle now worked to keep the details of his death in silence, but quickly the truth spread.

The night had passed quietly at his great uncle's home in the Marina, and like every new day his maid was right on time with his coffee, biscotti, and the latest editions of the

Chronicle and the Examiner. Giving a brief knock she then went to turn the knob to enter, but the door didn't budge. She knocked louder but not a sound came back in response. She had turned to his personal guards who sat near to hand. Marcus's great uncle always had assistants around, smart ones and strong ones. Already they had eyes on her and the door. Immediately the two took her place in front of the door to his bedroom suite, and after hard knocks then fists pounding and loud calls of concern, they both worked at pushing the door open. Shoulders braced against the wood they managed to wedge the door open enough for one to slip through. Once in the other was able to clear enough of the blockage to open the door.

The maid ran away, her nose covered, fear pushing at her eyelids, making them wide and bright with tears. The two guards identically covered their nostrils with suit covered arms to block the stench that permeated the room.

Wall to wall the room was filled with trash. Mounds of garbage in bursting black plastic bags. In the center of the confusion lay the body of great uncle Alfonz, his body barely recognizable. His limbs lay twisted as if grabbed by thick massive ropes, squeezed, and then pulled apart. From his mouth his engorged tongue protruded and where his eyes had been only empty blood-filled sockets remained. This was not all. His internal organs had been removed and where nowhere to be found. There were signs of forced entry through the balcony glass doors, and a path of filth trailed down the side of his great uncle's home, yet during the night there had been no sounds, no screams, or no evidence of any kind of trouble to be heard by anyone.

It was poorly surmised that a rival faction of the family or perhaps the Chinese or the Hispanics had made a daring strike against Marcus's people. Doors were locked and bolted. Windows shut and guns loaded as the strongest and smartest members hit the street searching for answers and payback. There was infighting. The vacuum created by his great uncle's demise left a whirlpool of instability as the next in line moved to take power.

During all Marcus said nothing but he thought many things....had the homeless man escaped and sought vengeance against the people, person, behind his recent accidental incarceration in a forgotten and abandoned hospital?...if so, how? The homeless man Marcus had seen was no specimen of physical prowess nor did he at any time appear to be a master of stealth, agility, and such violence that this act against his father's side of the family required.

No....what came to Marcus's mind was not human but some unimaginable creation. A horror dredged from fear's dark distances... a horror once erroneously called "baby" by a poor sick man trapped in a hole. To Marcus only its horrifying touch could generate such a gruesome scene as the one found in his great uncle's bedroom.

Over one morning's breakfast as his little brother watched tv he told his small yet formidable mother he was gay. Something good would come out of all this, Marcus was determined it would be so. He had lost some common fears somewhere in the days following that terrible night.

Of course, he kept his silence about the "baby". Speaking of such a thing would only create suspicion and stares questioning his sanity. This would all cause trouble for Marcus, his brother, and his mother, who already had enough problems when dealing with his father's family. A side of his family, he had decided, he would put behind him as he moved forward in his life...free of his cousin.

But remorsefully, not free from what he had done...nor from what he had seen.

Drifting on the fringes of the city the man shambles. His body still sick but slowly getting better.

He is free.

A small part misses a shopping cart, the good ones being hard to find, but he is feeling lucky, and he isn't hungry, and he isn't sleepy at all.

....and under the encrustation of grey concrete spotted black by decades of man's chewing habits, deep beneath the city streets, below the electricity filled metal veins, and the baked clay and brick conduits of sewage, titan coils of unnatural flesh stir and roll. Fat and forever gluttonous, lost in a madness of craving, the Child moves beneath the surface of the world on the trail of a lost morsel. Slowly it shifted the pressing earth around it, undulating and shrugging away the eons of dirt which hugged it like a quilt. It didn't care that once again it would know hunger, even starvation, in its hunt. It didn't worry, for it had learned many tasty things fall through the dark cracks of man's world to be reshaped in its stomachs. In time it would win, for it had more time than all the lives of man combined! And, for now, it was not hungry. For now, it was not sleepy...at all!

The Icosahedra Key

Volume One

Seen from the shore they could be easily mistaken for very dense, peaceful clouds majestically descended from their higher heights, to float upon the ocean's waves.

Amorphous puffy shapes of pale-yellow white...with reddish and pink hints within, rising and falling as the waves rolled.

They are not clouds.

Only off the coast of G'thik could the large gelatinous sponges be found, the environment giving them perfect conditions to thrive, and some unique fate, giving them their creation. Seabirds and other flying creatures often mistakenly land on their upper surfaces, resting in flight or perhaps drawn to a free and open nesting site, unaware of the danger. The doom to come. Landing only to find themselves stuck in the gripping flesh of the floating parasitic sponges, they are slowly drawn in... then, more slowly, dissolved and devoured. The water breathers also had no better luck. Fish, seeking shade from the brightness of the day and cooler waters, or erroneously seeking some semblance of protection from sleek and fast-moving predators, sheltered underneath the floating sponges, and suffered similar fates as those which flew. The yellow and red hues found in the flesh of these strange horror's coloring is simply a byproduct of their feeding and their slight transparency. The yellow: the countless undigested bones being digested slowly; the red: the countless microscopic drops of blood floating in misty clumps throughout their gelatinous flesh. All to feed semi-transparent organs.

For these unthinking monstrosities, the coastal waters of G'thik provided abundant feeding, and here, and only here, do these nightmares become gigantic in size.

Stretching as far as the eye could see, along the barren and mostly lifeless shoreline titanic arcing shapes, like the unfleshed ribcages of giants, now barnacled and dressed in seaweeds, protrude from the dark wet graveled sands in numbers not easily counted. A rich fog sits high off the ground, outlining the near perfect flat wet grey wall, a cliff's face, that lay many yards from the water's edge, and mere feet from the last rows of the strange upright barnacled forms. The cliff's top mirrored the vertical face of the great wall, a perfect horizontal line uninterrupted for hundreds and hundreds of miles, running without break in either direction. Obviously, it was a construction. Made by some now gone and great people. Its curving embraced the east and north edges of this foreboding land.

This is the coast of the G'thik, and its waters, the Thousand War Sea.

The sea crusted rib cages, in actuality the metal bones of ancient ships, preserved in some distant past and revealed as one sea receded and changed into another, told stories to the drifting thick grey above in a language of misty breezes pushing through their vertical forms. In its length the coast of G'thik had few open areas of beach where landfall could possibly be made, but it is not scarcity of shoreline nor monsters which has kept explorers and traders from the lands beyond the great sea facing wall, or for those with the spirit of entrepreneurship to create small settlements with docks and harbors where the coastline would provide. No.

G'thik was unforgiving and primal. Unexplored and unconquered. The last great uncharted area of the continent of Mu. Mu, only discovered 200 years ago, was not easily mastered by the first colonists and explorers who arrived there, but now much of the continent is known, and towns and villages were numerous, some of these towns a few decades from growth to the jagged silhouettes of cityscapes.

G'thik, a substantial mass of the continent of Mu's upper north eastern region, resists all intervention and exploration.

Many have tried only to be beaten and tortured by the unforgiving terrain. Jagged ravines of black and red volcanic glass; the vegetation more thorns than leaves, more poison than perfume; and the creatures, fearsome, masters of dwelling within shadows, flesh thirsty and quiet as death, all encircled the land where it was not guarded by the great wall. A band of woe forced many on bloody limbs to return defeated and forever changed. Of the ones who have made it through...silence! For no word, nor explorer, has ever spoke of succeeding...if any ever had.

Many had disappeared.

The lucky survivors pulled themselves from the cold salt rich waters or woke with bodies pressed harshly into the beach's tiny stones. Their numbers were few. All signs of the ship they had been traveling on nowhere to be seen.

Besides the many floating gelatinous sponges, the deep rolling fog that grew and breathed off the coast was the other known threat in this area of the Thousand War Sea. Alone a fog only slows things down, pulling ships and crew into a world more tense and far more precise. All eyes scanning mists for threats which materialize like ghosts at the edge of the vision, to become real and solid and dark in moments leading to a crash or if luck holds a rapid adjustment to a ship's course, to save life, limb, planks and sails. Close up threats can be seen....unless the threat is only one shade removed from the color of fog.

The storm was sudden. The fight long. And the course so far off to leave the vessel, *The Kellen Wasp*, ill fated, fog bound and lost.

It was with wounded sails that *The Wasp* collided with the sponge, a calf struck by a wolf, grey and dark with maturity. The ship's center buckled as the fore port side of the ship was instantly and partially engulfed. Wet wood penetrating and welcomingly gripped by the sponge's caustic flesh.

Scattered amongst the giant bones of the archaic ships littering the coast are smaller wooden bones. The wreckage of smaller ships. Modern victims of misfortune skinned or currently unskinned by barnacles and the like.

The six survivors of *The Wasp* sat, lay, or stood wearily on the sands.

"Where are we?" Jilliandria was the first to speak, her robes wet and clinging, fabrics darkened by moisture, glancing around her, both hesitant and unsure. She knew where they were but felt uninclined to utter the words, for this place had been the primary topic for discussion for many days on the recently abandon ship.

"We can only be in one place," the elf, Nighlus replies, his movements cautious, his sharp ears attentive, as he squats in the sand, touching the graveled ground, tasting the air for scents and sights. "The G'thik coastline."

"No....this is bad. We have got to signal a ship or- or build one," she awkwardly states, her hands twisting in the fabric of her cold robes for warmth and comfort, her long bright locks, hiding her ears, lay limp against her face, and her grey crystal green eyes shone bright against her tan skin.

Even the touch of the waters off this dead coast could be deadly.

Every few months the sponges go through what can only be called "spawning", releasing streaming columns of microscopic sponge spores into the waters. These minute spores stay in the upper surface of the waters, and, it is not unheard of, for wayward ships to sight mile long stretches of them. Their presence marked by waters turned a milky yellow green. Thick and viscous waters filled with the spawn of sponges. Fall into these spore rich waters and it is as good as falling into the embrace of an adult sponge or a pool of acid.

"No ship would be foolish enough to chance these waters to rescue so few, and going back out there in a poorly made craft would be death."

Gesturing, the elf's pale finger, draws his fellow survivors' gazes to the waterline and the terrain running parallel with it. Up and down, as far as any could see, thousands upon thousands of dying and dead, whole and rock ripped sponges lay. A soft minefield, able to burn and eat flesh.

"Disgusting," Jilliandria mutters gazing at the nearest decaying sponge mass rotting in the waves, her left hand instinctually clutches at the holy token of her god, a beautiful red haired woman's image engraved in a disk of copper hanging from a chain round her neck, usually hidden beneath her robes when amongst strangers.

"Like acidic snot monsters," said straight and far from elaborately, the short haired female human in worn and wet leathers chimes in.

"Crass but accurate Ms. Arrow," frowns the healer.

"The name is <u>Noc</u>. N-O-C. Save that formal shit for someone-!"

"We are not devoid of luck," Nighlus interrupts before the two start arguing again as they were want to do. "We all live...for now."

"Isn't that a little sliver of a silver lining in a fluffy cloud! On no wait. That's a death dealing sponge not a cloud!" Noc replies sarcastically.

Nighlus, momentarily lost in thought, or more truthfully trained to ignore the comments from his lessers, doesn't register the jape. His mind has wandered to his childhood, and stories told under clear night skies when the summer winds were cool, and the stars reminded every living elf of the Feywild, their first home, were the land at night was as equally lit as the roof of the world above.

"It is believed out in these waters, a sponge has lived for hundreds perhaps thousands of years. Legends say it's size is like that of a mountain, and within its flesh is the treasure of ten thousand ships."

"That's a lot of ships!" known for his quips and deficiency in common decency, the smiling tall lean half-orc, mottled green skin still glistening with seawater, Horak Shakundi, remarks from a few feet away, his fingertips and eyes exploring one of the nearest limbs of an ancient ship's ribbing.

"No sense pondering something that lacks validation or verification in our current situation."

The dwarf, missing his familiar plated armor responds, turning away from his scanning of the beach to face the other survivors.

"Sounds like something well beyond our pay grade."

Taciturn, efficient, and perpetually calm would best describe the dwarf, Ahlassiter Orekeeper, skin a deep rich brown, eyes a deep black. He was among those rare dwarves which kept their faces shorn, devoid beard and braiding. Whether for fashion or to rebel against his kind, he has not ever said and no one dare ask.

"First action, we need to get off this beach. If another storm comes in, we won't have to worry about being digested by those sea things. The cold driving wet winds that must plague this high north coast will be enough to rob us of both warmth and life."

"I think I can help a little with that," a soft voice speaks.

All eyes focus on the diminutive halfling, Gracis. She is missing her beautiful embroidered yellow and green robes which had lovingly complimented her deep tan skin. Her hands weave small rapid movements, making strange shapes by twisting and twining her fingers. These shapes blur and pull at the eyes of the others in a strange unwanted manner. Magic! A melody of sounds like a whispering breeze passes over her moving lips. Lips which oddly do not match the sounds pouring from her throat. She finishes. Silence.

Three of the party jump in surprise, as they feel their clothing warm...slightly.

"Cool!" Jilliandria exclaims, face glowing with surprise and joy, giggling. The holy symbol of her goddess, now pulled free from beneath her sleeping robes, bounces against her ample chest, catching the diffuse light of the grey dawn sky magnifying it. Like her present mirth it sparkles and glows.

The smiles given to her by the others make the halfling flush red. She tries to conceal her embarrassed wide smile at the appreciative looks.

Awkwardly, the little mage takes the praise.

"I can't dry our clothes, but if I keep using this spell, I can keep us warm...ish."

"One point for the halfling!" Noc grants, bowing deeply from the waist in the general direction of the wizard.

"Okay," the dwarf says, slightly pleased at even this minor success.

"No one else survived?" Jilliandria questions, she can't hide her sadness as awareness that many of those she had befriended on the voyage had most likely perished. Before she returns her holy symbol back beneath her robes, she prays with a saddened expression.

The survivors, to varying degrees, are touched with thoughts for the dead. The lucky six stand stunned.

"No. I don't think so," Ahlassiter answers.

"Whoa!"

The lithe and quick fingered Noc Arrow suddenly leaps ten feet to her left, one of her many small blades materializing in her right hand, her short auburn hair swaying as her feet impact the beach's gravely ground, as a tiny dull brown and red shape scuttles rapidly from the shadows beneath a few jagged rocks littering the sands here and there beneath her feet.

"What is that?!"

Gracis slowly begins to cross the distance to survey the patch of sand near her friend, her hands raised defensively. The hem of her warming robes catches on a heavily barnacle encrusted rock. In a swaying of arms, she maintains her balance, reaching back a hand to extricate her trapped hem. Making her way finally to the place the small shape had been seen darting, she finds nothing.

"I don't see anything."

"Of course not! Only took you 50 years to walk 30 feet!"

"Probably a crab," Ahlassiter comments, his brow beginning to crease with tension at this unfamiliar terrain, and its unknown variables and hidden dangers. "Let's move closer to the cliff face and at least put our backs to something solid before we make any decisions."

Still wet with saltwater, some beginning to shiver but not as strong as they might with the halfling's warming magic, the six survivors of *The Wasp* step and crawl their way towards the strange flat faced wall which runs the length and breadth of the G'thik shoreline.

Passing many of the remnants of the ancient's great ships, led by Nighlus, they make their way slowly without missteps, giving wide berth to the encrusted artifacts of the ancients.

Tanggg!

A sound. A rock rebounding off one of the ribs of the ancient ships shakes the five from their own thoughts and the constant sounds of surf, water striking land; of feet seeking purchase on damp rocks and shifting sand; of strenuous breaths and, occasionally, under the breath curses of those less nimble members among them as they worked to maintain their balance.

Five. Not six.

Already frazzled agitated and confused stares greet Horak's impish gaze, his right arm still up in a gesture indicating something had been thrown. Taking up the rear of the line, in his boredom he had taken to stopping every few feet to pick of interesting stones. His left hand, held close to his stomach, carried this collection. Besides Noc, Horak was the only other who had managed to leave the ship fully dressed.

"What?" Horak's pale yellow eyes stare back at the others.

"Do you really think that is the best idea right now?" queries Ahlassiter.

Horak stands silent, for a moment in quiet contemplation.

Tanggg!

Before an action or word could stop him, the green skinned sorcerer flicks out another stone from his collection. An interesting rock that in the poor light had had a pleasant green hue to his eyes, but upon further inspection only proved to be colored by a build-up of algae on white quartz, made the journey back to the ground.

"Those things pose no threat," Horak gestures nonchalantly at the nearest ship's rib. "See."

Five faces. Agitation growing. Even the normally jovial and prankish Noc stands with arms and hands tucked and wrapped against her body in disapproval. Her shivering and discomfort clear. A wet scavenger, hungry, and pushed into a corner she is not amused.

"Come on!" he smiles, his charisma flashing for these scared children. "Let's go!"

Horak walks between his stopped companions, merrily taking lead. Quickly, Nighlus follows, hoping to guide the crazed and annoying half-orc before his footsteps could lead them afoul.

Reluctant and annoyed, the remanding four follow.

"I wonder if this voids our contracts," Jilliandria mutters.

Two and a half weeks ago in the bursar's office of *Malgin & Willowfoot Cartographers* they had all met and been hired to take the long ocean voyage to the newly established settlements on Mu's south eastern territories. The alternative shorter route, south through the Zasfhr Strait into the upper reaches of the Ether Sea then immediately south east to the north west coast, passed through the warground of three great nations battling in the waters there.

The Adamantine War. Fighting for a recently discovered island. An island like many others, it offered enough space for habitation and some cultivation, valuable only in absence of other options. It was nothing special. Until the "discovery". A pure adamantium vein, close to the surface, upped the value exponentially, but still that is not enough for fathers and mothers, and kings and queens and nations to send their children, sons and daughters, men and women, to die in such a frenzy as to churn the seas red.

The vein was a deep running river! Immense. Estimated to be 30% of the small islands core...above water! Below it continued. Some think miles. The largest source of the rare metal ever discovered. Enough adamantium to make kingdoms....change empires.... or fund many, many, wars, and arm the soldiers to fight them.

The three greatest nations could not ignore it, nor could they afford for it to fall into another nation's grasp, for fear of the imbalance it would create in the struggles between them.

The war made it particularly difficult for smaller nations, uninvolved, yet having holdings and settlements that still required access to the newly discovered frontier lands of Mu, to travel there. No matter the state of things, they were forced to make hard decisions. In the case of Verus, a small yet growing nation, home to the prestigious *Malgin & Willowfoot Cartographers*, this made Mu inaccessible by the normal shorter route. Thus, the necessity for the longer voyage past the northern upper face of Mu, where wide berth is given to the coastal waters, and land beyond them...the feared and forbidding G'thik.

Tanggg!

"We may have to renegotiate new ones," Noc looks at the half-orc's back, cringing at the noise he is making and the damage he was making to the silence she kept well cultivated around herself when not goofing herself. Silence she had been perfecting since her first days at the guild, and even before then when life on the streets of Lwynkarr demanded stealth to survive the daily hunters of young unattended girls.

"If we survive this, we will be a lot more experienced!"

Tanggg!

"First part of survival still lies beyond this beach head." Ahlassiter grows more uncomfortable as they near the great wall. His senses taut and anxious are attended by a cascade of thoughts about the unknowns they would need to face and address in the coming hours, and in the days ahead.

Ponk!

Ponk?

No sooner than these last words are uttered by Ahlassiter, Horak, strikes another nearby upright and the sound it makes is markedly different. Nighlus freezes and raises a warning hand for immediate silence. The forward momentum they are making stops.

"Wait," his whisper pitched so it traveled no further than the most distant of their group.

"What?" Gracis whispers up to him from his left side. She has kept close to him as they have traveled.

Silence.

"There! Did you all feel that?!" Nighlus says quickly and a little louder than a moment before.

"Feel what?" Noc says a little too loudly from a few feet behind Nighlus and Gracis.

Pat-pat-pat-pat...

Another new sound.

The sound Horak makes, as he runs, approaches quickly from the back of their progressing group which has now halted. Once more he had fallen behind again as they neared the wall, but turning, everyone watches as the half-orc rushes through the center of the group.

"What are you doing?!" Noc yells at him as he passes.

Only three sets of eyes and curiosity followed the back of the running sorcerer.

"Running!"

"Why?!"

"....behind....you!....."

Whoom!

A large movement back towards the waterline, felt through the ground and through the soles of their feet.

Back along their path, what appeared to be a cluster of a great ship's ribs pointing vertically in the air, begins to vibrate and move....then bend!

Horak has awakened something with his last stone throw.

A cloud of dried sea life and beach, broken shells and bits of stone and seaweed, suddenly rains down as a creature unlike anything they had ever witnessed slowly rolled its flat body. Its twelve 30-foot-long limbs when unbent, which it had held up in the air in absolute stillness as it had laid on its back, come to rest on the sands to stand on pointed tips. Shelled and flat, it resembles a crab partly, its limbs and underbelly covered in a camouflage of dead seashells and barnacles, black green knotted tendrils of dried seaweeds. Its body was easily 15 feet across. Its limbs and multiple pincers and fangs spoke more of nimble spiders and chitinous scorpions that wept venom than of sea crustaceans. Unique to this coastline, it and its predecessors had adapted to fit this land filled with the husked bodies of ancient metal ships. Evolving a unique form, and a unique way to wait and ambush prey.

"Oh shit," the full elf speaks plainly, a first.

In a panic the remaining five flee after Horak. The muscular dwarf Ahlassiter scooping up the female halfling in mid stride.

"What tha-!" Gracis exclaims surprised by being dwarf-handled off her feet.

"We don't have time for your tiny legs!"

"My tiny legs?!" she rebuffs, her eyes double-taking from her unladylike position accusingly down at the squat legs of the dwarf's as she is jostled beneath his left arm.

"This way!" Nighlus takes the lead, the half-orc still yards ahead, and guides the fleeing group to the nearest section of ancient debris.

"Is that wise?!" the nimble Noc looks at him with eyebrows raised.

"Or only chance is to make it to the wall, and we can only do that now by giving that thing some obstacles."

Nighlus reaches the first uneven group of vertical columns, and quickly turns to guide the others up and through the debris.

"Be thankful. In the open we would be dead in minutes!"

"You really have to ease up on the constant optimism!" Noc quips in passing.

Her sarcasm does not go unnoticed, even by Nighlus.

The creature seems slow to locate what had caused it to wake. At the forefront of its shell a set of globular spheres, red and pink of tone, move and pivot around on short thick stalks. Drawn by the fleeing group's movements, the ponderous creature slowly turns, its paired eyes focusing on the terrain and its prey.

As the last member passes through the first patch of debris, the elf finally affords a glance at the monster.

It lifts one leg in the direction of *The Wasp* survivors....and begins to run!

"Holy shit!!" the elf cries out.

Nighlus jumps after his companions, yelling and gesturing.

"That way!"

The creature is fast. Faster than anyone of them could have imagined. The group makes it through the next vertical uprights and is moving well onto the next when the creature hits the first cluster they had just passed through.

Boom! KRAAAACK!

It was quick, but still a cumbersome abomination. It hits the debris with the force of a stampede. Warping and twisting the old metal, its mass and momentum cracks the antiquated materials, and the monstrosity wobbles before steadying itself. Its long limbs pick their way over what remains.

Up ahead the swift Horak reaches the wall, his eyes scanning the surface for a ladder or footholds. Nighlus watches him.

"Our companion has reached the wall."

"I hope he is looking for a way up for all of us." No sooner had Jilliandria spoke these words, than Horak, seen from a distance, puts one foot on the wall, then another, and simply begins to walk up it, as if it was merely flat ground. In a span of moments, he clears the top and is lost to sight.

"Son of a bitch!"

It is with surprise and some humor, that all the survivors around the priestess spare a glance to her in their flight...a few admirably.

"Don't act surprised!" Jilliandria yells still running "Being a half-elf means I am also half human!"

The nightmare of G'thik's coast is gaining ground, but clearly it has survived on prey weakened by the waves. Its evolution had given it superior camouflage based on the terrain, but not necessarily a body which moved masterfully across it.

Noc reaches the wall next after the vanished sorcerer and leaps, fingers and feet cat stretched to grab at any imperfections in the vertical surface. She succeeds and hurriedly gains more than a man's height from the ground below.

Its meal is escaping!

Kkkkkrrrrrrrrreeeeeeeeeeeeeeeeeeeeeeee!!!!!!!

The monster's piercing keen shears across the ground focused on the prey that is attempting to escape it. The sound from the thing, a scream, sharp and grating, high and alien, floods over them all as they all reach the base of the wall.

The sound is a torturous thing, ripping and ruining any calm the survivors had maintained in their mad dash to escape. Jilliandria drops to one knee and almost collapses but the forest warrior, Nighlus, bolsters her lifting her before she can succumb. Ahlassiter the warrior, strength his cornerstone, barely maintains his composure. He wilts under the cry, but the little mage clutches his side and looks up at him freeing him from descending further. This is not the place for weakness!

"Stay strong! Nighlus, can you get a rope up there?!"

"What rope?!" the high elf gestures round at their small and gearless band.

"Hurry! You are running out of time!" the most often cool and collected Noc cries out. From her advanced position on the wall, about 40 feet up, she throws a glance back along their escape route.

30 seconds.

Her mind, trained to be precise, can easily see how much time they had before it was too late. When the monster would be close enough to kill.

30 seconds!

"30 seconds!!!" her yell tells them with certainty and uncanny accuracy that doom would shortly be upon them.

Winded, Noc Arrow nears the top of the ancient wall. Sweat in small rivulets streaks her face cutting through the salt crusted to her skin. Almost there she thinks....as a rope falls past her, down from the top of wall to her companions below.

"What?!-"

"Climb people! Climb!"

Looking over the edge, Horak peers down. His face wears a cat-that-ate-the-canary's satisfied smirk.

"Son of a bitch," this time the looks of surprise are for the diminutive female magic user.

"See!" Jilliandria points and yells with a what-did-I-tell-you look, as if to counterpoint the look from above.

Fear can be an excellent motivator. Focusing the mind, pumping the body with energy just waiting to be used throughout the body.

Today, fear and desperation made grips tight and feet sure as the survivors set to climb.

The great creature watches as its quarry, a smooth line of closely spaced dots, begins to rush up the face of the great barrier marking the edge of its kingdom to that unknown kingdom above. Unknown and always present...taunting it. It did not like the wall, for here its might and influence ended.

Ahlassiter, protecting the rear, watches as his compatriots make it to the halfway point on the wall, one short span from escape from a spiky bitey crunching death. Next to him, the halfling stands ready to go next, up the rope the sorcerer had lowered.

Again, without asking Ahlassiter sweeps up the small halfling, and standing on the toe tips helps her gain a good start on the rope and the climb ahead.

He is just planting his feet when the cries from above catch him. Turning, he is in time to see the monster clear the last barrier of debris and the last stretch of open sand between it and the wall, and the warm living flesh that it would suck dry. Living flesh it would gnaw and rip till there was nothing left but patches of wetter darker sand.

Stupid! The dwarf is angry. Weaponless in enemy territory. How many things had he passed that he could have armed himself with? He questions how easily the training he had mastered in his old comfortable world so swiftly departed in the face of this alien creature.

He braces himself for the assault. He would make this creature earn its snack.

Meaty. This man-thing was meaty. Its keen eyes move along the small man before it. Yes. I will eat you! It sways as it takes the first steps towards this treat...cautiously.

The large rock which strikes its shell causes it to list dangerously to one side.

"Hey crab boy!" the voice of Noc calls down to the creature below, her hands already hefting another sizable stone to throw "You like getting stoned!"

The second stone arcs out on target. Noc nods her head, her hands a little abraded from the roughness of the rock she just tossed.

"'...getting stoned' really?" Horak looks at her pained and befuddled.

"Don't stop!" Nighlus shouts over to them, he kneels at the edge of the wall, reaching down he helps Jilliandria clear the last few feet. Below, Gracis, her small body struggling, clings to the rope. Her complexion pale. Wizarding doesn't prepare most for physical exertion beyond lifting rare overly large tomes of ancient lore. Honestly, even in her panic, she is doing surprisingly better than she could have imagined!

It will be later in the near future that she will attribute this achievement to the loss of her belongs, and that precious of all things, her spellbook, which had been as heavy as a small shield. Bound in soft exotic green leather with hundreds of pages, mostly blank, it was a gift from her beloved grandfather at her graduation from the academy. Her tears later will fall fast over this loss, but her sobbing will be muffled, as she lays in the night, curled around herself for comfort.

The second stone strikes the hard carapace of the creature, but it is prepared this time and quickly squats low on its many legs, absorbing the blow with a dull knocking thud. It is close to its meal and would not be denied.

Ahlassiter, one hand on the rope, back against the timeworn and salt licked wall of the ancients, casts furtively glances from creature to the ground around him. If fate would provide perhaps even with his missteps in the protocols of his training a natural weapon could be found.

He misses his great sword, well balanced and made of good steel, it had held a keen edge.

With this in his mind his eyes fall on the shape of a long barnacled object. Sweeping to his left he deftly kneels and rises with the object in his right hand.

In his hand even its weight is like that of his lost sword. Releasing the rope from his left, he grasps the object firmly in both hands and raises the improvised weapon in front of him.

With a rush the creature charges. The impact of each pointed limb striking the ground, dull and heavy hammers on the dense sands.

Phoooooom!

A fiery shaft, the length of a man's forearm, bursts two yards in front of Ahlassiter, scorching the moist dark sands, sending out a wave of sudden heat and light.

Both the creature and the dwarf react in surprise. The beast halts its charging attack. Its top-heavy body stumbling backwards, listing slightly to one side before regaining its balance. Ahlassiter spares a glance upward at the green hands, almost 50 feet above, still rimmed in a light of magic.

"You almost hit me!" he yells up at the half-orc.

"I know!" Horak yells down through cupped hands. "I was aiming at you!"

The dwarf would have responded if the voice of Nighlus didn't demand his immediate attention.

"Grab the rope and hold on!"

Putting the weight of his found weapon in his left hand, Ahlassiter raps the dangling rope around his right forearm and locks his grip. The quick jolt of the rope takes him off his feet as his companions work to lift his dense weight.

Above him all five of his allies had reached the top, and four of them now strain to extricate their dwarven friend from the beach below and the spindly nightmare seeking to eat him. Even with four, 3 average size humanoids, and one tiny, a singular dwarf is still a heavy prospect to lift.

Horak stands near the edge looking over.

"Pull!" he signals as his hands again weave an intricate pattern.

Quickly he strikes three of the first fingers of his right hand across the palm of his left. The gesture ends when he points down to the situation below. Sharp syllables like a match across a striker shoot from his lips, and once more fire lances downward.

Phooooom!

"You almost hit me again!!!" Ahlassiter shouts pressing his body against the wall as the fire narrowly misses him.

"I know!!!...This is exciting," the half-orc smiles at his straining compatriots.

The dwarf dangles 15 feet off the sands, his left hand holding firm to the added weight of his barnacled improvised weapon. He knows this added weight hampered his compatriots' abilities to lift him, but now that his hand grasped something that could be used to fight he would not let it go until he found better. More sorcerer's fire strikes near the base of the wall. Another attempt to deter the monster from nearing him.

It screams.

This close to the wall the sound is amplified, a screech over naked metal, but sharper pitched and accompanied by a gurgling wet sound coming from some place deep inside its body.

It has had enough.

Above Ahlassiter, his allies are stunned by the sound of this horror, and in front of him, the creature strikes.

The greatsword is one of the heavier weapons to use and master. Initially, it is unwieldy. Dragging around novices with each swing and strike they would perform, but, over time, muscles build, stances and forms are drilled in, and, if one survives this beginning phase, they can reach a point where the weapon becomes familiar and its use natural....in two hands!

One handed is another story.

The barnacled object in the dwarf's hand has a similar weight.

A greatsword was never meant to be wielded in one hand, yet there are still those rare users who through strength or other means can give battle this way.

Ahlassiter is not one of these, but now he would try to do what others had done. Using the hanging rope, the burly dwarf tenses his left shoulder drawing the heavy weight he carried in his hand away from his body and upward, and as the jagged pointed end of one of the abominations legs thrust at him, its aim set on the squishy center that most soft fleshed things had, Ahlassiter releases the weight of the heavy object down in a vicious arc, like a large heavy pendulum.

The creature is not expecting this.

The awkward barnacled object smashes into the approaching limb...and decimates it!

A clean cut! Ahlassiter is shocked and almost drops his prize in surprise.

Most of the built-up sea life amassed around his unwieldy found weapon breaks off....revealing a dark gray bladed edge underneath.

It is a sword! Ahlassiter cannot contain the smile and comforting surge this gives him. He is revived, emboldened.

A sword. Previously hidden under the encrustation of many decades. This is unexpected and welcomed with all the dwarf's being.

The monster draws back its severed limb, its tainted white fleshed interior revealed by the slice, as a stream of blue-black blood gushes out in spurting arcs, falling and hitting the sand below it. The smell of rot and sulfur fills the air. The flesh poison, hid always underneath the outer shell of the foul beast, taints the air.

Ahlassiter does not escape completely. He is hit with the unseen smell of the noxious odor. Tears immediately stream from his eyes, as bile rises in his throat. Even many feet above him, his allies suffer in the foul odors rising from below.

Its scream is long and sustaining, echoing off the wall's surface, a natural amphitheater to its pained cry.

This is a new thing for the creature. Searing pain! Bright and invasive.

Looking on in wonder, the dwarf is hauled upward. He continues to stare at the monster, now blindly tearing up the sand in its pain, listing from side to side, its wounded limb held awkwardly up off the sands, he gains the top and waiting hands of his allies.

Attaining safety and surprise of surprise, a weapon, Ahlassiter rises to his feet on top of the great wall. Around him the others gather. Catching his breath, he turns to look at the half-orc.

"Well?"

"Me?" Horak, hand to chest, innocently replies.

"Yes you!"

"Uhmmm...Yes?"

"Do you have, maybe something to say for yourself?" the dwarf waits, impatiently.

"Hmmmm...oh!" the sorcerer responds sheepishly shrugging. "Right...next time, run when I run, and...you're welcome?"

"Son of a bitch," Ahlassiter breathes out, shaking his head.

"Hey!"

Ahlassiter spares him no more time for a comeback.

"Come on, let's keep moving. Eyes on a swivel, stick together, and we can survive this."

The terror of the G'thik coastline stands almost stone still below. The flow from its dark wound begins to clot, and now only a trickle of its inky blood dribbles to the sand. The limb twitches spasmodically in obvious pain.

Its eyestalks look up. In the center of its focus, the six things of warm flesh and hot blood. It doesn't move. All six shudder with the same thought...a feeling. It would remember them.

"Let's go. We're losing daylight."

Each survivor moves away from the edge, one after the other till only Ahlassiter and Noc Arrow remain in the gaze of now unmoving monstrosity below them.

At first, they both think it is a trick seen in their own eyes, but what they witness soon is apparent. Initially standing still the beast begins to sway back and forth, its vision still locked to the top of the wall were they both stand. Gently it rocks back and forth, swaying as if to some unheard melody, like a sleepwalker on steady feet in an empty and silent house where no one sleeps.

"Creepy," the female human mutters.

"Yeah," after this recent brush with death, after surviving the traitorous water of the Thousand War Sea, the dwarf is numb.

"Yeah....you found a sword!"

"Come on."

"Bye bye creepy beach monster!" Noc says with humor, moving away from the edge. Below the creature looks up at the vacated space above it and is surprised when a moment later one last large stone strikes its shell. A parting gift from the giggling human female.

Rejoining the dwarf, Noc and Ahlassiter quickly catch up to the others, who had all stopped at the divide that marked the end of the wall and the beginning of the lands beyond. Together they all gaze for the first time on the land of G'thik.

The top of the wall runs flat and true, a perfect road high above the beach, moving off to their sides into the distance.

The great stone is unlike anything any of them had ever seen. On close inspection it appears as a mix of many minerals pulverized to small bits then bound together. Many colors held by a neutral base grey hue. Its creation a Herculean task made by some unimaginable people.

Where the wall top ends the land becomes full with vegetation and life. Large bushes covered in spiky pale-yellow leaves. Squat twisted trees with emerald bark and symmetrical alternating branches ending in clumps of downy leaves blue sky in color. Further, taller trees, some familiar, others strange. A tall species with a torus of horizontal branches, with monstrous flat burnt autumn hued fan-like leaves, seems to be the king in at least height, rising well above the canopy of its lesser cousins in the distance. The land slopes down in a vast bowl spreading out to a series of mountain ranges far in the distance. In grass plains to the south, animals roam in herds: small dark clusters of shapes moving together or gathered loosely, possibly feeding or resting, first evidence of things to hunt. Northwest and perhaps a few days journey from them, a great blue lake rules, taking up a large swathe of the nearer lands.

The sky above is clear, with only thin traces of the fog that grips the coast clinging to the areas nearer to the great wall.

Exotic and lovely and held in an eerie silence.

No wind sound, or bird cry. No grunts or growls of migrating and mating animals, nor the many meaning clicks and calls insects made which normally came with any land so full of green life.

"I don't like it," once again it was Jilliandria who first broke the silence between them.

"What choice do we have?" Nighlus looks at her questioningly.

"Maybe we should explore this wall- road, first?"

"It's so quiet," Noc states the obvious.

"Too quiet," Horak jokingly comments ominously.

"Shut up Horak."

"I don't think we will find better Jilliandria," Ahlassiter has learned it was best to speak honestly with the young naive healer.

Nighlus stands closest to the edge connecting the wall to the lands beyond. He stretches his hands out and feels no invisible barrier, but he does feel something. He draws his hands back.

"It is warmer...much warmer."

"Good," Noc hugs herself and shivers. Even she can no longer hide her dislike of the cold and damp they had all been subjected too.

All that stood between them and the lands beyond is the ancient wall's line of demarcation which cut across the unknown land before them. That and one step.

"Alright....one giant leap for dwarfkind," not one for being humorous most times, Ahlassiter steps over first, and sets his feet on the soil of this mysterious new land.

Immediately he is assaulted with the sounds and rushing heat of G'thik.

The impact is like the opposite of the beach monster's cry, but with an almost similar physical effect. He reels...momentarily.

The wind is sharp and hot and moist, rushing up the rise through the brush to blow the scent of rich life to him: plants, and flowers; the under scent of animals; all of it resting on a deep smell of earth, dark and fertile. Leaves rustling, limbs creaking, birds crying or singing, insects humming and clicking mandibles and wings. Far in the distance something big lumbers and breaks through vegetation with a loud crash.

Even farther something roars...maybe something small with a big voice. More likely something big and deadly.

Ahlassiter is drawn forward unthinkingly caught in this onslaught on his ocean abused senses, recently fed by the smell and sounds of saltwater, and the items saltwater rots and crashes against.

He begins to turn back to his friends when he hears something. A call. Then he sees it. A small figure, perhaps two to three hundred feet down hill, moving towards their position. Whomever it is they were in a big hurry for he could tell they were trying to run in the difficult terrain. The distant figure begins waving its arm at him. Ahlassiter raises one hand and gives a quick saluting wave back. He jumps when he feels a presence by his side.

The sorcerer in his black robes, now stands at his side, smile wide waving enthusiastically at the advancing figure.

"A local!"

The dwarf holds his ire. He had not said if it was safe to cross.

It is a break in protocol, and Ahlassiter knew he would have words with the impetuous half-orc sooner rather than later. Following Horak's lead, one by one the others cross the line, also discovering, thankfully for their sanity, G'thik is not a ghost dead land of quiet. Two still stood, doubtful to take that last step.

Nighlus and Gracis. Both had their reasons: one, calculating. This unknown place...was a trap; the other, frightened. Held back by a feeling they would all die here...horribly!

....actually they both felt the latter.

"What is he saying?" Jilliandria eyes watching the unknown humanoid approach.

The small figure, now recognized as a human man, has gained ground, but still struggles to reach them. He continues to wave his arm, rather emphatically now, and is yelling something but is still too distant to be understood. Among them, Nighlus, trained in the Great Elven Forest, Simberael, was the member most gifted in perceiving, but he is still standing on the other side of the invisible barrier which prevented the sounds of land to touch those of sea, so he could provide no guidance as to what the approaching man was trying to communicate.

"I don't know. Everyone be on guard. Watch your 6." Ever cautious the dwarf grips his new weapon tightly, fingers biting into the encrusted layers which still encased the weapon's grip, eyes on the figure, he monitors everything else within his sweeping vision.

Gracis steps across, against her better judgment. Even in this short time from their first meeting she trusted her new friends, at least a few of them, and would not be separated from them no matter her fears. She would go with them and make herself useful. She is afraid to be alone, left behind.

Ahlassiter steps a few feet in front of the others, ready to meet with either friendship or violence the approaching figure.

"Stop!" the figure is heard to shout.

The short human male, not young by any means, but still a decade or more from being wrinkled and old by mortal definitions, can now be heard clearly. His skin would be pale if not redden by unprotected years under the sun, and his mouth is a field of yellow stained teeth, with a good number either missing or broken. His wears odd leathers and hides, feet shoed in short tough boots of grey black skins that just cleared the rough grasses as he strode quickly towards them. In his waistband the hilt of short sword is clearly visible. On the opposite side, rising above his left shoulder, a light and rustic shortbow sits. His left hand clutches a walking stick, jet black and glossy, and as thin as a cane reed, long in length, it reaches up to his chest. Slung across his right shoulder a bulky satchel made from a dull coarse brown fabric, an object made for use not beauty.

"Did he just say 'stop'?" Jilliandria states.

"Stop him!" the human male shouts again.

"Him?!" Horak looks around curiously.

The approaching human male is less than 20 feet away, when Nighlus, the last of their party steps through the barrier and into the mystery of G'thik.

"Don't let him cross!"

Breathless the stranger stops a man's length from Ahlassiter and the rest of the survivors of *The Wasp*. Bending over, he rests his hands on his knees, the sweat beginning to drip from his brow to the tip of his broad nose, and to the ground at his feet.

"Too....late," he gasps out.

"What is 'too....late'?" Horak pantomimes the older human with hands on knees. "I mean-"

"Who are you?" Ahlassiter, cuts across the half-orc's comment. His authority is not to be denied and his voice demands answers.

The stranger, still bending, raises his right hand, index finger pointing loosely up at nothing above. The gesture classical and understood as patience as he catches his breath to reply.

"Mmmmm..." the human man clears his throat with a swig of water from a flask he has pulled from the bulky sack at his side.

"Hello...I am Qeta Sape," he exhales breathlessly "Welcome to Yet-al....mistakenly called G'thik. It is a harsh land, but as you can witness with yours truly...survivable. Make the most of it....for you will never leave."

"What the fuck?! Is that a threat?!" the statement by the newly arrived stranger immediately draws Noc Arrow's ire.

"Wait! Hold it together," Ahlassiter says raising his sword to ward off the threat of this man's implied words "Qeta Sape speak openly and plainly! What do you mean by that last part? If you think to hamper us, I assure you, you will find us more than equipped to defeat you."

"Hahaha...no-no-no! Let me finish. G'thik, as you call it, lives up to all the myths you have heard. And ain't it a shame, like every dumb cunt-"

"Hey!" Jilliandria immediately voices offense at the term, with Noc and Gracis casting deadly looks at the human man.

"Oh! My apologies. Not many with manners will you find here. Every dumb...peasant? Person? Yeah, I think that is better. Every dumb person who comes here to prove themselves something special released from there mum's womb. A 'true' hero to break the riddle which is this accursed place. Seems Yet-al is like a beacon for the foolish and the arrogant, myself included. I have been here for 30 years and studied all the history this place has to offer....and I can say that since the end of the Yet-al empire...No one has left."

"No one was left, of the empire? Alive you mean...after the ending?" the words come out puzzled as the halfling studies Qeta to see if she is right about his meaning.

"No. That is not what I said. No one, now or before you lot, has been able by foot, hoof, wing, scale or tail, magic, or divine intervention been able to leave Yet-al. Once anyone, anyone, steps beyond the great sea wall or the range of mountains that encircles this nightmare to the south and west, no one ever leaves....though they all try. Thousands have tried. Tens of thousands I would reckon! And the failures in that attempt equal that same number.

"Once entered no one has been able to leave this land for over 3000 years."

"That is not possible," the lean priestess of Sune says once more instinctually gripping at the holy symbol beneath her robes.

"Oh my dear, it tis! Go on. All of you. There is the way back to the beach," Qeta Sape gestures back behind them. "Try to leave."

They all do.

One by one, they all try, but each encounters the same thing...something strange and frightening. No invisible barrier presented itself to stop their movement forward, merely as each step took them further and further back across the upper portion of the great sea wall, the world in front of them grew whiter and whiter, and conversely colder and colder. Cold like a cavern of ice where no wind touches and no light has ever shined.

Nighlus, accustomed to taking risks as a scout for his people, walks the furthest...eight long strides, before backing up from freezing and deep unyielding void.

"The curse of Yet-al," they all look at Qeta Sape "You accepted it as yours the minute your feet touched the soil. Tried to stop ya."

"Fuck," the half-orc gets no disagreement from the other survivors.

The bellowing roar, heard a stone's throw away, shakes them from these first miserable moments in this prison called Yet-al, previously and erroneously known as the lands of G'thik. The roar belongs to a large head, bony and pale, seen a short distance away, which easily tops the short vegetation of these upper slopes. Not one of them is interested in seeing the rest of its form.

Ahlassiter the dwarf sighs.

"I wish I had a rocket launcher."

One week prior.

"No. You may not play a dragonkin." Bill Owen sat at the large conference table. Laid out before him in a small arc, his precious books, paper, pencils and erasers, various notebooks, a new tablet, and a pile of many-colored dice. The players sat close by on either side of the long folding table. Six players total. Three to his right, three to the left.

The air circulating through the room was cool enough to be too cool. A large industrial AC's hum, located some place within the vast structure, drifted through the air ducts to them, loud enough to comingle with the hum of the fluorescents over head in intensity.

Bill made a note to ask for some warmer lighting, or better yet, a warmer place in more ways they just temperature. Somewhere less utilitarian, spartan, antiseptic.

Dragonkin. It was inevitable. Bill had been expecting it. He knew it was coming and he had a gut feeling who would cross the line first, to ask for special consideration in their race selection. He was wrong.

Phillip Shoji. Chemist. PhD, fluent in 4 languages. Hobbies: growing crystals and surfing. Who in college for 3 years had gathered with some fellow grads weekly with beer, weed, whiskey, pizza and wings, and the beloved tomes that Gygax helped to make, to play, The Game. It wasn't him.

"Oh, come on, give me a good reason," pouts and pleads the man farthest to his left. Dr. Francis Indra Shrivinda. A tall lean athletic man with short wavy black hair against soft brown skin, and a face long use to getting its way.

It was a rebuttal from childhood, lacking maturity. All charm, and one step from a tantrum from being told we can't have something, even though we really really want it (foot stamp! frowny face).

Bill was slightly surprised by this request for this particular race, for as far as he knew Dr. Shrivinda had no prior experience playing the Game. It was more likely the good doctor had been doing some Internet research to give himself a leg up in his choice of character races.

It was usually the folks with prior Dungeons & Dragons experience who gravitated to the more exotic races. The motives may vary. They look cool. They can fly. Or, like Dragonkin, they can expel a blast of one element or another: fire or lightning, perhaps frost or acid. Which element all depends on what type of dragon, by "means", impregnated the humanoid half of the coupling.

After the birth of Dungeons & Dragons into its first fully playable form the creator's, along with coming up with the individual classes and professions, also came up with the racial archetypes players could choose from:

- Human
- Elf
- Half-elf
- Dwarf
- Half-orc
- And, Halfling (a clear nod to Tolkien's hobbits).

 At the time, this small yet diverse group of races was more than enough to fulfill the average player's desires, but the game itself was designed and created in such a way that it was not only necessary but natural that the game mutated, changed, and grew. Things were malleable. DM's, initially called "Judges", naturally began to adjust rules and added and created new elements to enhance their game sessions. With the rich source of mainly fictional fantasy literature, and some films, filled with exotic magic items and even more exotic creatures, DMs and players began to work out ways to introduce new races from these rich mines of fiction, or from their own fertile imaginations, and concurrently how these additions would work within the great game.

Since this beginning, the number of books, and booklets, known as "modules", which have been produced to aid and enhance the game is monumental, and contained within their pages a cornucopia of playable races with varying skills and attributes. Races with abilities ranging from natural camouflage to teleporting small distances...to breathing fire.

Bill Owen thought it was a beautiful thing.

Beautiful with a high chance of difficulty for the DM, adjusting challenges in game scenarios for a player who would have a "more powerful" character race when compared to the other players characters. Dealing with jealousy, as almost inevitably one player or more will feel cheated at the missed opportunity to play a stronger, cooler, race.

What normally would be a challenging combat for a new group of players at the lowest level, one, just one exotic race, can make the same combat a cakewalk, and, diametrically, if you adjust the combat difficulty according to this one exotic race you can inadvertently make it more difficult and deadly for the other players, which is not the goal of a DM to have most of your players meet untimely demises.

"At this point in time this land is not fond of dragons. Listen, if-hey, everyone!"

The other players looked up from their tablets and their character building to meet the eyes of their DM. Next to each, or in front open to some page, sat shiny new Player's Handbooks, the main resource for information for all players of the Game. Bill had purchased them for these new players as a welcoming gift for the journey they were beginning together. This book was the first cobblestone to a storied road, and to the tale they would create together.

Here, and eventually, "elsewhere".

With all eyes on him Bill continues.

"Like the world around us, the world you are entering has a history. This is a world your characters have been living in for years. In the case of adult elves decades. And like our reality, this world is a place where the past trials and triumphs have shaped the present. Certain races on one continent live with amenity, one among many, but on another can be loathed, reviled, persecuted and even hunted.

"In this world, two hundred years ago, dragons waged war against humanoids on two of the major continents. Continents with powerful kingdoms and long memories. Kingdoms with colonies and settlements well beyond were their lands meet the water or other natural barriers. Who here wants to be a living walking reminder of war?... genocides? The cruel deaths of loved ones?"

The concept obviously appeals to no one.

"Dragons are Nazis."

"Dragons are <u>Nazis</u>?" All emphasis on the last word. Assuredly he had heard wrong...but no, Dr. Shrivinda had not. His desire to be a dragon lays on the floor, a childhood snow globe, a broken dream, all bits of glass, clumps of floaty white bits, and a puddle of water.

Bill lies.

"Yes. They are"

The overly large hangar, where they have gathered in one of the interior rooms meant for pilot briefings, vibrates as a jet roars close by, in the unseen sky above them. Destination: unknown.

CHAPTER 1

"Do you have everything?"

Fumbling keys. The sound and impact of a backpack being slung over a shoulder, full and heavy. The familiar press of a dice bag in an inside jacket pocket. All normal things for William "Bill" Owen. Except today with his familiar armor and equipment was a newly pressed baby blue dress shirt and a black tie free of wrinkles.

"Yeah I think so!" he yelled to his mother in the living room. Browned bread with butter, a single egg over easy, a dollop of sweet grape jelly artificially colored, the smells of breakfast lingering in the air in the house they shared.

It's rare when opportunity comes knocking. Most knocks were either soft and selling something, or hard and demanding entrance. For Bill, his present opportunity knocked with manicured hands and email to follow up. Offering him a chance at a dream job...well "dream job" at least as far as he could presently tell.

Bill did not have an average job, nor did he have an average paycheck. He was a social celebrity. Hundreds of thousands of media service subscribers followed his every action with keen interest and feverish intent. He had gained access to a new world, where popularity and income can come from doing the thing you love the most and streaming it live, audio and technical glitches withstanding.

Bill played Dungeons and Dragons... And more specifically he DMed for groups online, three times a week with three different groups in three different settings. His uploaded videos did much better than the average up and coming hip hop artist's or brand-new pop sweetheart's videos ever could. Bill was a Dungeon Master, a DM, a titled well-earned and cryptic to the uninitiated. Average assumptions are this is some specialist title for those into BDSM.

His work had led Bill to this very morning, rushing out the door, to make an interview for a job looking for him, and others like him.

The new company had approached him about some great project where he would be a Dungeon Master for an undisclosed group of professionals. Professionals of what he had no idea. Perhaps for TV or a new RPG supplement company looking to mine the best minds in roleplay. It sounded interesting, and vague, which intrigued him, but then it also sounded too good to be true and possibly insane when they told him how much they were willing to pay.

There are office spooks in Manhattan with sharp suits who made less than what he would be making if he landed the position, but money had never been a great lure for him as it is with many others.

"Bye mom," he called out, as he passed beyond the door's threshold. Bang-click! He could hear his mother's muffled good luck through the door as he made his way down the front steps. The air was slightly chilled and deeply scented with the smell of water saturated pavement and wet dead leaves, aromas which played with the wet dark earth scent pervading everything.

"What?"

Bill couldn't stop himself from saying it, so he said it again.

"What?"

Almost immediately he imagined Samuel Jackson's character in Pulp Fiction yelling back at him "Say what again!!".

"How would you feel about going into space?" Mr. Harrison repeated the question from across the boardroom table, surrounded by expectant faces, some in suits, or in something trendy and polished enough to be considered good enough to socialize with those finer fabrics.

The address from the email had led Bill to a beautiful new building, standing high and mighty against an October sky. A new and constant reminder of the growing beast the city was becoming, wired and electric, glowing and pulsing, a constant valley with ever new and expanding horizons.

Bill was surprised when he was directed by the kind face at the front desk to the top floor, which, in his experience, is only reserved for the cream of the crop, the top of the cup. All sweet and luxurious. A height most self-professed nerds never climbed nor reached unless it was to deliver a package or a pizza.

The elevator doors had bloomed open and he was then directed by another kind face behind another reception counter to a waiting area. He was not the only one waiting. He was greeted by some familiar faces. Fellow colleagues in storytelling and world building. DMs....Dungeon Masters.

He immediately recognized men and quite a few female DMs, chatting with each other with smiles and embracive gestures of comradery. He gave a quick smile and wave to one. Mark Sherlock, a DM from across the pond. They had chatted once at a convention a few years back. Among the best out there, Sherlock had a vivid imagination and a great heart. The Game was better for people like him.

"Oh shit!" Bill almost blurted out loud. He knew them all, but what made him almost shout, stop, and turn around where two men jokingly discussing something with each other. One large and portly with a gleaming smile, the other tall and lanky with a long braid of hair trailing down his back.

Merlin Matthews, a wiz with voices and stories, and Percy Christopher, wit and wisdom manifest...both perhaps the best DMs the online community could provide.

Of course, they would be friends Bill thought.

The best rivals always are.

And of course, they would be here.

Bill immediately lowered his own value when he compared himself to such an illustrious group. His prospects dimmed like a fading Light spell in a dark cave surrounded by growls and evil sickly yellow eyes.

The interviews began, and, one by one the room of prospects dwindled.

Some seem to hit a revolving door. Rising from their seats, walking through the doors, only to be spit back out mere moments later. Most of their faces reflecting confusion or impatience, all except for one.

Matthews walked in and walked out, almost instantly, his face a transparent veil to the anger burning in his eyes. The glowing royal treatment he garnered in our community obviously dulled the minute he stepped into the room of cool air and cool personalities not impressed by anything other than revenue, Bill assumed. His portly waddle only amplified the indignity of not being chosen. Without a word he ushered himself to the elevator, pressed the down button, waited for the doors to open, walking in the second they did and turning, his eyes staring at something other than the nervous and questioning eyes of those of us still waiting.

Ding!

Bill imagined as the doors closed Merlin's days to follow would be vengeful...to anyone with the misfortune to be a player in his games.

Percy Christopher's interview was longer. Longest by far, twenty seven minutes, and when he left his face held no anger or disappointed...he only looked, puzzled, as if an encounter in a dungeon had gone odd and left him with more questions than answers, a pouch devoid of healing potions, and a treasure worth nothing.

Bill was summoned and with a mind whirling, he entered the room.

What followed started with basic questions: name; birthplace; education; employment current and past.

Next the questions were about his Dungeons & Dragons experience: when did he start playing; how long he had been DMing; preferred editions; what were his favorite elements of the game; how he dealt with difficult players; techniques for fostering teamwork; how he handled creative blocks to keep an adventure going; how well can he adapt to shifting player dynamics.

Then their questioning got odder:

Mr. Owen, any problems with tight spaces?

Any problems sleeping in noisy environments?

Dietary issues? Religious needs?

Bill, any sensitivity to smells?

Longest time spent indoors.

Longest time without physical contact.

This is personal Mr. Owen but we can assure you it is important, but what are your sexual preferences?

It was at the 20-minute mark the interviewers all looked at each other. Then the strangest question, from the main interviewer, a Mr. Charles Harrison:

"If you could, given the chance, would you ever go into space?"

His stomach had rolled and his repetitions of "What?" only made the head interviewer lean forward, eyes expectant, voice slower, calmer.

"Have you ever had a desire to go into outer space Mr. Owen?"

"I mean...well...sure!...Hypothetically speaking," Bill's words clumsily spill forth. "It is a dream a lot of people have, but actually going? To be honest as an actuality I would be scared shitless."

"And after defecating completely, what would you say?" smiling, Mr. Harrison asked. Bill started to laugh nervously, but bit down on his tongue, when the looks around him reflected only seriousness without anger, though a few of his interviewers hid smiles with hands or opened folders.

Was this a joke?!

"Honestly, I don't know."

Silence.

Bill's mind suddenly spun. Did he just blow his chance?

But a chance at what?!

To go to space?! The idea was ludicrous.

What did any of this have to do with the game that had possessed his life from morning to night and back again. The game that had molded him into the man he was today. Bill's stomach lurched, like the moment of freefall on a rollercoaster ride. A cat suddenly materializing in empty air, arching through the clouds, ungrounded, spinning, claws ready to grab at anything solid.

The dream!

Over a year and a half ago Bill woke with a start in the low hours of the morning before sun and daily activities called him to naturally awaken. Hands clutching his bedspread, heart pounding and breath pumping. The dream he'd awakened from, had been vivid and quick. A minute, no more, which had left him shocked and oddly determined.

A hallway. Industrial...sterile...spartan. Ending in a small open room. A chair, but not a comfy one. No, it was all struts and strong fabrication. The bustle of activity around him, centered on him. Lab coats and technicians, clipboards and tablets with displays of time, temperature, heart rate, checklists. Bill was in a panic.

He was being prepped for space.

The red spacesuit covered him from neck to toe tips. His spherical helmet lay just off to side. In as little as 1 hour he would be launched upward against the pull of Earth's gravity...and he was "scared shitless"! Inwardly he was in a panic. The thought of prolonged confinement was suddenly both claustrophobic and idiotic. What had he gotten himself into?!

Even in his dream panic a part of him had rallied.

There was no going back. There was only up. Up and away from all things familiar and safe. Space is not ever safe. He had known that in the dream, and yet he had set his path's course unerringly towards this goal. Was he ready? Probably, but now his whole being cried no...but he would go, nonetheless!

He had awoken, surprised and excited, with the fear a faint gossamer structure underneath his determination. Determination to live up to the responsibility he had been given by those who could not, or would not, go.

Now. A room full of unspoken expectations.

"But given the opportunity," Bill advanced, the faces around him waiting. "Hell yeah!

"I'd go in a heartbeat!"

Bill got the job....sort of. He was told next would come 6 months of training and medical exams. In addition, he would be working with the Team, the group selected to play, on building an adventure, 2 days a week minimum, each gaming session 2-3 hours in length. This was presently the most time that could be allotted under the tight schedules of each astronaut. Two other DM candidates would be going through the same treatment. At the end of the project one candidate would get the green light and the other two would go back to their lives, with one caveat: to be prepared at any time to move into this DM position if something unexpected happened to the first DM's ability to run a game or to go on the trip.

Thee Trip!

14 astronauts including himself. 14 including Kermit, a frog sent to study the effects on aquatic and terrestrial creatures of zero Gs and love earth gravity. Amphibians were the select choice for their ability to breath both water and air. 14, because superstition nonetheless held its shadow over a few and 13 was not an acceptable number for such an auspicious venture. 4 years: training, launch, arrival, and return. Mars and back again Passepartout!

Mars! Perhaps his red spacesuit dream had been a premonition. He couldn't honestly say, but now it felt like one.

A grand adventure. An adventure fraught with obstacles and hidden crises. The biggest two difficulties besides the unforgiving vacuum of space: isolation and confinement.

The mental toll could be far higher than the physical. Catastrophically so. Suicidal thoughts in a fragile ship coursing through unknown space was a danger.

Potentially, to the rescue came role-playing games(RPGs). Namely "Dungeons & Dragons". The parent of all RPGs.

The data was officially in.

What keeps people going: in the midst of strife; longing; sickness and accidents, and the recovery from sickness and accidents; or, the mind crippling boredom which can quench positive thinking, and often fed and fueled our weakest thoughts, causing them to grow and blossom.

Such flowers kill in the great vacuum.

Many occupations. Many individuals in constant suspension between rock and hard place situations. Divorcees. Parents in child custody battles. The imprisoned. Slow death sentences, medical and otherwise. Public school teachers!

Many glues holding them together. Most with intoxicating side effects, but a few glues without much physical sacrifice: Sports fans. Bonded. Supportive and dedicated. Diehards. But often too aggressive, and the downtime between seasons created a vacuum of its own, even with fantasy sport leagues and social media to fill it; art fans and artists. Media, from film to graphic novels, from songs to poetry. Enriching and life affirming but with no template to bond individuals according to likes and preferences.

Get a group of fans together and you can create lifelong bonds...but usually no creativity. No expressions beyond adoration of their shared obsession.

Many areas in society where we get together and stay strong. Strong enough to get the job done.

But space exploration needed more.

Mars needed more!

One group stood out. Dedicated. Creative. Supportive. No off seasons. No time between albums or volumes. A group with an activity that made them change schedules and family holidays to allow for continued play. A system that even as we aged, even as our lives fell into turmoil, players turned to as a lifeline and problem solver, a salve against the mundane. Walking away empowered and excited for what was next. Pushing through all obstacles to get to the next session...to continue the adventure!

It was a game....A mutated child from the war tables of war reenactors and history buffs.

Dungeons & Dragons.

Bill knew well the ladder of hope, stability, and perseverance weekly game sessions gave to people. The mounds of shit and shitty people one endured every day, and every week, just to play one more game of make believe with paper, and pencils, friends, and dice.

Dice, aka "die".

"Dungeons & Dragons" didn't require much to play it. It never did and never has, never will. Its simplicity was its biggest sell. No need for large screens or precious computing space. Which saved energy on long space voyages. Energy needed for other systems necessary to keep them alive and on the mission in a metal home thrusting through the space between worlds.

There is a strength needed to look Death, capital "D", in the face every instant yet stay on task unphased. An astronaut needed more than simple run-of-the-mill releases and distractions, to travel further than any human had traveled before.

Perhaps D&D could be that release and distraction.

They were lucky to find him.

In fact, Qeta Sape said it to them numerous times as they all made their ways across the unfamiliar terrain. The area they were currently traversing consists of squat bushy trees, a little below head height at their tallest with short green needles in clusters at the end of every branch, and a scruffy, no more than boot high, grass, green at the base fading into a light tan. Further on, more of the same, with black and dark grey irregular boulders here and there in clusters.

"Oh yes! You are all incredibly lucky to find Qeta! I was about to head back. These lands would have sorely tested you. Night here is....difficult."

There was no well-used pathway Qeta Sape guided them on but the direction he was moving was clear. Southwest.

"Tested?" inquired Gracis the halfling wizard her small legs doing their best to keep up with the group.

"...uhmmmm." He gave them a look that said there was more to be said but he was perhaps weighing the price of saying too much.

In fact, Qeta Sape is not very forthright with any answers to any questions put forth to him. Pressed for answers, succumbing finally to their barrage, he informed the party his guidance to the nearest settlement was a gift, free, but by the nature of things in this land things given for free, such as information, was a rarity most would not give.

Answers cost. Everything has a price.

The shipwrecked group had lost most of their belongings to the waters and their deep depths, yet miraculously the sneaky one still had her coins in some undisclosed location on her person. In a flash, two shiny gold pieces appear in Noc's hand.

"This is all I have," she says quickly thrusting the two gold coins against the chest of the dwarven warrior, not making eye contact, and even more quickly, turning away from the rest of the party.

Most do not believe her.

Qeta Sape can't hide his pleasure. It is apparent gold pieces have more value in these unknown lands.

Lips freed by his luck and Noc's gold, he began to answer all. All he knew and all he was willing to guess or hazard a theory about.

This was a harsh land where no one group controlled more than a small area. Most children did not survive childhood and most mothers had stillborns, so the population remained at a constant level never growing but never truly declining. The creatures, the flora and fauna, was different from what could be found in the world beyond The Rim.

The Rim is what they call the circular stone wall that visibly circled the north, northeast, and east coastlines, and apparently the whole land, in a ring of ancient perfect stone, though in the areas to the south and west the Rim was covered in curving mountain ranges.

Work is hard to come by if you didn't have skill and talent or strength, and if you had no skills and no talents, or no physical prowess those work opportunities became even fewer.

Qeta Sape is not a strong man. Neither is he skilled and/or talented.

He survives by perseverance. Foraging and gathering what he can. Taking those few jobs nobody skilled or strong would take. When asked about these tasks Qeta refuses to elaborate.

Then he begins to speak of the world that awakened...when the sun slips below the horizon. Shaking his head, he looks on the rolling earth and strange vegetation surrounding them as if at the sight of some past and tragic war field, which still holds many bad memories and still fueled nightmares. Saying here had been much terror and death.

"You were very lucky to find me," he says again, even more proudly of himself, yet he can't hide the undercurrent of sadness in his voice, looking down at his feet momentarily.

No stars shown over the lands of Yet-al when sunlight vanishes. Only a vast red glow called the Coldfire, that tinted all here in many shades of blood, both fresh and dried. Things normally white or pale in normal sunlight grew rich with pink and lavender hues. Deep dark violets lived and beat in the heart of every shadow. And red! Rich royal and ripe red wove it all together.

No one traveled the land at night by choice, and anyone caught out in the open without some covering or protection, would either die from the weather or from the monstrosities and madness that thrived under the starless red sky.

Sape assures them more succumb to madness under the night's horrid light, than they do to any inclement weather, or encroaching breathing or unbreathing creatures.

Those who do survive the assault upon their optic senses then must face a bitter unforgiving cold, pressing down on the living as forcefully as the night's damning light. Cold which froze the breath on ruby lips.

The Coldfire. An illuminating illusion of fire, bringing no warmth.

As they journeyed, they still met no discernable paths or trailways.

"What's that?" Noc said suddenly, for just coming into her sharp perception's range is a stretch, a stripe, of dark earth, a pure line moving across the uneven terrain ahead.

"The Great Road!...mmmm, actually you could call it Only Road. Some do," Qeta said calmly.

Drawing nearer all the party feel a gut familiarity as they lay eyes on the Great Road.

"Asphalt?" the small halfling voices, looking curiously at what lay before them.

Near to black, its surface was made of small stones, equally dark, which had been flattened and pressed as if by a hot heavy iron. It moved across the land uninterrupted by no tree or stone. At first it appeared flat, but on close inspection was ever so slightly rounded, higher in the middle pitching lower at the edges. From edge to edge its width stretched some 30 or so feet.

"Ass fault? I suppooose it could be described like a fault, the ass crack of Yet-al," Sape replies curiously nodding.

A few smiles pass among the newly shipwrecked and recently found.

"The Great Road is an artifact from Yet-al's far distant past. It wanders over the land's entirety and has many branches."

"Where does it lead?" the half-elf Jilliandria asks, unable to hold back her curiosity.

"Nowhere! Nowhere at all," Qeta answers, raising a hand up. "Hold your questions, let me explain. Undoubtedly at some distant point in time this road and its many branches led to 'places', but not anymore. Follow it all you want. Spend your entire life doing so. You will only find dead ends. Many dead ends. The middle of a forest or the edge of a lake. A cliff wall. A tree! Not a magical one sadly. Not ancient. Simply a tree! More likely you will find your destination in some open expanse of nothing but grass and grazers."

"Got it. Loud and clear, but why did you call it also the 'Only Road'?"

"Because it is."

Qeta Sape goes on to explain that any work building roads, or trail making, was always gone by morning. Erased under the gaze of Coldfire. Naturally occurring changes stayed. Things, other than roads, built go untouched. But anything made resembling a path is not allowed by unknown powers to exist. Unknown powers that were the true rulers of the strange land the group found themselves traversing.

"We say it is because Yet-al can never be fully mastered."

They all stand at its edge unwilling to step on it, the memory still fresh of the Rim and its imprisoning enchantment.

Qeta Sape quizzically glances at his wards to his right and left, a befuddled frown and raised eyebrows lifting his lips while lowering the corners. He steps on to The Great Road and walks a yard or three before turning. None of his charges have advanced.

Sheepishly, scratching just behind his right ear. "Not everything is trying to kill you here. Many things are quite harmless. This is just an extremely well-crafted and made from unusual materials road....as you say, 'ass fault'...yes, nothing more."

In seconds, the party has joined Qeta Sapes in crossing The Great Road. Horak, had however, stopped, and kneeling drew a dagger. A plain and simple thing, owed by many common folk, a bladed tool no more. Inspecting a patch of the road's surface he slowly begins to lower the blades tip. His intention is obvious, to test the strange surface. A breath before he can strike his mark, he is halted by Qeta's sudden cry.

"Noooooooo!!!"

The cry catches all of them by surprise. The half-orc sorcerer, dagger now white knuckled in hand, rocks back to land on his backside.

"No!!! Don't ever. EVER! Harm the road....EVER."

Horak nods shaken, staring into the wide fear filled eyes of Qeta, and for the first time shows he is also not immune to fear. No one moves and no one makes a sound, except the wind and animals in the distance. The moment of tension passes.

"Good! Let's continue, shall we!"

With a smile, as if the moment before had not just occurred, Qeta turns and continues his mission of guiding the group to the nearest settlement, his current home, the Arh Cleft.

"Wait," Jilliandria worrying queries the back of their departing guide "What would happen if he did?...Mr. Sape?"

Qeta keeps walking, either ignoring the question or pretending not to hear it. Slowly the survivors of *The Wasp* follow.

They continue. After a time, the small mage approaches the side of their guide.

"Sir Sape-"

He laughs and cuts her off.

"You're cute."

Awkward Gracis blushes at the comment.

"Beware who you call sir or lady here sweetie. I do appreciate the curtesy, but I am only Qeta. Sape to most."

"Qeta?" the halfling continues "Why do most know this land mistakenly as G'thik?"

With a quick shoulder shrug Qeta mutters a hmmmm'ed "I dunno."

"Nobody does deary."

An hour later they catch sight of their goal. At least Sape said as much for the group of very tired survivors saw no discernable settlement in the terrain ahead.

The Arh Cleft finally appears as a shadowed line in the terrain moving away to south and a notched path that leads down into it.

"Good we made it in time. Coldfire will begin soon. Wait here and watch," it is not a question. "...but do not watch for too long."

Qeta Sape their first contact in the lands of Yet-al doesn't stop moving as he speaks and disappears down into the Cleft.

"You all must see...you all need to see...I do not."

They wait.

Their conversation is at first only small talk but quickly a silence descends on them.

Then, finally, the night's assault begins.

The stars vanish with the sun.

It is wrong. Something sick and twisted had betrayed and tortured the natural order of things, for as the sun slipped with its last light beyond the edge of Yet-al's farthest distance...Coldfire ignites.

Eyes wide. With shock and fear. Horrific betrayal. Open lips, parted mouths. Suddenly dry throats, tight and hard to swallow. Red washes over them, and it can not be held back.

"Oh my Goddess," Jilliandria whispers breaking the silence, and as if given permission, the creatures of this ghastly night begin their cries of predation, mating, and dying, shrieks and shrill whistles, guttural roars wet and hungry.

The party quickly turns away retreating down into the Cleft until it is only the dwarf and the sorcerer left, bathed in the red wrought night. The sorcerer for some reason starts to smile, grin. Glancing to his right he looks down at dwarf, then turns back to gaze upon the dread of G'thik.

"Cheecheechee hahaha!"

The dwarf is silent. He turns and heads into the unknown sanctuary of the Cleft, as he does, he mumbles under his breath, immune to the humor of the half-orc.

"Yes...we have been lucky."

From behind his DM screens Bill reached down and hit the switch on the power strip besides him on the floor, depriving electricity to the four lamps he had rigged around the room. Twice he had been surprised with the amenable behavior of the officials and staff around him to babysit him and his "task". He thought requesting the game sessions be held away from most base activity, in the small on-base home they had provided for him, would require a few phone calls held over hours or maybe a stack of paperwork filled and submitted and submitted again for approval, but he was relieved when his request was met with almost immediate agreement and approval. Of course, they said yes. It made sense they said. They really wanted it to work they said. The money had been spent and certain people needed to be kept happy, but in the project ahead nothing small really mattered. What did "matter", was anything, anything at all, even things as far out there as roleplaying games, that would raise the stats for a astronauts to survive, both physically and mentally a very long journey in space, which could kill them or drive them insane, and the subsequent stay on an alien world, that could also kill them or drive them insane.

Tragic deaths were not an option. The public's fears and ignorance had derailed the space program already once before...twice before. A third time could be catastrophic. In more ways than one.

The red-light bulbs in the four lamps went dark, and the room with it.

Another power strip beside him, and another flipped switch, and the normal soft ambient lighting revealed and return the players and Bill to the game room and normal reality.

"Oh, thank God!" the lead biologist of the mission, Cameron McDowell, breathed out at the return to normal lighting. She had the look of someone finally freed from a tense filled situation and the breath holding it had induced.

"Nice one DM. I approve," the ever-engaged chemist, Philip Shoji uttered with an approving nod.

"I was not expecting that," Cpt. Irwin stated, blinking strongly to help his eyes adjust to the change in color and luminosity within the comfortable room.

"I don't know if I could handle more of that red lighting," said the brown skin woman from her seat on the left of Bill. She had barely any accent betraying her origins and her birth country, Mexico. He was perhaps a little surprised astronaut Arlena Blair was bothered by the red light. Her years in the Navy meant many nights under red lights, a system used to protect sailor's eyes from adjusting out of night vision.

"That was cool....and horrifying."

"Wait....you're not going to use them every time we play?!" Sharon Douglas gestured at the red bulb lamps in horror. Her short blonde hair had looked pinkish under the red glow.

"Who knows a night on Mars might look similar if we didn't know better," Phillip couldn't help but smile.

"Oh! The RED planet! Bill?! Was that your plan? A Mars simulation...kinda," a look of understanding played across Arlena's face as she voiced her summation.

"Haha...no. This was a onetime effect Sharon," Bill pointed at the lamps. "And Arlena, we all know Mars isn't red like Yet-al, but Mars is still classically known as the Red Planet, and the lighting naturally, both day and night, will be different from we know here on terra firma."

"Closest I've come to a night like that is one under a blood moon," Sharon remarked.

"Hey gold hoarder! You've been holding out!" Dr. Shrivinda turned an accusing gaze to the Mission's biologist. It had been assumed by all the players that done of their characters had any gold or valuables after the rush to survive the sinking of *The Wasp*...an assumption proven wrong.

Without missing a beat Cameron responded.

"I have no idea what you are referring too."

Francis didn't believe her.

"Come on! Deception roll! I'm right. Bill?"

"The term would be 'Deception check' not roll. Your character doesn't know, and in game knowledge is the guide here not out of game knowledge. Which is why we have Insight checks, and it was only the Captain who succeeded with the check with a nat 20," Bill looked at the pilot "Did you tell him what you learned of the rogue's deception?"

"No," Cpt. Irwin, the enigmatic pilot and leader of the mission replied. "No, I did not."

"But I know!" the doctor countered and complained.

"*You* know," Bill started. "Your *character* on the other hand, is blissfully ignorant. D&D has some aspects like gambling. You don't show your cards. You play them when you need to. Sometimes you see the bluff. Sometimes you're the one being bluffed. In this case, your character is at the table and failed to see the bluff made by Cameron's character."

This earned Bill a warm smile from the team biologist and a frustrated gaze from the doctor.

"But <u>this</u> isn't poker, so just as there are times where you shouldn't show your whole hand, there are also times, to maintain peace and fair play and to keep it a group activity, you have to show all. A player solely about their own agenda is not fun to play with."

Bill and the doctor locked eyes, for a moment. Bill hoped the message was received...but he doubted it. He already knew who was possibly going to be that "one agenda" player.

THE ONE RINGER

A slice of homemade pie.
A hot summer evening touched by a gentle breeze.
A basket of playful kittens.
A great blockbuster on opening night, tickets in hand, near perfect seats (perfects seats would entail being friends with the director, an evening of cocktails, and a private screening in a mansion).
Or a simple natural 20.

That is Ar.

Ar short for Arlan. Arlan Novack.

James had met Ar early in his collegiate life at some gathering just off campus one Spring evening. The day had been uneventful like many others before. Steady streams of faces mostly young, mostly bored; a few faces in lucky blossom, lit my some new passion to mark the badge of "doing" and "becoming" and "discovering"; all shifted and collided in tides and swells marked by time and rooms with chairs and the paths that connected them.

Bill had never had any major social issues prohibiting him from connecting with others. No autism or rage issues. Neither was he disposed to be morose or melancholic. A tad arrogant, perhaps a little too smart, at least he thought so...he was not out of place with most students his age and the various gatherings where they tended to congregate. That evening at the party, like most back then, the self-entitled and the vain swapped wide grins and handshakes, aggressive hugs and dull clinking plastic cups filled with sloshing liquids: clear, or yellow, or pink, amber or dirt brown. Spilling enough to add to the miasma of the already sticky kitchen floor. House Cleaning would need to be fired. Another facsimile of a would-be DJ choked the air, forcing his version of what was danceable and cool on a majority of accepting ears. Better would-be DJs stalked the edges silently with eyes narrowed, downgrading the event with each bad track.

Dance majors were in attendance, "expressing" themselves. Easily spotted for their exaggerated limb movements and sudden pirouettes. In corners, small groups debated themselves into them. Agreeing and disagreeing. Agreeing more. All nods final.

Bill always had a gift at noticing things that stood out, not the big things, but the small. He also was talented in spotting things trying to hide. His Perception check were exquisite.

His first sighting of Arlan was accompanied by food: pepperoni and sausage, peppery fatty meats; a basil rich generic tomato sauce; mozzarella, an oily frozen landscape of brown and gold crusted bubbles in a circular sea; the close to burnt scent of pizza dough;....and the sensation of a still warm slice smacking him in the chest.

In one hand she had held a plastic cup. The other a pizza slice, plate-less. It was as a friend snatched the cup she was holding that she went on a stumbling trajectory towards Bill's clean shirt emblazoned with the great aquatic logo of Fishbone.

"What the?!-"

Bill barely managed to comment before the inebriated female partier mumbled something. An apology? He had no idea for quickly she had been dragged away and he was left the victim of a hit and run party foul of pizz-ianic proportions.

Snatching napkins Bill was just about to start the attempt at shirt salvation when just off to the right he heard someone say, not loudly, but somehow loud enough to be heard over the din of the party.

"Crit fail."

The speaker was right.

And the speaker, was Arlan.

A tall and lanky guy with dark skin and shoulder length rivulets of dark brown dreadlocks.

For the next 3 hours Bill and Ar chatted about everything, but mostly they discussed their love of "The Game".

Arlan was born into a family of Bohemians. His mother, Claudette, was an accomplished pianist and playwright, whose last two plays had received good reviews, and who was forever determined to have her next play be off off-Broadway. His father, Maverick, who was not named after the 60's popular TV show baring the same name, was a university lecturer, and was rarely home. Theirs was the house where each day something or someone new was occurring or visiting. Daily deliveries and pickups left the front foyer of their home, an ever-fluctuating landscape of shapes.

Ar was a free spirit by upbringing. Wrongs were rarely met with reprisals, rather curiosity, questions, and mild impatience in his household. His parents were busy people.

Most days after school when he was only a boy, he would gather the more interesting shaped arrivals in the sitting room. He would play games of what-is-this-shape before opening them to be either surprised or justified in his astute observations and deductive reasoning. More than not most arrivals were books or magazines.

One day, a package took his fancy. He knew they were books. Multiple books, but their size was odd. Too rectangular for what he would consider art book, books highly prized in his household. Too big by far to be fiction or nonfiction hardbounds. It was with a leap and a hope he settled on a series of European graphic illustration book, which in his mind were the best, because the art would be cool, and he would almost be guaranteed that some of the subject matter would be adult.

"Dungeons & Dragons?"

Opening the package, the titles told him little and only increased his curiosity, so he opened the books, one by one.

The great game.

This was Ar's introduction. He didn't play at first, for it took months to get a decent number of friends to show interest, and then a few more months to get one of his friends to volunteer to be the Dungeon Master, the linchpin to adventures into imaginary worlds.

Ar was a player, not a DM....the idea of developing scenarios appealed to him, but he lacked his mother creative genius to pull off the delicate art of storytelling in a roleplaying setting.

Ar loved being a player. A character in someone's story. He loved wearing masks, playing at being someone else, somewhere else.

Bill completely understood, and years later after college, when he started running games again, he remembered his strange friend. He had been running 3 different games at the time, and his newest was not going well. It was a classic tale of players: over-acting; rampant bad jokes; players doing things "fir chits n giggulls", which often involved the murder of innocent NPCs(non-player characters); and no one really listening, to him or each other.

For Bill Owen this was new, and absurdly frustrating. He had a natural gift at improvisational storytelling and found many creative ways to draw players in and awaken something in them they hadn't known needed awakening. The Game can change you, for the better....but only if you play it right, and yes, Bill would say to anyone, there is a right and a wrong way to play. Anyone who said otherwise was probably a shit player.

It was after one particularly bad gaming session with this group, at home contemplating the best way to terminate this game, when Ar sprang to mind. Going to social media he located the most recent post from his college compadre. The post, dated 3 days prior, had Ar at a local art show for a mutual college friend. An event Bill had been unable to attend.

He reached out to his old friend.

Some guys don't change. Ar was an ever-growing art installation unto himself. His once smooth face was now covered in a thick mustache and beard, his head of hair trimmed respectfully. Owen couldn't help but smile.

"I don't know what to do Ar." He had said to the screen "Guess I've had it lucky. Almost inevitable if you think about it. Ever game can't have an Arlan Novack."

Or could it?!

The next day Owen got a hold of his old friend and explained his idea.

Ar was on the next plane out.

It worked.

By the time Ar arrived Bill hand already fleshed out the prototype for his game saving new player's character. It was not an easy thing to develop, for the ultimate goal is for each player, or character, to value this newly introduced character in such a way that the gameplay changes positively, for most often one characteristic will attract one player but repel another:

The cute and wounded.
Bunny with broken leg.

The strong and uplifting.
Action hero...Rambo...John Wick?...maybe not.

The beautiful and compassionate.
Mother Teresa...or Gwyneth Paltroy? Oprah or Ellen!

The helpful and empathetic.
Dr. Oz....or a beloved teacher.

The wise and fatherly.
Ram Dass...or Herschel, from The Walking Dead

Oh!
The super-hot and flirty.
Sebastian Stan. Sophia Vagara. Evangeline Lilly.
Leonardo!

Classic archetypes, personas, that people gravitate to, and any given one can have aspects of the other, and the right one injected into a scenario can bring unity to the divided, focus to the distracted, wisdom and compassion to the foolish and callous.

The trick was deciding what persona, what being, would rally this game's players together, and bring out their better qualities.

Once Bill had the dynamics worked out, the rest came easy.

He started first with the character's class. This was simple. Bill based his choice on the player with the abilities not being used properly or not at all. The human fighter. The difficult player. The quintessential RPG problem child.

The guy playing the fighter had spent most of his time using his character to attack and intimidate any and all townsfolk, livestock, and trees that he came close to. In fact it was when he was testing his blade on a grove of young sapling apple trees, that a farmer and his eldest son tried to stop him, that he drew down on them, killed the father, wounded the son, then proceed to butcher the late farmer's four cows. The farm was part of a district with more than 500 citizens. The party was quickly apprehended, and it was only luck and the fact the farmer had attacked first(a deception) which had saved one if not all from the gallows. They did not get away without some punishment. The fighter was branded on the left side of his face for his crimes, of which the offending player commented on with only one word.

"Cool".

Bill wasn't surprised. In a novice group there was always one player who acted out, like a troublesome child. The one player who suddenly couldn't stop from making everything into a potential comedy bit, from one-liners to innuendos of the most juvenile sort to hideous puns!; the player who doesn't listen to any of the hints and clues and then cries when their character suffers a misfortune, or more than likely causes another player's character to suffer and/or die; or like this particular player, who just seemed Hades-bent on attacking the weak, which wasn't new, but always surprised Bill when players did this in the Game!

Being a bully was always an odd choice in a game populated mostly by the bullied.

The Game had always been a nerd thing. For geeks and dweebs, spazzes and poindexters. For the most often shunned...the most often bullied. Here when given the opportunity to at least pretend to be a hero this player chose villainy, to be a bully.

The Owens's didn't come from wealth. His family had had a life where every now and then the family toes, skimming above the poverty line, dipped beneath, and in those deeper waters bullies were always to be found. In part Bill turned to the Game for what his world didn't have enough of. He didn't need any more bullies...he needed heroes!

This third game he was running at this time had a bully, and the rest of the party either lacked the confidence to stop, the interest to educate him, or merely egged him on.

Ar's character would be the cure.

Race was another easy choice in designing this minor messiah to a dying game. The party member who lacked the most confidence was the female elven druid. This was not a fault of the character; it was all a reflection of the player herself. If the Ar's character was another elf it could give her a partner in crime, especially if this new elf came from the her village and they were longtime friends....and surprise surprise, they were!

It was Ar's idea to have three saying from their elven woodland home which when started and uttered by one, the other could finish, or join in chorus and complete.

It was enough. Owen added a rescue/revenge mission of the only NPCs the party liked, and "Project Save the Game" began!

The injection of Ar's character didn't take immediate effect. It was only natural for there to be an immune response to what Bill and Ar were attempting to do. One or two of the players must have guessed Ar was only there to babysit their gameplay, but if they knew anything they said nothing. The fighter immediately felt threatened by Ar's elven barbarian who raged and threw hand axes like a madman with great effectiveness.

The fighter initially tried to get Ar's barbarian to join in the violent hijinks, but soon realized that wasn't going to happen. Ar played it well, never chiding the fighter for his actions, but also offering absolutely no support of his behavior. He quickly would defuse situations which prior to his joining the game would have led to violence. Slowly, the others followed suit, and the player of the abusive fighter, slowly, stopped.

Then an ambush in the night almost claimed the barbarian and it was through the fighter's skills that the party knew Ar's character was in trouble. The scene of the barbarian on the ground surrounded by attackers slinging racial slurs and kicks was all it took for the fighter to finally act the hero. He had secretly developed a need to have the approval, notice, of Ar's barbarian and Ar himself. The double tap was the reveal these were villains hired by Ar's character's own brother. The fighter immediately hated this family betrayer. This flaw in Ar's otherwise perfect character, brother against brother, appealed to the fighter.

In real life the fighter's player had a brother, and Bill had uncovered, they were often in opposition of one another.

"baseball cards
board games
collectibles
comicbooks
role playing games."

The Glowing Goblin's window proclaimed in pride and precise painted letters that it was not a place for your average human. Which was brought home even more by the cornucopia of strange miniature figurines in mock battle displayed in the front window. In fact, if you needed a more geek fantastic store you would have to look elsewhere much farther than the city limits of Houston. Parked out front the NASA van was drawing more attention than the strange shop.

"Oh shit!" the young woman behind the counter exclaimed as he entered.

Bill Owen was not surprised. Everywhere he went, no matter where, if it was a bastion of nerdic vices he would be recognized. Upon entering *The Goblin,* the woman had immediately given voice to her surprise. Her exclamation made most heads in the establishment turn, and almost every eye widened.

"Oh wow, Bill motherfuckin' Owen!" by her large grin and wide eyes it was obvious to Bill's astronaut entourage the odd fellow they followed was more than just some nerd, but a person who had his own notoriety, at least within the world of the Game.

"Yep," Bill blushed slightly, as a few with him smiled at an obvious fan of his. "Hi, how's it going?"

"How's it going?" the store clerk couldn't hide her exuberance "How's it going?! Fucking great! Bill Owen just walked in the door! Wow!"

This made Bill laugh.

"Well I am pleased to make your day," he paused squinting at the young woman's name tag which she had personalized with stickers and sparkles "...Allison."

"Oh wow. Can I take a pic?"

She quickly pulled a cell phone from beneath the counter. Bill could see a few of the customers had followed suit. He could see one of them was already videoing the sighting for proof to any future naysayers.

"That's fine, but first, I have some new players and they need die. You think you can help them?"

"Of course, of course. This way."

Allison came from behind the counter and guided the group to an area not far and still within sight of her station near the front door.

"Here you are! The dice section!"

In row after row, behind the glass of two upright and one horizontal display case, lay a vast array of dice. Bill had been to a lot of similar establishments but was immediately wowed. Someone had been terribly busy. Dice displays can be a riot of colors, with no rhyme or reason. Transparent dice sharing the same space as opaque dice, which shared the same space with dice that sparkled or glowed or did both. Here at the *Goblin* someone was not going to let that happen on their watch!

Spread out before them was a dice rainbow that moved from edge to edge within the displays. At the edges, to left and right, were black dice which flowed into blue which flows into purples into reds into oranges into yellows, with the white dice at the center, and the organization didn't end there. Each ring of color started with opaques to transparent to sparkles to glow-in-the dark die.

"Wow!" Bill commented. "Now I am one impressed."

"Really?!" it was evident by her immediate glow, this was Allison's work, for she beamed like Faerie Fire in a dark cave.

"Really! I think you should be immensely proud. Most would buckle at such an endeavor."

"Thank you Mr. Owen"

"Please, call me Bill."

"Oh wow, thank you Bill. To be honest *The Law of 20s* was one of the reasons I did this."

Allison knelt and looked through the glass of the three display cases.

"Hahaha, now you honor me again, Allison. I just introduced these new players to the *Laws*. I hope they can find their sets here that they will keep and use for the rest of their lives."

Allison looks at the group with Bill and raised an eyebrow. Their NASA themed attire not going unnoticed.

"We aim to please here at *The Glowing Goblin*!" she rose and flourished with arms spread the establishment around her. She once more focused on Bill. "I owe you a big thanks...Bill. *The Law of 20s* changed my gameplay completely. I had over 15 sets of dice, and if I didn't start following the *Laws,* I would have had many more by now. I was able to whittle those 15 down to 3, with only one twenty-sided...with a few cheap 20s as backup support."

She winked conspiratorially.

"Congratulations and thanks....I know for some of my critics the *Laws* where a little difficult to stomach, if stomached at all. Maybe they are a little too esoteric, but it was something I developed over many years and it was my hope others in the D&D community could benefit from them. More suggestions than laws. And to be honest, I really just made them for myself."

At little sheepishly with a little laugh Bill finished by saying.

"I also got a little tired of players blaming their dice and 'jailing' them or downright torturing or destroying their die because of a series of unlucky rolls."

Bill looks at the beautiful array of dice in the three display cases and gently places a hand on the glass top to peer deeper at their colors.

"It's not their fault."

The day before.

"The what?"

"*The Law of 20s*," Bill answered Francis' quizzical look.

"And what exactly is that?"

Bill had been a D&D player for most of his life, first beginning his adventures in elementary school with small breaks here and there, and in all that time he had rolled and purchased lots of dice, and been witness to many more rolls and dice than his own. It was almost inevitable for players to form interesting relationships with their die, for when it came down to it the dice had more control than the DM and the players combined. They said yea or nay to all that could or would not occur.

Dice were magic.

A few years ago, during a rough batch Bill had invented *The Law of 20s*, almost in memorandum. Returning to his mother's house for a visit one year he was greeted by several boxes laid out on the garage floor. His mother had gathered his old things, to see what he wanted to keep because the rest was destined for charity groups or a landfill.

Sitting with beer in hand Bill went through each box methodically pulling out a few cherished items: a trophy, an art project; and anything not worth keeping he would spend a moment reminiscing with before sipping at his beer in gratitude and then putting it in a box for the Goodwill or a bag for the trash.

Of those things meant to be held and cherished till the time's end what he prized most was placed lovingly in a box by itself. Most of the things in that box was related to the Game.

Old maps and miniatures; binders and notebooks of adventures and ideas; photos; a few worn and weary menus from pizza places and Chinese restaurants, kept for pure nostalgic reasons; and of course, the holy texts of his religion...

The Player's Handbook.
The Dungeon Master's Guide.
The Monster Manual.

Battered and beaten, and mostly held together with wishes and duct tape and teenage memories.

Amongst these items there was one thing he didn't put in the box, or in the charity pile, or the bag for the fully unwanted. This thing sat in his lap partially over his left thigh. It lay relaxed and a little dusty. Colored a deep burgundy but faded in spots to lavenders and tans.

A dice bag.

It would have been perhaps prophetic if in the last box, at the very bottom, Bill would have found it. Like a sign from the divine....but no. In the third box he searched, right at the top, it had been found. Bill's ooohhhs and aaahhs came out spontaneously as he snatched the bag up and pressed it to heart and lips, and for a precious moment he held it with a fondness which made him rock forward then back, eyes closed with a wistful smile.

Then he remembered, and a melancholy clutched at him as he muttered.

"Damn."

The year was 1998, and Bill Owen was entering his sophomore year in high school, and summer had been a fruitful one of work and D&D, and his bank account was the fullest it had ever been, so it was no surprise to family and friends for Bill to come home with some new treasure from the local gaming store.

The weekend before the first day back to school Bill left his house just after 9:30am to get to the game shop when it opened at 10:00, which was early for most weekend stores but any good game shop always served double duty as a spot for gamers to game. Usually in some backroom dedicated to the community, so early weekend hours were normal.

Bill had no purchase plans in mind for anything specific, he only wanted to bask in the glow of the place before Monday, and the return to classes, and the boredom they fostered set in.

The bell above the door ringed a greeting that day and his feet made the transition smoothly from grey faded black gum dotted pavement...

....to deep red short fibered carpet which ran wall to wall in his home away from home.

He was greeted by the man behind the counter with a hey-what's-up, a receding hairline, a greying beard, and an ever-expanding waistline.

Wes Kilpatrick, proprietor and owner, and a staunch supporter of all things gaming, unless said game required a monitor and a keyboard or a, in his words, "no-joystick".

He was a local hero to some and savior to others, to most *weird,* for behind the doors of his establishment a nerd could feel *normal.*

"What brings ye in this fine morning Sir Owen?"

He enjoyed handing out titles and speaking old English...especially when renaissance fair season rolled round. It had.

"School starts Monday," Bill responded with a shrug.

"Ahhhhh," this was enough of an answer for Wes, who well understood the weight the world placed on young shoulders who had the unpleasant task of surviving school, and a community of overburdened educators and judgmental peers.

"Unnecessary evils."

This was just one, among many, sayings Max had...personalized:

"No good DM goes unpunished!"

"A copper saved means you need better treasure."

"The path to the dungeon is paved with good people!"

Max's world was completely his own. Beyond judgment and critic. Colorful and rich it danced to his tune and gave him all he ever needed.

"Anything new?" Bill Owen the younger had asked

"Verily ye knoweth that answer!" Wes had replied.

New products came in regularly. Modules and supplemental books, which offered new lands for players to venture into, filled with new and hopefully novel flora and fauna, magic and mystery. Dry erase maps either tiled in squares for close encounters and dungeons, or hexagons for terrain and geography. New role-playing games, either developed by established companies, or new upstarts who sought to prove equal to the great Game. But mostly what came in were pewter miniatures and dice. Lots of dice!

For DMs, the main drug of choice were the miniatures, but for players their first addiction was the dice. Always the dice. In a way the dice played surrogate to the gems and jewels found in many imaginary treasures within the Game.

"Even got some old die today. An offload from another shop."

This had peeked Bill's interests.

"Where?" he asked Wes.

The next hour was spent going through this box, and when he left, Bill was the proud owner of a new module and one old 20 sided.

Bill loved the color green. All kinds of green, emerald to forest to deep, and anything that looked like jade had his admiration instantly. Semitransparent, like a pool of green milky water, jade always came to mind when he thought of magic.

Jade was enchanting. The old 20-sided was just such a color.

He remembered, on that day heading home, holding the 20 up to the light of the sun and being surprised to see that the light penetrated to the heart of the dice, creating an almost kaleidoscopic effects as yellow green rays danced and spun within.

What next followed was a season of glorious games, one after another, and each one was marked by the rolling click of his new jade colored 20. It gave him criticals, "nat 20s", at the most opportune times, and when crit fails happened, "nat 1s", they always seemed to lead to some of his best creative improvisations to save the day.

He loved that dice!

Then...somehow...he lost it.

As he neared graduation and college, and his gaming seemed to naturally taper off, between one day heading from a game to home and the preceding days that followed, it had vanished, for at his next weekend game, one of the last gaming sessions of his high school days, reaching into his dice bag his fingers couldn't find it. He remembered pouring out all the dice in a pile before him on the table, hands and eyes sifting and searching, and seeing not one trace of the jade green he had become so familiar with. He grew angry with himself for his buying habits as he rifled through a quantity of dice he did not need, most he never used. Each unneeded dice a stranger blocking his eyes from his cherished 20. He next checked his backpack, vomiting out its contents in a mad hope, but he already knew....it was not there.

The fate filled game, a week prior, had been held at a local diner which had proved friendly to his small group and the money they would spend over a couple of hours congregating there. He knew, somehow, he had lost his beloved die there.

After school, the next day, he returned to the diner. Talking to the wait staff and the owner, a buxom red-haired middle-aged woman who maintained a steady rotating crush on this or that high school boy, he was pointed to the "Lost & Found" box. In it he had found nothing except the lost things of other people.

His imaginative mind immediately crafted the most likely of scenarios.

Closing time. The cleanup. Floors swept and mopped. The refuse all gathered up and tossed in trash bags, which were then tossed in the dumpsters outback. Dumpsters eventually lifted and hauled away by a garbage truck a day or so later. He thought maybe it had escaped and sat in one of the two dumpsters, but the thought of rummaging through either of them even with gloved hands was vastly unappealing.

He did it anyway and found naught except the overwhelming stench and clinging touch of garbage juice.

Gone, gone....all gone.

This marked his first and last break from the Game, his attention set on his new life in college and all its myriad distractions. Distractions to distract him from a loss not many could understand.

Years later, in his mother's garage, surrounded by his familiar and mostly forgotten past, his old bag of die laid across his leg, he remembered, and in the remembering he came up with the first law of 20s:

Protect your 20 sided.

For every group he guided into the Game he would initially introduce them to the basics of gameplay, and very quickly then to his "*Laws of 20s*". Which were more guidelines than laws. Laws bear punishment if one breaks them. Guidelines were more forgiving.

Like his other groups these astronauts would be no different.

The Laws of 20s

1.) Choose only one.

2.) Accept every roll.

3.) Find the surface best suited for your 20 sided dice.

4.) If rolls are bad, switch hands and/or how you roll.

5.) Periodically purify your 20-sided dice.

6.) Let no other hand touch your 20-sided dice.

7.) Love your 20-sided dice, for it is a pure vehicle of Fate.

8.) Do not boast of your 20-sided dice's prowess.

9.) Do not ever threaten your 20-sided dice.

10.) Do not ever blame your 20-sided dice.

11.) Avoid demands. Let your 20-sided dice be free, do not impede.

12.) Avoid all practice rolls.

13.) A roll...is only a roll...when it stops on its own.

14.) Your 20-sided dice is your companion. Respect it as such.

15.) Protect your 20-sided.

16.) Use it only for its intended purpose.

17.) If your 20-sided dice jumps from your hand or hits the floor, question what your character is about to do.

18.) Roll with conviction.

19.) Focus your mind completely...but gently also.

20.) Don't spend too much money on your 20.

Ahlassiter stops before entering the Arh Cleft. He waits for Horak. Patiently. He had been taught no dwarf should ever be left behind... Even if that dwarf was a very annoying and lanky half-orc.

Allies being a commodity here he thinks it best to keep Horak close. Also he waits, as a measure to protect those in the party who could possibly be affected by the sorcerer's actions. Particularly if those actions could be seen as negative to the natives, and possibly arouse their anger.

Natives who held sway on whether the group's nights were sheltered in a safe place, or out in Coldfire. Sape, their guide and first contact, did show telltale signs that he might not be worthy of complete trust, but his dire warnings of what an exposed night could do left Ahlassiter with no doubts.

Sape's fears were very real.

As a sorcerer Horak had been taught to be unafraid of the unknown, to embrace the hidden, and glorify the different, but even with this training, and his natural bravado, he quickly turns away from the horrid night, noticing the dwarf's sudden absence at his side. It is hard to contain the shudder passing through his body as he turns his gaze from a land drenched in red. It spoke of defilement, destruction.

"Kali," he mumbles softly under his breath, as he walks to the steps leading down into Cleft. He walks past the dwarf. His smug smile returning to his face.

"Miss me?"

Without pause and following close behind, the dwarf replies.

"No," and both descend together down into the first civilized place they had found in the enigmatic Yet-al.

It is with some wonder and thanks as they step below that there is an immediate change in the light from the world above. They pass some invisible demarcation, like the surface separating air from the waters below it, and move from a dark bleeding red sky to a more natural tone of a deep blue night. Looking above they expect to see a red tinged sky, yet they both find a normal night sky, and its natural darkness. A deep and dark blue ribbon punctuated with cool sparkling stars.

Casting an even cooler glance at the still upwardly gazing dwarf, Horak hides his wonder.

"Magic" he says matter-of-factly, passing by Ahlassiter. "An illusion. Nothing more, dear dwarf."

The condescension is not lost on the dwarf. Not wishing to feed the half-orc's arrogance, Ahlassiter says nothing.

Here, the Cleft, was the first clear example of the control that could be gained and maintained by those seeking safety and community in Yet-al.

Below them at the first major landing waited their guide and the rest of the party and drifting from below the sounds and smells of life rose to greet them. People: their calls and laughs, a cry of pain, footsteps and fast running, the general din that accompanies large gathering. Rich earth smells and water on stone. The smoky scent of cooking fires and grills, rich heady oils of fresh meat and vegetables sizzling and popping over open flames. Undernotes of exotic spices and herbs swimming in rich sauces. The foul invading shit and piss smells underneath it all.

The survivors' minds immediately turn to food and bellies which hadn't had anything in them for more than a day. Their last meal, a night before in the galley of *The Wasp*. Salted fish and porridge, and hardy vegetables that could survive long voyages without spoiling was something they had all just been getting use to when the wreck happened.

Here and there, a scream of some animal, or a humanoid, rose from below. It was hard to tell.

"You will be needin' lodgings. Tis ill advised to sleep in the open. The deeper the night, the darker the actions of those who steal in it."

The Arh Cleft was a natural fissure in the earth. A long deep rip into the flesh of Yet-al that descended a few hundred feet downward and ran for many more in a general north to south direction.

Sape guides them down, moving past the first landing into the first level of the Cleft.

Eyes upon eyes watch, and mouths behind hands whisper at these newcomers, for their unfamiliarity, and perhaps for the fact they travel with a man like Sape.

Soon more than eyes follow. A few, then more and more feet, drag their bodies after Sape and his charges. New people were a rarity, and, against their nature, it brought out long held in check unquenchable curiosity from the citizens of the Cleft. Soon Sape was hard pressed to move forward as those ahead began to block, then question:

"Who are these?"

"Where do you come from?!"

"Sape! Where did you find them you basterd?!"

"Do any of you come from Feon?!"

"Anything for trade?! Bring it to Orget's Goods!"

"Orget's sucks! Everyone knows if you want a good deal ya go ta Orgen's General Store!"

"How dare you Orget! I'm tellin Ma!"

The two men, brothers, proceed to push and shove at each other, until an overly large woman with grey white hair breaks them apart with several smacking blows to their heads. Ahlassiter presumes this is "Ma".

Soon all forward movement of the new arrivals comes to a halt as they are hemmed in on all sides by the curious and the questioning.

"Oh shite!"

Qeta Sape spins in place, looking at his new companions apologetically.

"No worries," he smiles awkwardly at them, then turns and addresses the crowd "Please! I assure you all will be made clear, but right now please let us pass! These new citizens are undoubtedly hungry and tired."

They were.

"Now, let us through!"

Whether he is heard by the crowd it matters not as the surrounding crowd suddenly surges and several cries of pain rise from the back as a formation of men and women in dark green cloaks and worn chainmail armor push through with jabs and quick sharp strikes from the truncheons they all carry in their hands.

"Move it! Clear out!"

The forward most figure bellows from an overly broad chest, made more broader by massive bosoms she did little to conceal. Dressed like the others, except for a small silver emblem pinned to the right lapel of her cloak, she easily cuts a swath through the curious onlookers.

Not overly tall by any means she is still an impressive figure. Her skin light with eyes to match, the only other characteristic of note, besides her natural endowments, is a long thick blonde braid, which trails well past her back and almost to the ground at her feet. A braid which swings behind her as she comes closer.

With one last blow from her truncheon the crowd finally gives way.

"Who here wants to spend the night in the stockade?!" the woman roars. Fear greets her question on all sides "Now I suggest...you all go about your business."

Spoken like advice, it is still clear this is an order. The crowd slowly disperses. A few sullen and a few perturbed of that number, drift only a short distance away, curiosity still holding them near Sape and the newcomers.

"Greetings Commander Olisar!"

Sape bows deeply to the woman leading the truncheon wielding guards.

"Sape." Her reply is only mildly polite, touched with a modicum of respect as if she were addressing a slug she had found on her doorstep that had forgotten it was a slug.

"Let me introduce these new friends. They are recently shipwrecked, and-"

"Hold your tongue!"

This she says as if the slug had surreptitiously spat at her, so in response she crushed it under her booted foot.

"Come with us."

Turning away the survivors can only follow, as they are quickly encircled and shepherded by the other guards to follow their leader, Commander Olisar.

No further locals block them as they are unceremoniously led deeper into the Arh Cleft at a rapid pace, and any deviation, forever slight, was met with a scowl or a jab of a truncheon to any exposed tender bits.

Or for a female halfling a strong nudge of a big booted foot.

"I beg your pardon!" Horak voices emphatically his disapproval.

The booted guard in question, is a particularly small and stout fellow with pale yellow eyes like a foul night predator. As is his nature, the half-orc had begun to lag, his own curiosity slowing his steps as they moved through the strange unfamiliar community, so he is closest to Gracis when the incident happens.

"Beg dis you orc!" the reply comes with a shove to Horak's side and a middle finger raised to sky and the sorcerer's complaint.

"Orc?! You bastard! Is it not obvious I am no full blood representative of those foul creatures? You should well make an effort to-"

Is all he utters as the squat man flicks and strikes his truncheon against Horak's exposed wrist.

"Owwww! You dick!"

"Trouble back there Relin?" the voice of Olisar launches over her shoulder in mid stride.

"No commander," his pale eyes fix on those of Horak. Pale eyes which do not blink and do not care. "Is there?"

The veiled threat is window clear.

Horak contemplates an immediate reprisal even as he sees the look Ahlassiter gives him. The look is stern and foreboding and pleading, but it is the gentle tug on his robes near his knee and the eyes of the gentle halfling looking up at him imploringly, ultimately, that kills his desire to harm the pale eyed human...for now.

"No," Horak bows, arms outstretched to his sides, then comes up with a glowing smile, full and wide and tusked, that expresses to all he holds no ill will. "Of course not. Sir Relin was only protecting us from ourselves. Being newcomers."

"Good" the commander remarks and continues leading them. Ahlassiter waits for Gracis and Horak to pass him before he follows taking up the rear. There would be no more stranglers and no further altercations if he has anything to say about it.

The half-orc, smile still affixed, looks into the dwarf's eyes as he passes him, and in those eyes Ahlassiter can see the matter was far from over, and that the guard Relin has offended the wrong person. The dwarf's jaw clenches and relaxes, as he confirms his decision to watch the sorcerer closely.

Without the pressing crowd the survivors of *The Kellen Wasp* are once again able to bask in the sensory assault that was the Cleft unhindered. The walls of Cleft run with quartz veins, and granite, both black and grey green, and here and there rich ruddy reds of iron rich ores. The Cleft's populace had devised ways to carve into the walls making tunnels and walkways, open spaces and modest homes, and where the granite proved to hard they hug suspension bridges, paths. Quite a few smaller structures hag off rock faces similar in shape to bird's nests accept built for medium size or smaller humanoids. The Cleft is a riot of colors. Fabrics lavishly dyed in yellows and blues, orange and purple past them with every step; and plants, in small and large potted plants and in tilled earth terraces, spread their green everywhere. But not much red, which is logical. They even pass a place like an amphitheater surrounded on its walled sides by mirrors and large glowing cylinders of impure glass, giving light and life to a small underground forest and an even smaller underground pond. Here can be seen lovers and friends, parents and children, mostly unsupervised.

"Bats!" the half-elf Jilliandria screams as a fluttering group of dark shapes launches just above her head from a nearby tree and shuttles their way through the air and across the enclosed park.

"No. Not bats."

Noc Arrow has a fondness for all things that flew. Even bats. What she doesn't have a fondness for are those who are easily scared, especially if that person was a fellow woman. Hard fought had been her way to be respected and acknowledged by that lesser yet fated to dominance group called males.

"I assure you they are not."

She makes it a point as she passes by the half-elf to step on her heel.

"Ow!" Jilliandria cries out.

"Sorry. Bats."

Noc eyes round in an apologetic look of innocence.

More minutes pass as they are led deeper into the outlandish undercity and slowly one smell demands their attention. It is Nighlus who first notices, and he rapidly determines its source. Cloying and fetid it rises from below, past the brighter lights of the Cleft above.

"Oh my God!" the healer blurts out.

"Oh my crap more like it" the female halfling raises a sleaved arm to cover her nose.

"Where do you expect the refuse and waste to go, or more pointedly, fall?" Nighlus gestures down to the unknown that waits below.

The Commander is neither bothered by their comments or the intense smell as they head downward, deeper still. It takes all their fortitude to maintain their composure. Perhaps having empty stomachs saves them from adding to the stench with offerings of what food from the night prior still lay digesting in their bellies.

In whispers, Sape informs the party that this is where the Cleft's second level begins.

They descend through smoke, oily and moist, air filled with the smell of many unwashed people and fire. A dampness that they can sense but not yet see, at some yet undetermined level below, said a body of water must exist farther below. Filling the bottom of the great Ar Cleft, and obviously aswim in the effluence from the populace above.

The atmosphere shocks the group as they go deeper. The half-elf and half-orc fair the worse. Both attempt to cover their noses from the offensive air with the hems of their robes. Jilliandria can't help her response as her eyes grow wide with trepidation at the situation they have found themselves in. In her sheltered life she has rarely been to places such as this though her oath and path kept her in service and contact with the less fortunate, but always within the confines of temples dedicated to her goddess. Temples ranging from humble brick and clay structures found in many small villages across the realm to the grand temples which arch into the skies in the major cities, glowing glass edifices lit from within and edges trimmed in the finest woods and metals. Temples where she was always protected. Temples which were always clean.

The half-orc makes no attempt to hide his disgust, as he vainly seeks to avoid all contact with the people and the walls nearest him. If he could, he would not even touch the ground his shoed feet walk upon. Already his feet have sunk into puddles containing all manner of things he would not imagine.

Noc is unshaken, sparing only a harsh smirk for her sensitive compatriots. She is the only one who appears to respond positively to the experience, her shoulders relaxing as she smiles at the sights and sounds around her. It is only the elf's sharp eyes which catch her hands at play over her person, nonchalantly and seemingly without intention, but, now being somewhat familiar with her and her "talents", he knows each hand touch is to reaffirm the position of this dagger or that, and also the positions of the many darts she had secreted all over her person.

You would think as they descend, the areas they pass would be less crowded, but like every place that humanoids populate there had to be a "special" place for the poor, the destitute, the unwanted, and the unloved. A demographic that was always larger in number when compared to the fortunate and their numbers.

This is where the Cleft kept them.

Here the poor far outnumbered the middling and the well-off who lived above. Here is their place, to fight and struggle, to starve, grow sick, and die.

The truncheons of their escorts again found cause for use. No pressing and curious throngs needed to be pushed back. No. This overpopulated space meant that each inch had to be fought for and that it is almost impossible to move without brushing up against someone, or something. On all sides and underfoot they made their way through people. Crying. Dead of eye. Mewling. Gibbering. Hissing. Coughing. Screaming. Sullen. Hateful. Eyes and filthy hands. Young and old. Here life is for those with fingertips unkissed by fortune. The unskilled and untalented these people are not. Viscous snarls from men and women who could give the commander and her group a fight none would forget said that physical prowess is not rare here. Here and there craftsfolk weaving, carving, or sculpting fine works which, if given opportunity and access, would afford themselves and their kin a life devoid of such hardships.

No. Some hidden laws kept these people in check and down here in squalor. Long held grudges. Prejudice. Mistakes of station. Perhaps an unwanted advance by a powerful upper leveler that was rejected. Many the reasons, without any clear justification to why most found their beginnings and ends here. And below a lake of shit.

Finally the motley group pass a point and all activity and people are left behind, Within a short span they all halt.

Thankfully for the survivors of *The Wasp*, they went no deeper or nearer to the stench below, and now stand face to face with a massive door, more wide than tall, set with bands of cast iron and a small grate at eye height.

"Oh no."

It is a gasp though it is uttered with as much volume as a whisper. The nearest to him, Noc, looks immediately at the returning to silence Qeta Sape. On his face, conflicting emotions wipe clear anything he had been thinking prior to their arrival at this edifice. This new predicament ripples across him. Realization, excitement, and dread colors his eyes and his skin grows pale. Ahlassiter Orekeeper stares at him attempting to get his attention, but Qeta refuses with downcast eyes and silence to look at any of them.

The Commander Olisar raises her truncheon and strikes the door in a quick succession of taps. Even in the close proximity to the constant din of the 2nd levelers, the shepherded group could hear the strikes echo beyond the door's frame and all along this deep, dark, and unseen area. They wait for a few minutes, growing more and more uncomfortable for what possibly awaits them beyond the heavy door. The massive hinges creak drawing all eyes, as the thick and overly wide door swings inwardly open.

Expecting some huge and haggard humanoid the group is surprised to be greeted by a frail yet well attired human male, a few seasons out of his youth.

"Commander."

Olisar nods silently and gestures at the group behind her.

"Master Vellis is expecting you."

Without another word the unassuming youth steps to the side and gestures everyone to enter, and without any word the commander steps in and the group is forced to follow pressed and prodded by her subordinates.

Passing over the threshold before them, they are lead down a tunnel perhaps 12 feet in width and 10 in height, well-lit by lanterns. Orange ember, yellow and red light swimming, casts sharp and obtuse tones on polished stones and well-kept dark walls and floor. If they hadn't seen it with their own eyes they would not have believed they had not just passed through such a wretched area filled with such poverty, for beyond the door is a well-kept tunnel, the air clean with the wet smell of washed stonework, and underneath that, fragrant vegetation from some unknown source lingers. Behind them the massive door shuts with a loud thud.

They continue in the quiet the door creates. The door closing off the world they had just left behind.

The tunnel, after 20 yards or more, comes to a heavy wrought iron gate patterned in swirls and geometric symbols. Here both Horak and Gracis pause, their eyes drawn to the arcane shapes crafted into its surface. They both can sense the magic woven into the hard metal and know without the proper incantations and mystical gestures one would be hard pressed to find a way through it....or out from behind it.

The frail yet eloquent young man, who had been trailing behind them all, excuses himself as he passes to the front and stands before the closed gate. From a belt at his waist he produces an ornate key from a large dark leather pouch. Fitting the key into the lock, he stops, neither removing the key nor turning it. For one breath or more he does naught else, merely waits, then he raises his hand to the key and gives it a satisfying turn ending in a profound and clear click. The gate opens, and a torch just beyond ignites exposing a landing to a descending flight of broad and shallow stairs that spiral out of sight.

Once all pass beyond the gate, the youth retrieves the key and shuts the gate once more. He turns the moment the gate gives a duller click as the magic held in its frame rebolts the lock. He moves to the front again and with no gesture silently begins to walk down the curving stairwell, another torch ignites a few feet in front of him.

"Let's go."

The Commander nods the order and begins to follow the young gatekeeper. The survivors of the ill-fated *Wasp*, hemmed in by guards, follow.

The stairwell starts off in a clockwise direction but after one downward turn it immediately turns counterclockwise for one turn. It repeats this pattern two more times. Noc, feels as if she is gliding down the back of some great serpent, frozen in stone. Torches continue to ignite ahead as they proceed and draw near them.

Coming round the last curve in the stairwell, the pathway down straightens and continues to descend for 100 feet before ending, and with the last curve, sounds and scents dance up the steps to greet them. Birds in night song; water playfully splashing on stone; air moist and heady with the perfume of flowering plants and rich resin filled trees. Life. Green life.

Most in the group assume, inaccurately, that perhaps they are once more near the surface, and to some open to the air space, but most also quickly realize this to be an impossibility having so recently descended down deeply into the Cleft. Nighlus once again recognizes more, sensing and knowing open sky lay a hundred feet or more above them possessed by a red sky.

The party reaches the end of the large stairwell and find themselves in a large open space under a night sky. The release from the pressure of walls and people cause them all to relax briefly. Before them, the stoned floor continues for several feet before meeting the beginnings of a lush garden lawn surrounded by a squat stone wall. At the center of the garden a three-story mansion, clad in wood boards painted white, sits. Its windows, filled with light from within, illuminates the gorgeous garden and the night in glowing orange lamp light. The path of stone they all stand on, wide enough for three carriages to sit side-by-side, continues to the left and right, eventually wrapping around the large garden and home.

"It isn't real," the forest warrior asserts.

The strange comment draws puzzled expressions from most of Nighlus's allies.

"What?" Jilliandria asks confused.

It is Ahlassiter and the small Gracis who immediately grasp his meaning, for looking closer at their surroundings both see the truth. They are not outside, for glaringly obvious the red hue that plagues this land at night is missing, and also the cold bite that they know accompanies it. No. They are in a large cave carved square, and like the fake night that drapes over the Cleft, it too is painted with only the illusion of night by magic or some other means.

"What?!" Frustrated Jilliandria casts look to each around her. She grows more impatient when she recognizes she is the only one who doesn't understand the place they have found themselves in.

"We are still underground Jilliandria. We are looking at another sky illusion, like the one which hides the Cleft from the red night above." Gracis speaks calmly, her words straightforward. All now understand.

"Master Vellis is waiting."

The gatekeeper, servant of Master Vellis, waits on the stone walkway that leads to the front entrance. He shows no sign of impatience, yet his attitude and bearing hints at an employer who prefers for things to be perfect. A person who does not like to wait.

Without a glance towards her charges, the Commander Olisar steps onto the path and follows the young man towards the front entrance, and all wisely go along. Passing through the garden the survivors of *The Wasp* relax a bit more, encompassed on both sides by nature's beauty, found so deep here below the earth's surface. In this faux night the blooming flowers fill the cool air with aroma, and a demonstration of colors from soft blues to vibrant yellows perform across a deep green backdrop. This garden is well tended and blessed under the care of those with a natural affinity for things that grow from rich dark soil.

Arriving at the entrance, the front doors are elegant creations, carved by a master from a dark wood like ebony, and here, once again, Horak and Gracis both notice more signs of infused magic.

Without break, the doors open before the young gatekeeper, and behind them, two matching servants in blue livery hold them open waiting.

Stepping across the threshold the weary and sea salt burnt group, and their escorts, find themselves in an entryway. It is with no doubt that each survivor knows they have found themselves in the home of wealth and power. The domain of some high ranking member of the Cleft's unique society. The floor is tiled in white marble with pale veins of blue running through their surfaces, and in the golden light of a grand candelabra, that hangs high above each, the tile shine. To the left and right, doorways lead to other areas, and next to these doorways, twin stairwells arc up and along the walls to meet at a landing and double doors some twenty feet above. Nestled in between these stairwells at ground level is a large ornate fountain brimming with water lilies and other flowering water loving plants. After the assault they had just come from their nostrils are now equally overwhelmed by the beautiful perfumes exuding from the green life held in the fountain's clear waters.

On cue the upper landing doors open and all eyes turn upward expectantly. Each envision: *here, here! A grand entrance for a persona who would impact their lives positively or negatively without doubt!*

The "persona" stands clear on the landing above. Her baring is regal. Her skin flawless and pale, and in her arms...a stack of folded linens. Her royal blue uniform, in color scheme, matches those of the doormen. She jumps a little when she sees all the eyes on her from this group of strangers, those both military and road weary.

"This way."

The survivors of *The Wasp* and their shepherds turn and regard the gatekeeper, who now stands in the open doorway to their left.

All follow as they are led into what appears to be a sitting room for guests. Armchairs and chaise lounges sit near to walls painted in soft greens. The group doesn't stop as they are led across the room to a carpeted hallway that turns to the right. They are led down this hallway and they pass three doorways before they reach the end and a pair of closed doors.

Both Horak and Gracis can't resist looking at each other in surprise as both stand in the glaring magic that shines through the door. A light they both know without question the unmagicked of their group cannot see, but in this instance they are wrong. Sune's worshipper, Jilliandria, stands motionless, mouth slightly agape, eyes wide, her right hand clutching her deity's holy symbol held on the chain round her neck. The raw magic that pulses just beyond this door is palpable. Each pulse passes through her, and she is rocked to her core knowing not if this power offends her Goddess.

The gatekeeper, true to his title, opens the doors with flourish and efficiency.

WHOOOSH!

The party is struck with the pressure release that had built up behind the doors that separated two different ecosystems: the mansion proper and the room beyond these doors. Like a greenhouse the room before them exuded clean heat and moisture untouched by rot. Now all present experience raw magic's telltale tickle upon their skins as the doors stand wide open to reveal a large round room bathed in light and life. Here the smell of the outside garden is amplified. Jasmine and rose, gardenia and cedar, and moist warm air blows out on them. The room before them is tiled with the same milky white tile as the antechamber, and here also is another fountain, not as large or as grand as the previous one, but beautiful, simple, and clean, filled with crystalline water sparkling and vibrant, lit from a source below the waters. Almost all, even the guards, lick lips. Commander Olisar controls herself. All are suddenly thirsty, like lost wanderers making sight of an oasis after a harsh trek through a harsh unflinching desert.

The gatekeeper steps to the side, bowing and gesturing for all to enter.

The Commander strides in, soft booted soles softly padding with each step. With no reluctance the survivors enter also. The room is inviting and comfortable, though hot, and perhaps 30 to 40 feet in width. It is the first real place where rest, and safety, could be a possibility for the weary group. Sophistication and healing dwells in this new land contained in this odd room. Rest they may want but the room is assuredly a place of work, made apparent by a large desk which takes up most of the room's right side. Ceiling-to-floor bookshelves lined the walls, holding many tomes and scroll tubes, curios and study subjects, and in every open space available green life flourished. Crawling verdant vines trail up every wall, weaving a brown and green tapestry, that partially crossed the ceiling to twine around three glowing globe orbs hanging a foot down from the high ceiling's center. Each gave off an even light that was neither too cool nor too hot to the eyes. Small trees in miniature, made so either through training or magic, are held in manageable sizes for inside spaces. Mosses, spongy and damp, and minute and delicate plants, fill every other nook and cranny.

The survivors of the ill-fated *Wasp* finally focus their eyes on the occupants, who stand at the center of the room in mid discussion.

Three figures, so different from one another that only in the oddity of these surroundings did they fit perfectly together. A perfect portrait. The party quickly fill with questions wanting to be answered but they all utter no sound in this sacred domain.

Obviously, the being who stood with his back to the group, the survivors and their escorts, was the aforementioned Master Vellis. Black hair deep as night flows down his back, straight and perfect. His stance is regal, his height tall, body lithe. Back curving like a dancer poised to leap he wears a well-tailored suit with tails. Three tails to be exact.

Hanging betwixt the two dashes of fabric that denoted the "tails" in a suit with tails, is a third appendage.

A real tail. Pale purple, part snake yet thick like a many jointed finger. Long and sinuous, it played at his feet. Rising and falling, tipped with a deep purple barb, the tail tip looks sharp. It reflects the light like a dark insect's polished carapace. Two inwardly curving midnight blue horns jut from the sides of his head. Hard horns ridged and gnarled.

Two figures stand before him.

First a diminutive and developed in age human female stands paying them no mind. Her eyes and ears focus on the Master as he talks to her, who bends forward slightly to listen to her quiet replies. At first glance you would think she is a dwarf for her short stature, but her slim body speaks not of that stocky robust race. Every plant in the room faces and reaches for the glowing orbs above, but for this small woman the light that she turned her world to is this half-demon man.

The second figure draws looks of wonder and gasps of surprise. Fear even colors a guard's face who has never seen the like. Whether this fear is for both the master and this creature none could say without asking her.

It stands, near ten foot tall, its head nearly touching the ceiling, and its focus is neither on the small woman or Master Vellis.

Its four jet black eyes, perfect glossy spheres held on stubby eyestalks, gaze with absolute unbreaking focus on the visitors. It stands on four limbs but has a physique that says when necessary it can stand on the back two, solely, to rise at least a few more feet in height and intimidation. It is not made of flesh, and in its veins, if it has any, perhaps something flows more similar to sap than blood. It sways slightly as if in some unseen breeze, a susurration of leaves covering its upper body, calming to the ear if one wasn't already quaking in fear at its physical presence. Its body is plant colored, all greens and browns. A creature birthed, sprouted, fed and fostered by sunlight, clean water, and rich soil. Skin the sheen of supple creeping vines. Thick and rough bark patches that could easily act as armor. A sculpted mass of roots the barrel of its chest.

Awake. It stands regarding the survivors of *The Wasp* coldly.

A living, sentient, plant. Intelligent, for it suddenly speaks.

"Vellis."

It speaks as an equal with no deference for the title "Master" Vellis holds.

"That will be all Foruna. Thank you."

"As always Master Vellis," the short greying woman appears deeply pleased as if the simple gratitude from this master had a heavier importance. Sparing a glance at the visitors to Master Vellis's private rooms, the glance slows when she looks at the weary travelers, new to the lands of Yet-al.

She spares a full pause on the even smaller than herself halfling magic user. The look is an appraising one, measuring some unspoken quality that the taller yet still short woman found reason to notice and perhaps value. Near expressionless she passes across the room and exits through a door tucked between two of the biggest bookshelves.

Before the door clicks shut the horned and tailed regal being turns to address the group.

He is a beautiful man...being....person.

His tail's pale purple coloring continues upward and covers most of his body from what can be seen. The color on his face is even lighter. Covering his cheeks and the bridge of his nose a spatter of pale-yellow spots like freckles. His soft smile sparkles, barely hiding his sharp fangs. Unnoticed before, in his right hand, but clear now, he grasps a walking stick. From first appearances it looks like a giant blade of the greenest grass, unwithered and living. Noc Arrow and Nighlus both voice their immediate deductions.

"Druid."

"Tiefling."

They have not once heard their companion Nighlus speak in harsh tones, or have they heard any emotion color his comments or replies other than calm assertion or mild amusement, but here they notice a new shade to his tone. Part disgust and part hatred, he does not hide his animosity.

Master Vellis either is oblivious to the animosity or chooses to ignore it. It would be safe to assume with his weight and power, it is the latter.

"You have come a long way."

Melodious and smooth as a whisper his voice filled the room like fine and precise chamber music.

"Though you may not feel it, due to the quality of your reception here," he loosely gestures at the Commander and her squad. "I welcome you. I am Qren Tu-at Vellis, and for the sake of brevity I will be as truthful as I may, given the cards I hold and the ones you do not."

"Sir Vellis-"

"Master."

Ahlassiter begins to speak but is immediately cut off by the plant being. It was not a question, the word...."Master". He is being told.

"Ahhhhh...this is my colleague. He has a name, but only he may offer it...if he chooses. Him you may call 'Sir'."

"I misspoke. Master Vellis." The dwarf bows his head slightly in acknowledgment.

"It is no matter. I understand free folk are not accustomed to addressing an unknown as such, but I will assure you...

"My title is earned for the mastery of my craft."

This statement will broker no questioning or judgment, and it is said with such profound honesty, all knew it to be truth.

"Commander," the eloquent tiefling addresses Olisar. "That will be all."

With a curt satisfied nod, the Commander turns and begins to leave the room, her troops rapidly moving to follow suit.

"Please," the word is spoken oddly as if only newly acquired in the Master's vocabulary. "Take Sape with you. Thank you for your services Qeta."

"But-"

A withering black stare from the eyestalks of "sir" silences Qeta immediately.

"Ah-uh...yes Master Vellis."

With a bow, a furtive glance at his recent charges, and reluctance, Qeta Sape moves to exit, and is soon surrounded and guided from the room by truncheons and dour expressions.

Ahlassiter immediately is adrift again, uncomfortable, because for all of Qeta's arrogance, he is not a threat and is quite easy to understand motivation wise, and at this time he was the closest thing to a friend the survivors of *The Wasp* had in Yet-al, but now he is gone.

"You all must be thirsty and tired. Please," a pause. "Water and do help yourself to the bowl of fruit."

They all turn and look seeing a side table set with a pitcher of water and glasses; fruit shaped like plums but of a yellowish hue in a crystal bowl. This offer of hospitality is seized immediately as all, except the dwarf and the full-blooded elf, head over. Jilliandria is the first to bite into the strange fruit and is instantly thankful, for as the sweet clear juice runs down her throat, they carry a pure and potent energy, which invigorates her as it washes into her center. The others soon follow suit as they see a flush of color return to her cheeks and the weariness in her eyes vanish.

Ahlassiter and Nighlus hesitate, but reluctantly take the offerings as the refreshed half-elf presses them with full glasses and two of the beneficial fruits.

Drinking the water and eating the proffered fruit both are instantly appreciative they put caution and pride aside as they too feel a haze fall away from their strained bodies. Profoundly they realize they all had been nearing collapse, drained by their recent trials. Surviving the doom that had brought them here.

"Now to business. If you will follow me...please."

Please. The word truly sounds foreign coming from Master Vellis's lips, though the group senses it is not from any arrogance but from his inexperience at its use. His world is a region where all common platitudes were unnecessary.

Master Vellis does not wait for a response. Against the far back wall, opposite the entrance they had used, is a door. Stepping to it he opens it to reveal a corridor, and passes through, and one by one they all follow. Noc first, followed by Gracis, Horak closely after, and Jilliandria. Ahlassiter and Nighlus bring up the rear. They are only a few feet into the corridor when they hear the door shut behind them. Both turn and resist the reflexive urge to jump in surprise as the plant being, Sir, follows, deathly and quiet.

Here the smell of water and vegetation, once again, intensifies as they proceed forward. Notably they feel the humidity, water in small particles in the air, grow.

"I am sure Qeta Sape has been an 'adequate' host and has afforded you some information on the lands you now find yourself in, so I will not bore you with thee obvious.

"Yet-al's 'civil' settlements are neither numerous or generic. Each has their own unique qualities. Most, if not all, differ in how they combat and close off the night and the harm it brings. Caves...lots of caves, hold a few large communities like the Cleft. Each with their own flavor. Man-made structures of stone and wood, with a few large enough to be considered castles. Underwater dwellings. One place like the Arh Cleft, is a gargantuan hollowed out tree called Obrus far to the south. Perhaps you will visit. But most places where we," Vellis encompasses them all in a gesture. "...can live, here, are small dismal things, where savagery and cruelty are the common coin, so you must know..."

Here he stops to face them all.

"...you are lucky to be here."

Silence.

"Yeah, Qeta told us as much."

Horak had been unusually quiet, ever since the painful altercation with the Commander's crony, and he now chose this tense time to break the silence with sarcasm rather than wisdom. Master Vellis pauses. All fear the half-orc has said too much and overstepped the rules of propriety. But the soft honest smile that briefly visits the master's face says otherwise.

"Hmmm-hmmm...I suppose he has! And he is right.

"Yet-al is a monster. I know for some of you," he spares a glance at the elven ranger Nighlus. "This may be hard to accept from a tiefling, but it is true."

Gracefully he continues down the corridor and shortly it opens on a large chamber with the exceedingly high ceilings. Walled on three sides each wall is marked by doorways and stairs leading to other doorways and stairs, and chambers that must lay beyond. Far across the chamber's floor, where a fourth wall would be, the great room appears to open into a vast space which drops below the floor line. Everywhere there is activity. People moving here and there in groups and pairs. Pushing carts. Carrying equipment. A few wagons even move across the floor, horse driven and loaded down with goods and supplies. One would think all were equals if there wasn't a very noticeable difference.

Most wear shackles, and a smaller number do not. Amongst this smaller number about half have weapons dangling from belts.

"You are also lucky if you can fulfill a need here that others cannot fill, of which I and my domain most certainly do."

They all travel across the large chamber, to the shifting clanking sound from the shackled limbs of shackled people moving about, and soon reach the edge of the room that opens on a massive cave. Far below, the floor of the cave, some 100ft down, is taken up by a large indoor marsh. The ceiling above this repeats the same night sky illusion that lies above the master's mansion and garden. It is with ease all can imagine that in several hours a false sun will rise bringing a sky of day replacing this one of night.

Moving amongst the reeds, waterways, and many cultivated patches men and women work, tending to the many fields held within the marsh. Far across, dotted with numerous openings and walkways connecting them, is the cave's back wall. Even from this distance the survivors know these openings to be cells.

A prison.

They can't deny it for they cannot put a lie to the truth their eyes see before them.

It is clear Master Vellis is a master...a master of imprisoning men, and women...and children, for keen eyed Noc and Nighlus can clearly see the small shapes of children, human and otherwise, moving in the landscape below.

Their host, his tails, both flesh and cloth, sweeping dramatically, spins from the view below and faces them directly. He raises his arms broadly.

"Welcome," his smile opens fully, his sharp teeth glinting, "...to Level 3."

~End Volume One~

www.ingramcontent.com/pod-product-compliance
Lightning Source LLC
Chambersburg PA
CBHW060932030726

47503CB00003B/570